ISBN: 978-1-913463-00-7 (print edition)

ISBN: 978-1-913463-01-4 (ebook edition)

For W - more than anything

1

H e died alone. In all fairness, it was how he would have wanted it, had he ever thought about death. Sadly, other aspects of his final few minutes were far from favourable. But then no-one would choose that end, if they knew.

He had seen many others die. He had counselled them beforehand, preparing them for what he thought might happen. He had even assisted in their deaths, if he was totally honest. It was part of the job after all, playing God. Not that they talked about it, but it was. Now he was no different from Mrs Goodwin or Keith Shepherd, or any of the others he had watched as they left this world. Now they were all equal.

He tasted metal and gagged, but his throat was too dry. No saliva came. He tried to lick his lips, but his tongue was lodged like a slice of cured ham pressed hard against glass. His lips twisted. His mouth splintered and tore. He moaned. His eyes were wide and darted wild like an animal.

Surely none of them had suffered this? He knew that there was no going back now. The flames came in waves, blistering and wracking at his chest. His breath was spasmodic. Little air entered. His body heaved with the exertion. He could smell burning. Like seared bacon.

Sweating, he reached up and tugged helplessly at his necktie. Despite tearing half of the buttons from his shirt in his urgency, he gained no relief. His skin was cold and wet. Like the scales of a fish. His hands shook. He looked down and saw blood and pink vomit.

Still, the fire licked and teased. He was tormented by the pain. No words came. Twice, maybe three times, he tried to call out. His mouth was a yawning hole. He had left pressing the emergency buzzer too long. Bubbles and foam came, but nothing else. No-one would hear him drowning in fire.

He grabbed blindly for the sink. Instead, he fell. Crumpled and foetal. He was beyond wondering if someone might come.

He was on the floor now. His body was no longer his own. Privative reflexes continued. He twitched and thrashed, but was completely unaware.

His mouth was now a crevasse of ugly blistering skin. His eyes stared at the door, unseeing.

2

Dr Cathy Moreland looked up from her computer screen. Her eyes were alert, but her mind was tired. She had been rubbing her right temple when the knock came, a habit she was prone to indulge. It was as if she was trying to sooth away her overactive thoughts, but it rarely worked. The door, which had already been ajar, slowly opened further and Brenda looked in.

'Have you got a minute, Cathy?' she asked, and without waiting for an answer, entered.

Cathy smiled sardonically at the practice manager, Brenda, who was dressed conservatively as always. A floral dress covered her ample figure, and the heavy make-up and sensibly low block-heels completed the picture. Brenda must have been in her late fifties. Married and childless, it seemed that she devoted her latter years entirely to the practice. She spoke little of her husband, who Cathy knew only by name. She was a private woman, all in all. Efficient and private.

Brenda was smiling at her. Her face looked like a soft marsh-mallow. Irreverently, Cathy imagined the billowy pinkish-white foam, depressing under her teeth, the layer of sugary dust, clagging on her tongue. Stop it, she told herself, that kind of nonsense wouldn't do.

The doctor moved around her desk, positioned to the left of the room and angled so that both clinician and patient might sit without barrier. This layout suited Cathy's consulting style well. She was accommodating to her patient's needs and saw medical decisions less as those to be made by herself as an authoritarian, but more in partnership.

The room was on what was considered to be the least desirable side of the building, with the other consulting rooms across the corridor looking out onto fields. Cathy observed only the comings and goings in the carpark. Had she been given the option, she might well have chosen it anyway. Her room felt light and airy, and between patients she would occasionally amuse herself by people-watching from behind the blinds.

Turning at the door and glancing across to the window now, Cathy spotted one of her practice partners, James, jogging back from his car carrying a bag, his suit jacket flapped in the wind. Cathy smiled and shut the door. Brenda, she saw, had already settled herself in the chair offered.

'Well?' Cathy said expectantly, sitting down once more. Since returning the week before, she had felt sure that there had been a shift. There now seemed a veil of forced-civility between her and the staff. Everyone had been very welcoming and kind, but it all felt rather false. Of course, she had known that returning after such a long leave of absence would be hard, especially given the circumstances, but she had hoped things might have relaxed by now.

Cathy didn't quite know where she stood currently. Neither of her partners had spoken directly with her about the situation since she had come back. James, the more senior of the two, had come in on the first day and had given her an almost laughable speech about taking control of her life and making a difference to the rest of the community, or some such drivel, but as yet no-one had mentioned the big taboo. That, she supposed was to be discussed at this evening's meeting.

Cathy finally broke the silence. 'It's this evening, isn't it, Brenda? The meeting? What have they said?'

Brenda looked up sharply, her eyes wide and unblinking. 'Nothing, Cathy. James and Mark don't tell me their business. You of all people should know that by now.'

Cathy laughed, knowing this to be a lie. Brenda wrote the minutes for the meetings. She would have already prepared an agenda.

As she sat, she studied Brenda closely. Was this why the practice manager had come into her room? Had she wanted to forewarn her about the decision? Perhaps her two partners had already discussed everything in her absence and had decided to send Brenda to do their dirty work. She couldn't blame them if they had. Not after all that had happened.

The practice manager, who had been part of the team since before Cathy had joined, looked back at her. Her face, Cathy decided, although more tired than when she had first started all those years ago, was still rather beautiful. Her eyes were an unusual pale mauve. Cathy found herself transfixed by them for a moment. Brenda smiled at her. Her eyes crinkled. Cathy thought that she saw compassion. That must mean bad news.

'I wish you'd just say,' Cathy went on. 'It's better to prepare me. Surely you owe me that?'

What if, during her three month absence, her partners had decided that they would ask her to leave, or worse still, rather than this, she would be requested to demote to staff-grade? Perhaps they were going to offer Linda the partnership. Maybe Linda had done so well during Cathy's time off that they felt she was a better bet than Cathy herself. They would put the down-grade to her, as a kindhearted offering. She would see the

embarrassment and pity in James's eyes. Mark, her other partner, would be more abrupt and offhand. Once he had made a
decision, there was no point in talking it over.

Cathy liked and respected both of her practice partners, they
were excellent doctors, but how would she be able to carry on
working alongside them, knowing that she had once been their
equal? But she wasn't completely crazy. She wouldn't stand in
their way if that's what they had decided.

During her three month's enforced leave, Cathy had thought
often of her colleagues. She had needed the time out to rebuild
her strength, but had felt guilty for it all the same. She had been
given no other option though. Things had become so bad that
she was, by that stage, a risk to herself and her patients. The
illness had swept over her so fast. She had tried to conceal much
of it, but by the end, her erratic behaviour was becoming impossible. There had been complaints. Cathy cringed when she
recalled the language she had used during consultations.
Thankfully though, for the most part, she had scraped by
without incident. She had, in her heart known what was wrong
when they took her to the hospital. She wasn't so far gone so as
to miss the tell-tale signs. It had still come as a shock though,
having the diagnosis confirmed, and then there was the awful
spell as an inpatient until her medication kicked in.

Over the years, Cathy had looked after several patients with
bipolar disorder. At the time, she felt that she had done a good
job showing them respect and compassion, as she did with all of
the people that she cared for who were in mental disarray.
Having stood in their shoes since however, she saw things somewhat differently. Gone was her selfish fortitude and drive, and in
its place, was a vulnerability. This might, on a good day, lead her
to a greater understanding of her patients. On a bad day,
however, the deeper empathy and insight might completely
crush her. Cathy was still to be tested in this respect, but she

knew that it must eventually come. There would be a patient who would rock her foundations and challenge her professionalism.

'Linda isn't coming, is she?' Cathy asked, unable to hide the note of paranoia in her voice.

'Linda?' Brenda asked. 'No, she's not been attending any of the business meetings while you've been away, only the clinical ones. Oh Cathy,' Brenda suddenly said with genuine feeling. Cathy looked up at her and then back at her own hands. 'Please,' she went on, 'don't jump every time we're due to have a meeting, expecting it to be something bad. I'm sure Mark and James just want to discuss practice business. Of course, they'll want to ask how the week's been for you, but don't read too much into that. We all just need to adjust to one another a bit again.'

Cathy sighed and continued to study her hands. Her fingernails were short, but around them, the skin was dry and splintered. She caught at an edge and picked it, revealing a capillary bleed that only lasted a second before she covered it with her thumb and returned her attention to Brenda.

'How have you been finding the week anyway?' asked Brenda. 'That's really why I came in. Not to break some horrible news to you, if that's what you're thinking.'

'Fine,' Cathy said, shortly. 'I'm frustrated not to be doing more, but it's fine.'

'If it's getting to you that much, you can do some of the insurance claims in-between your patients. I've been nagging the boys to do them the whole time you've been away. I think they've been dumping them on poor Linda to be honest, rather than bothering themselves.'

'Poor Linda,' Cathy said rather cruelly. 'I'm sure she coped admirably.'

'Yes, well Mark's been given an earful from me while you've been away. That's another reason I wanted a word. All that carrying on with Tracy. You'd have heard about the two of them, I take it? I didn't want you to get a shock or put your foot in it. Horribly unprofessional to be dating a staff member, and when his divorce is barely settled.' The practice manager sighed. 'It's not been easy, while you've been away, you know? Not for anyone.'

Cathy nodded. She had never been desperately fond of Tracy, their newer practice nurse. She had seemed a little too flashy, and eager to offer her assistance at the most noticeable times. Their other nurse Irene, was quite the opposite. She had worked for the practice for over ten years now, and had performed her duties quietly and apparently without the expectation of gratitude or fuss.

'Yes, well it caused a bit of a stir initially. You'd think they'd be grown up enough to conduct themselves with some decency, but apparently not.' Brenda said.

Cathy laughed and glancing sideways, found herself automatically scanning her computer screen. Finally, her next patient was in the waiting room.

Brenda got up.

'I'll let you get on,' she said, but turning at the door, she paused. 'Cathy, don't be so defensive. James and Mark aren't perfect either. None of us are. Just give it time.'

3

'Morning ladies,' Fraser said, walking into the shop. He often arrived a little later than his two assistants Anna and Sarah, allowing them to open the front door. Giving them, as he said, a little responsibility. It was essential that the girls felt valued and part of the team.

The two girls had been speaking in whispered tones behind the counter. Sarah turned and smiled brightly at her superior.

'Morning Mr Edwards. Anna was just saying that one of the regulars who gets a dosette box has died up at the court.'

Fraser came through the shop and removing his suit jacket, hung it behind the door at the back of the shop. He replaced it with a freshly laundered white coat. 'Who was it?' he asked with some interest, for despite working in the job only four months, he already knew the customers, and especially those elderly patients who required a box of weekly prescriptions to be made up so that they would receive the correct dosage.

'Mrs Gregory,' Anna replied. 'Expected, I believe.'

Fraser shook his head and tutted. He moved around the desk and began to leaf through the pile of prescription papers waiting to be made up. A certain one caught his eye and he sighed, shifting his spectacles further up his nose. They were out of olanzapine and would have to order more before he saw to that one.

As the years passed, Fraser had gained a reputation for being a rather detached, but undoubtedly talented, pharmacist. With experience and skill, he now afforded some significant respect from those he worked with, and if a doctor was to telephone the dispensary in which he worked, he would almost always impress them with his knowledge of the patients and his memory for the medication they took.

Only the other morning, Dr Longmuir, a scatty, old GP from the local practice, had phoned through to explain an error in one of his prescriptions. Fraser had of course already spotted and corrected the mistake. It happened all the time. These doctors, having attended five long years at medical-school, seemed to be increasingly less able to understand the intricacies of pharmacology. The number of simple errors that he had to modify on their behalf was unbelievable. The buck, after all, stopped with the dispensing chemist and not them, so if a patient died of an overdose that they had prescribed, he might get the chop also.

Fraser reached up to the shelf and found the preparation he was looking for. Opening the box, he carefully counted out the correct number of tablets and printed a label with instructions for administration. He smiled to himself. It was not a medication he personally rated, but doctors were stuck in their ways. If they kept up to date with the advances, just as he did, they might well find themselves in a better position. Recognising that despite his youth, he was becoming more jaded, Fraser shook his head.

Sarah came through at that moment and he nodded to the girl.

'I'll be seeing to the methadone measures later, Sarah,' he said, catching her eye. 'I meant to say to you earlier that I had noticed your care in dealing with the schedule three drugs this last week. I saw your attention to detail and was very pleased with the way you double-checked with me.' Fraser paused deliberately to allow the young pharmacy assistant to absorb the compliment fully. 'That kind of consideration in this job does not go unnoticed. I wanted you to know.'

Sarah thanked her supervisor. Quietly, Fraser continued with his work. He had studied long and hard to achieve this position and was now quite settled in the comfortable setting of Glainkirk, a small market town in the Scottish Borders. As he went about his business that morning, he reflected on how fortunate he had been.

After finishing his degree, Fraser had originally chosen hospital pharmacy as a specialty, but the work had proved hard and unrewarding. The rigour of enforced deadlines, added to the sheer volume of work, resulted in a somewhat unhappy and lonely spell. Fraser found that he hated being treated as a subsidiary. Within the vast hospital, he was all but a number on a timesheet.

In an attempt to console himself, and inexpert at dealing with a substantial pay-cheque, having only recently qualified, Fraser resorted to lavishing his earnings on things to cheer his empty life. A new watch, an expensive jacket, and so on. He dated one of the student nurses briefly and took her out for dinner and impressed her with his intelligent repartee and extravagant lifestyle. Despite appearances though, inside, Fraser felt quite lost.

When during this difficult year, Fraser received the news that his father had unexpectedly died of a heart attack, the young pharmacist returned home briefly. He found his mother pale, frightened and naturally distraught, but more shocking was still to come, for it seemed his father had been living for some time far out with his means.

Fraser had assumed that financially, both he and his widowed mother would be quite secure. On a hard day at the hospital, he had even found himself considering how he might deal with his inheritance and had rejoiced in the fact that he might be quite comfortable from now on. However, as it turned out, after several months of wrangling, the family home was sold to pay off debts and Fraser was left with next to nothing and his mother only a small allowance. In many ways, this moment was a defining one. Having seen the hash his father had made of his own affairs, Fraser was bitterly determined to propel himself forward, out of the drudgery of his past.

It was during this spell, having failed to gain sufficient results to elevate his mood through alcohol alone, that Fraser first experimented with prescription medication. It was by no means difficult to procure. A small quantity of a low-dose opiate-based tablet was simple to come by as he was handling them regularly enough. During lunch break was the safest time to perform the sleight of hand. The first pill he ingested was whilst still at work, and he was surprised to find that for the remainder of the day his mood was significantly raised, so-much-so, that he invited one of the sonographers in the corridor out for drinks, an impulsive and unprecedented move for him. Having enjoyed the positive results the once, Fraser stole, not regularly, or sufficiently to become addicted, but frequently enough to see him through the rest of that month.

At this point, Fraser's habit might have been nipped in the bud. He knew that what he was doing was wrong and he despised himself for his weakness. But due to the dissolute nature of a junior doctor who happened upon him in the pharmacy whilst he was procuring another batch of tramadol, things took a somewhat different course.

'Naughty,' the young medic had whispered as he walked by Fraser, shuffling along the aisle.

Fraser had frozen, having assumed that he was quite alone and unobserved. How he could have been so reckless was unfathomable.

'Oh, don't stop on my account,' the man had said without turning. Fraser bowed his head and saw that behind him, the doctor was reaching up to one of the shelves to remove a box of allopurinol, a gout medication. 'I know the temptation is very real,' the medic continued quietly. 'I've seen you about and we spoke in the common-room before, didn't we? You asked me about the cricket scores. We should catch up some time again, Fraser, isn't it?'

Fraser stood motionless as all of this was being said.

With that, the doctor marched from the pharmacy, the medication he legitimately required for a patient, held in his hand.

For the rest of that day, Fraser struggled to concentrate. What had the man meant? Did he intend to blackmail him now he had caught Fraser red-handed? Fraser had, by the evening time, decided that the only thing for it, was to admit everything. When questioned, he would declare his guilt and take the wrath of his supervisors. It had, after all, been for personal use. With extra supervision, he might continue to work, and following a couple of years, he might be trusted to continue on, unregulated. What a foolish mistake to make though, and right at the beginning of his career. Fraser felt quite sick about the whole thing.

He didn't encounter the young medic, who he now knew to be called 'Jackson,' for almost a full week following the unfortunate incident, and during that time, Fraser fluctuated between relief at possibly having been given a reprieve if the doctor waived the event, to deepest despair at having the thing hanging over him. Repeatedly, as Fraser walked the long corridors of the hospital, he thought he chanced a sighting of the medic. With this, he found himself going quite cold and his hands beginning to sweat.

As it happened, in the end, they met in the lunch queue outside the hospital canteen. Jackson greeted Fraser as an old friend, a sentiment that Fraser struggled to match, wishing to do nothing other than throw down his tray and run from the place. But knowing that he could no longer go on in such a manner, Fraser found himself sitting with the junior doctor and eating his lunch of steak and gravy pie in the man's company. They talked of generalities at first, but after Fraser had lain down his knife and fork, he felt at least somewhat reassured by the other man's demeanour. Surely if he was going to expose him, he would have done so by now, and why sit and chat with him in such a manner if he intended on telling his supervisors?

But Fraser was to be surprised, for the young medic who had now also finished his own meal of macaroni cheese, a glutenous mass of sticky orange, leaned forward and smiled.

'A little suggestion,' he had begun, and after only a few minutes of hushed discussion, Fraser's heart sank as he understood what Jackson wanted.

'It needn't be much,' the doctor said, leaning back. 'Just a bit here or there for my friends. I'd hate you to get into bother on my account.'

Fraser grimaced. 'Can't I pay you? Or I could give you the stuff to hand around.'

But the man had laughed and told him that he wasn't handling a thing. He wouldn't be termed a drug dealer himself and had no intention of becoming involved in a scheme of the sort Fraser proposed. He had no plans to jeopardise the long and exciting career that lay ahead of him.

Fraser felt nauseous, knowing that he had personally endangered his own.

The plan was that Fraser should procure a small amount of

either diazepam or tramadol. The junior doctors struggled to sleep when coming off night-shift, Jackson said, and a few of his friends living in staff accommodation had in the past, popped the odd pill to good effect. It might be thoughtful to offer them a helping hand given that their job was so taxing and important.

'Why can't you just help yourselves?' Fraser asked. He had, after all, seen the medic taking legitimate medicine for a patient, and countless other doctors came down to the pharmacy to do the same.

'We could,' Jackson agreed.

'I'd turn a blind eye if you did it on my shift,' Fraser offered desperately.

'I think it's too risky, Fraser,' the man said. 'I'd hate for anyone to get a whiff of it. You keep your end of the bargain like a good man, and everything will be sweet. What's today? Wednesday. Well, Friday evening might be a good time to receive our first delivery. Staff accommodation is the best place to hand it over to the troops. We'll be waiting for you, Fraser. I'm so glad we managed to catch up for this chat.'

And so, for the following year, Fraser was tied into the most horrifying agreement. It seemed that the pharmacist would never free himself from the contract. Several times, he considered throwing himself at the mercy of his supervisors and confessing all. If he lost his job, what did it matter? He was ruined whatever happened. But repeatedly mollified by the young medic who reassured him that what he was doing was of such insignificance that it should be forgotten, he continued. If he did express his desire to stop, and once he declared to the junior doctor that he was finished with it all, the man became quite nasty. Fraser was in no doubt at all that if he spoke out, he would be hauled up in front of his supervisors and nothing could be said in his defence. Jackson's scheme had been now going on for a full six months. How on earth might Fraser excuse himself, even if he declared that he was blackmailed into the thing? No, the medics had been too clever for him. They closed ranks anyway at the sniff of trouble, Fraser knew that. All he could do was to see it out until the end of the year and hope that he might move onto another post and forget the whole sorry business.

It was with great relief when he did finish his job in the hospital and said goodbye to the dreadful predicament to which he had become bound. Thankfully, Jackson had no idea to where he was headed, and Fraser felt sure that his troubles were at an end. It was back to community dispensing for the world-weary pharmacist and by this time, he had qualified to take on a supervisory role himself.

He had found exactly what he was after in the small market town of Glainkirk where he now stayed. He had been in the position for nearly five months. Southern Scotland, although not his first choice, was pretty enough when one left the poverty behind. Most importantly, it was far away from the hospital in which he had worked and for a time, Fraser was quite content.

Glainkirk High Street was undoubtedly rundown. The residents, a mix of farming folk, or families long followed through from the old tweed mill days, made up the majority. Once you settled in Glainkirk, it was often said that you wouldn't leave. Fraser had heard this statement several times since arriving and wasn't sure if he considered it in quite the same light as the proud inhabitants.

Often, when the shop was quiet during those first few weeks, Fraser would look out of the window. Glainkirk was his ticket to freedom, and yet as he watched the purposeless amble of the elderly with their chins jutted out in resolute defiance at progress, he found himself falter. Rallying himself though, he knew that the move had been for the best. Although he would have dearly loved to work his way up the ranks of hospital pharmacy, he knew that things could never be the same. No. Glainkirk was the most sensible solution to the problem. It was here that he would set up his home.

Come eleven o'clock that morning, Fraser, having worked hard to clear the stack of prescriptions awaiting his attention, saw that the first of their methadone-prescribed customers had entered the shop. This side of the business was par for the course in such a town, and Fraser, although not delighted to be involved, did not mind. He had managed methadone dispensing for hospital clients on countless occasions before. This time, was the first where he was entirely responsible, however, but the accountability did not faze him. He was quite confident in his own managerial abilities.

Kiean Watts had been on heroin for most of his adult life. Aged forty-seven, it seemed unlikely that he would ever free himself of the drug. Two years before however, his psychiatrist had instigated a reducing regimen of methadone in an attempt to get the man back into a more controlled dosage. Fraser, having dealt with him and innumerable others, knew that this would never be the case. Kiean continued to take both heroin and methadone quite openly, and his prescription had not been dropped for many months now. Kiean was affable and no trouble to the pharmacist whatsoever. He turned up every two days for his dose of drug-substitute and took away with him a second dose which he was trusted to self-administer orally every other day. Come weekends, he was given two sealed doses to take home to see him over the Saturday and Sunday.

'How have you been over the weekend?' Fraser asked the man as he led him through to the private consulting room in which he saw all such customers.

'Not bad, not bad.' Kiean said as he always did.

Fraser, with his back to the man, rolled his eyes. 'Come through and sit down, and we'll go through the usual. It beats me why we have to be so formal when your prescription hasn't changed in the three months that I've known you. All this paperwork and we know what you have every day. Are you still thinking about reducing?'

The man snorted.

'Those doctors are all a bunch of hypocrites really,' Kiean said. 'Started me on the stuff, but I don't think they want me off it at all. I reckon they get paid extra seeing people like me anyway, so it's in their interest to keep us on. I'm not reducing anytime soon, no. I've got enough trouble as it is.'

'Is this enough then?' Fraser asked. 'Are you using the heroin way above and beyond?'

'Sometimes I have to,' the man said. He rolled up his sleeve and Fraser saw the bruising and track-marks. 'Groins all to pot now. I'm using my feet some days.'

Fraser was genuinely shocked. 'Have you spoken to the doctor and asked for an increase in your methadone?' he said, but Kiean shook his head and laughed.

'Nah, and I'll not bother with that,' he said. 'Don't worry about me. I'll make do with what I can get. Unless you're offering me more on the side?'

Fraser swallowed. Taking a deep breath, he smiled.

'That's a rather unprincipled suggestion if you don't mind me saying,' the pharmacist said.

Kiean laughed. 'Worth a shot,' he said. 'I thought you and I had a bit of banter going these days and you'd have a laugh.'

Fraser nodded. 'No, I quite understand and I can see the difficult situation you're in. I can see your difficulty,' he repeated slowly.

There was a long pause, during which Kiean obviously struggled, weighing up if Fraser might be trying to catch him out. 'So, you might be able to help?' the addict eventually said.

'Oh, my goodness, no. I don't know what you mean,' Fraser

answered brusquely. Closing the control drug register and getting up, he walked to the door. 'I'm afraid there's been a misunderstanding, Mr Watts. I'll get you your day's dose and tomorrow's as usual and we'll say no more about this.'

When Kiean was gone, Fraser stood alone in the back room. His hands shook and he wished that he could settle his nerves with a drink. It had certainly been a temptation, but he wasn't going to start up all of that nonsense again. He had messed around with mild sedatives and painkillers, but section three drugs were quite a different league. Dealing with doctors was one thing, but actual drug addicts was quite another. No, Glainkirk was his new beginning. His fresh start. What possible reason could there be to give all of that up?

4

———

'Where is she?' said Dr Mark Hope, a small involuntary twitch pulsing by his left temple. Cathy watched the muscular tic with interest, having never noticed it before. She wondered about Mark's blood pressure. All eyes were now on him, and the doctor, apparently aware of the fact, seemed to grow in height. 'We need to get started,' he repeated. 'God knows, she's been off the boil recently. Made a balls up of the alarm system on Monday and had to get in the engineers.'

'She came into my room earlier,' said Cathy. 'I think you should give her a break, Mark. It's a rotten job at the best of times.'

Mark snorted and folded his arms across his chest.

It seemed that the plans for the business meeting had changed, and much to Cathy's dismay, the entire clinical team had gathered upstairs at the end of the day. Irene and Tracy, the practice nurses, sat together at the far end of the table, in deep discussion, and Linda, to whom Cathy had now taken an irrational dislike, was beside Brenda's empty chair. Linda caught Cathy's eye and grinned at her. As they had walked up the stairs together earlier that day, Cathy had imagined Linda tripping and face-planting on the sharp step edge. She imagined her nose bleeding and one of her front teeth dislodged. Perhaps it was the illness, but Cathy found such thoughts coming into her head with surprising frequency. Sometimes she felt guilty, but as she entered the coffee room with Linda intact beside her, she had smirked to herself.

Cathy glanced at the clock. It was now gone six-thirty and already the top light in the conference room was on, a sign that autumn must be drawing in. Outside, the sun was dying. Positioned upstairs and at the back of the building, the room offered its occupants a strip of sky. Oranges and pinks decorated the clouds, which themselves ran like wispy vapours. Cathy wished that she could paint. She would have painted that sky with such enthusiasm, layering the lowest cloud with a forceful stroke, and then the next coating, an almost pure white, the tips, a flush turning to a deeper, more permanent glow. Below them, she could hear the back door being opened and then banged shut. Her eyes blinked inevitably with the jarring sound. Several car engines were started; the reception staff leaving at the end of another busy day.

Cathy looked across at Mark, who was now drumming the table with his fingertips. Had he always been this bad? Cathy couldn't remember it being so obvious; the impatience, the rudeness. Mark was only ten years her senior, and having worked together now for almost five years, Cathy thought that she knew her partner well. Perhaps her absence had only served to highlight his intolerance. Had she never gone off sick, she might not have noticed the gradual escalation in his ego. Strangely, as Mark had seemed to grow, her other partner James, who now sat beside her, had apparently wilted.

She leaned in towards James. 'Why does Brenda want us all here tonight?' she asked quietly.

Mark, although sitting opposite and knowing the question was not directed at him, answered before James could speak. 'Your first week back, Cathy. Bit of a party,' he snorted. 'Not really,' he laughed. 'It's a significant event analysis first and then the business meeting. Brenda's been trying to tie us all down for ages, but the nurses have had meetings of their own at lunchtimes and there's been CPR training going on. I think it needs doing before the re-evaluation next month. You tell her about the significant event, James. It was your one after all, wasn't it? Bit of a blunder from what I heard. Getting on a bit, and making mistakes.' This final caustic remark was made directly to Cathy in an exaggerated, hushed tone.

James shook his head sadly but didn't speak. It had become worse between them, Cathy thought, glancing from one to the other. Even before she had left, things had been tense, but the increased workload inflicted upon the two of them due to her absence had clearly intensified their dislike for one another.

James was nearing retirement now. Cathy watched as he spun the ballpoint pen between his elongated fingers. His hair was now quite grey. His face had a weathered look, as did his clothes, which although perfectly smart and well-pressed, were worn and tired as their owner.

Dr James Longmuir had done his time. He was one of the more respected general practitioners in the area, having worked both as a trainer and mentor to some of the junior practitioners over the years. Regularly, he was asked to attend dinners and meetings, holding close associations with the Royal College of General Practitioners. Cathy wondered if this annoyed Mark; to know that his partner was acknowledged as one of the 'wise men' in higher circles. She thought it probably did. Several times in the past, he had made scathing comments about James's repeated absences to attend college conferences. Cathy saw things somewhat differently. She had only been in the job six months when James had lost his wife. She herself, had been taken on as a new partner following the retirement of her predecessor and had witnessed first-hand the strain that the bereavement had had on James, and the force with which he had thrown himself into his work to combat it. Had Maureen still been alive, Cathy wondered if James might have retired far sooner.

James looked sideways at Cathy, perhaps sensing her thoughts upon him. 'How's it going then?' he asked conspiratorially, ignoring Mark completely now.

'Fine,' she replied firmly. 'I hope that you think I've been doing alright too. I know it's early days ...'

She studied his face and saw nothing but affable geniality. 'Good, good,' he said, but Mark was getting impatient.

'For Christ's sake, where is bloody Brenda? Irene, go and round her up. We can't be kept waiting like this.'

The senior practice nurse hesitated, clearly unsure if she should pander to this offensive request.

'Well?' Mark challenged. 'Above taking orders are you now? We pay your bloody wage.'

Irene slid from her chair, her face a deep, mottled red.

'Some of us have a life outside this practice,' Mark said in defiance, seeing both Cathy's and James's raised eyebrows.

Fortunately, poor Irene was spared the indignity of finding the practice manager as the door was opened. It was clear that Brenda had overheard Mark's final comment.

'Sorry to keep you waiting, folks. I got caught up downstairs,' the practice manager said apologetically, entering the room and immediately going to the seat she always took at the far end of the table. She quickly opened her notebook and finding what she was after, smiled around at the group. 'Finally, we're all in one place,' Brenda said. 'I just have a few points to go through that involve the whole team.'

Brenda spoke about an age-old issue of staff forgetting to turn off lights when they left, and their apparent thoughtlessness over the heating in their rooms.

'All I ask is you think to switch your radiators off at the end of the day. I've said it time and again. Linda, you don't come in on a Wednesday or Thursday some weeks, and your heating came on with the rest of the building for two full days unnecessarily.'

Linda nodded, but Mark was clearly growing bored and Brenda moved on. She discussed a problem that all the practices in the area were having in trying to obtain locums. 'This means we're relying on residual staff to mop up any short-fall, I'm afraid,' she said. 'I hate to ask it when your holidays are sacred, but if either doctors or nurses feel that they want to pick up extra sessions having not booked anything already in the way of trips away, then please let me know. It's a blow to all of us, but a real problem all the same. You'd be paid locum fees of course if that helps.' This suggestion was met with the expected response. Cathy looked around having heard the murmur of concern, but from beside her, James spoke.

'Put me down for my week off Brenda if it helps. I'll take the Monday, Tuesday off and come in the rest of the week. That'll do me fine.'

Dr Mark snorted rudely and Cathy saw Tracy smile across at him. 'Short on cash at the moment, James?' he asked. 'I'm sure we'd cope without you, wouldn't we Cathy?'

Cathy glared at Mark and Brenda held up a hand. 'We'll talk about details later. Mark, you know we need a certain number of doctors in the building. James, come into my office in the morning after you've had a think. I hate putting people on the spot and I know everyone needs some sort of a break. Now,' Brenda sighed, 'onto the significant event. James is going to present. Can I remind everyone,' Brenda paused and looked at

Mark, 'that this is a no-blame culture and our significant event analysis meetings are a learning opportunity for all, not just the person directly involved. As always, we allow the full presentation without interruption and then we can discuss. Agreed? Excellent. Thank you, James, if you're ready?'

While James got up and struggled with the computer, Mark turned to Brenda. 'I suppose you've seen they've been at the sign again, bloody vandals?'

Brenda looked concerned. 'The sign?' she asked.

'Yes, the bloody metal plaque at the front of the building with our names on it,' Mark said in exasperation. '"Dr Hope – less" it reads. Get it sorted, Brenda. It's a damn liberty. If I catch who's been doing it, I'll skin them alive.'

Cathy was sure she saw a smile twitch on Irene's lips.

Ignoring this exchange, James pressed a key repeatedly. He looked up from the screen over which he had been bent and smiled around the room.

'I'd like to discuss the matter of a simple prescribing error that could have had very real consequences had it not be dealt with rapidly,' he said.

James was a likeable and gentle figure. As he spoke about the mistake and the actions that he had taken to correct it, Cathy sat in respectful silence. In many ways, her senior partner was the reason that Cathy enjoyed working at the practice. He held the place together with his high standards, warmth of character and steady wisdom. Thinking back, although initially drawn to Mark's charismatic self-assurance and wit, Cathy had always felt safer in James's company. It had been he who she had gone to first when she had a problem.

The presentation lasted approximately ten minutes. Rather than coming over as a fool or a careless prescriber, James highlighted the need for honesty in owning up to a mistake. It was something that impressed Cathy greatly. The team discussed the case in-depth, with Mark making some good and well-judged points without apparently feeling the need to make a snide comment or jibe at James, at least for the time being. When finished, they were clear on the safe-guards required to prevent a further error occurring, and Brenda was tasked with transcribing the case and sending a copy out to all of the GPs for their approval before submitting it for the re-evaluation team in a month's time.

'Well James, on behalf of everyone, thank you very much,' Brenda concluded. 'Everyone happy?'

'Oh, quick query about the coils and Implanon list,' Irene said. 'I know you need to get on, but I couldn't catch you all together. Linda's been doing the list for the last few months.' Irene smiled at Linda.

'Yes,' said Linda, taking over. 'I don't know what your plans are now that Dr Moreland's back,' she said apologetically. 'I'm happy to continue with them, of course, but I wasn't sure about booking folk in.'

'I'll re-start the contraceptives and minor surgeries,' Cathy said firmly.

'Perhaps we will discuss this at the business meeting?' James cut in.

'She's not a bloody child, James,' said Mark, clearly forgetting his good form, 'and we can't treat her like an invalid either. If she's fit to come back to work, then she should be allowed to get on with it. Jesus.'

Suddenly, his face a deep red, James slapped the table with the palm of his hand, making them all jump.

The rest of the practice staff looked at him, dismayed. But ever the professional, Brenda stepped in.

'Now folks, I think we should begin the business side of the meeting,' she said.

The nurses and remaining non-partner GP, Linda, looked relieved.

'Thank you for coming everyone,' Brenda concluded.

Cathy and Mark still stared at James in astonishment. The rest of the clinical team left. As she passed his chair, Cathy saw Tracy reach out a hand and touch the back of Mark's neck. Linda was the last to leave and as she did so, she rolled her eyes and mouthed 'sorry'. Cathy hoped that she fell down the bloody stairs on the way out.

Brenda, choosing to ignore the awkwardness, moved on as if nothing had happened. She smiled around at the remaining three partners. 'Right, on to business. First, I'd like to say how delighted we are to have Cathy back.'

5

After a blissful hiatus, the monotony soon began to kick-in. Like so many before him who had achieved their dream employment, Fraser found only disillusionment. Glainkirk was not what he had expected and if truth be told, he was unutterably bored. He certainly didn't miss the atrocious situation he had found himself in at the hospital, but he longed for the faster pace of labour and the mental stimulation of working within a busy team. It seemed that having lived on adrenaline for over a year, he was dependent on the rush. Ruefully, he looked at the methadone-users who came in and found that he envied their quick fix. But he knew that he must rapidly stop with that kind of madness. He must knuckle down and make the best of what he had. His situation was enviable. He had security and reasonable wealth, not to mention, the respect of his two assistants.

No, excitement, was an unnecessary and overrated commodity. He reminded himself of what he had left behind; the sleepless nights, lying in the narrow hospital bed in the staff accommodation wing, listening as the junior doctors returned from their shifts. Sometimes they would tap quietly on his door and wake him, simply out of devilment. When he did go to answer the door, breathless and shaken from his fitful sleep, there would be nobody there. Minutes later, on returning to bed, he would lie his head on the creased pillows and hear their laughter echoing along the corridor.

It was madness really to feel anything other than happiness now that he had escaped. His pay as a supervisory dispenser was not bad at all. He had finally signed the papers to secure a property on the Langholm Road this last week. Although it was a busy stretch leading out of town, the house, a three-bedroom, detached, was set far back due to its large garden, and there was ample parking to accommodate his new car also. Things were certainly on the up, so why then, Fraser asked himself, wasn't it enough?

He continued on for a number of weeks, pushing the feelings of discontent to the back of his mind and making polite comments to the shop girls, Anna and Sarah. Day-in-day-out, he would dole out the tablets and tonics as everyone expected. He moved into his new house and began to slowly do it up, spending his weekends in builders' merchants and homeware department stores. He toyed with the idea of writing a research paper. Perhaps he should get in touch with one of his classmates and see if there were any study projects requiring assistance at the nearest university. Maybe if he applied his talent in this direction, it might satiate his restlessness. On one evening, he even sat down at his laptop and opening up a blank document, began thinking of titles for a novel he might write. A murder perhaps, with the perpetrator being a fiendishly intelligent organic chemist. Fraser closed his computer screen in self-disgust. Had it really come to this after all? He considered how things might have been if had listened to his father and followed in the family tradition of law. Perhaps if he had, his attention might have been kept, and his head steadied.

Throughout this disappointing time, Fraser continued to see Kiean every other day, such were the man's requirements for his prescription. He had given the matter a good deal of thought, having been shocked at the desperate man's half-hearted suggestion of Fraser giving him an 'extra' dose on the side. In spite of all that had happened, Fraser found himself actually momentarily considering helping the poor soul out in some small way. Offering him an additional measure to tide him over when times were tough. But when he thought of it, it was an utterly absurd idea and would end in much the same manner as the previous predicament he had found himself.

All the same, late one Friday evening after work, cosseted in his immaculate house, jaded beyond belief and slightly dazed on whisky, Fraser keyed in the question on his computer. It took only a matter of minutes to find that the illicit trade in prescription drugs was buoyant, to say the least, particularly in the green, sickly tincture which he was considering. Fraser closed the computer screen in horror at what he had contemplated and then opening it up again, he rapidly deleted his search history. What if someone was to find his computer and see what he had been researching? Dear God, what was he considering? And why would he? He didn't need the money. He was settled and content. The tablets in the hospital had been bad enough, but methadone was quite a different thing altogether.

That night, Fraser struggled to sleep, and when he did finally manage, he awoke confused and frightened, convinced that he had heard a knock at the front door. Too afraid to get up, he lay still and listened for what seemed like hours. But he had been mistaken. It was because of the whisky he had drank earlier, of course. His father always said the amber liquid only led to madness. Fraser settled himself down again, resting back in his bed, and eventually drifted off. That night, he dreamt of terrifying masked figures pinning him down whilst holding syringes of poison to his veins.

But despite his dreadful night, going into work the following morning, Fraser walked with a bounce to his step. He had parked by the old tweed mill, long since converted to flats, down by the river so that he could enjoy the longer walk into the centre of town. The crumbling high street took on a new energised atmosphere and the huddles of leisurely, ancient shoppers that spilt from the pavements in absentminded conversation, no longer riled him as they had done the previous day. Side-stepping out into the road to pass, he raised a hand to a regular customer. Yes, things, after all, might be quite alright, for he had awoken knowing finally what the problem really was. He was lonely of course, and needed to find himself a good woman. And she had been there in front of him all this time. If only he had bothered to do something about it.

By the time Fraser had reached the pharmacy shop, he had all but made up his mind. He would ask her out that day. Sweet, gentle, innocent Sarah. Now he thought of it, he had known from the start that she was for him. Her mild, friendly banter while assisting him to measure out the liquid medications. Her studious accuracy in checking the dosette boxes. Indeed, it was obvious that they were perfectly matched.

But ever professional, Fraser knew that his love-life must wait. He set to work as always, dealing with the mountain of repeat prescription requests, and discussing over the telephone several minor prescribing errors with the GPs who had written them. The morning passed quickly and it was soon eleven o'clock and time for the methadone-users to arrive at his door. Fraser set aside what he was doing and collecting the control drug register notebook, he went through to the back room where he saw all of the clients who required a confidential consultation. Kiean was first, as he always seemed to be, and smiling at Sarah as he passed her, he led the man through.

'Come through Kiean, you know the drill,' Fraser said, barely looking at the man.

The addict followed him, and before the door was shut, Kiean, to Fraser's utter amazement, began to shudder, as if gasping for air.

Initially, Fraser thought he was having some kind of a fit and made towards the door to shout for help. Only then, on properly observing the man, did he realise that the methadone-user was sobbing uncontrollably.

'Oh goodness,' Fraser said, quite unsure what he was meant to do. 'Sit down Kiean. I'll get a box of tissues if you wait a minute.' He left the room, glad to have some space to think. Re-entering, he found Kiean more composed. 'Now then,' Fraser said. 'What's it all about?'

'I shouldn't make such a fuss,' the addict said and rubbing a grubby hand across his face. He seemed to pull himself together a little and grasping the tissue offered to him, blew his nose noisily. 'Bad news today. I just heard a good friend of mine passed.'

Fraser, who was still standing, lowered himself to the chair opposite. 'I'm sorry to hear that Kiean. Was it unexpected then?'

'Cancer,' Kiean said and blew his nose again. 'Too young, but God, I'm sorry to carry on in front of you, Mr Edwards, really I am.'

Fraser smiled. 'It's fine. Honestly. I lost my father a couple of years ago and even that, all this time on, still gets me occasionally. Now, if you have your prescription, we'll get you sorted in that way at least this morning.'

Kiean fished in his jacket pocket and then began patting himself down. Fraser's heart sank. Please don't let him say he's lost the prescription, Fraser prayed. Suspiciously, he wondered as he watched the drug addict go through the motions, if the story had been a rouse all along. Fraser watched distantly as the man removed his coat and jumper and then began rooting through his pockets, all the while muttering that it must be somewhere. He didn't have the prescription, of that Fraser was sure and he doubted that Kiean's friend with cancer had existed either. Fraser felt as if he had been taken for a fool.

'Well, Kiean?' he finally asked as the man stood before him, repeatedly apologising and reiterating that he didn't know what had happened to the damn thing. 'It should have been a triple dose as well Kiean, because it's Friday.'

Kiean nodded. 'I know. I honestly don't know what I've done, Mr Edwards. You can phone the clinic and ask them. They left the prescription for me to collect this morning at nine as they always do. It hasn't changed. My dose, I mean. It's the same as it's always been. I must have dropped it at home before I came back out, I had to go back to get my fags. I'll bring the script in on Monday and you'll see.'

Fraser shook his head. 'You know I can't dispense without it, Kiean. Give me a minute and I'll call through to the clinic and see.'

Fraser left the man and did just that. To his surprise, it all seemed above board. Kiean had collected his prescription at nine-fifteen that morning and his dosage hadn't been altered. The doctor suggested that he fax across a duplicate prescription to cover him for the weekend, as withdrawing from the quantity he was on, would undoubtedly be dangerous.

Fraser returned to the room and told Kiean that he would indeed be receiving his medication after all. The drug addict seemed pitifully grateful and must have thanked Fraser a good six or seven times before he left.

As Fraser closed the door, he had a dreadful, sinking feeling in his stomach, but he dismissed this. He had checked with the clinic and it was as the man had said. As far as Fraser was concerned, he had the faxed prescription which was undoubtedly legitimate and all was well.

'I heard you ringing the clinic,' Sarah said as Fraser came through to the front of the shop. 'I hope Kiean wasn't any trouble.'

Fraser pulled himself together and nodded. 'Just part and parcel of the job, I'm afraid. He lost his prescription, but it's sorted now. I got the clinic to fax another through and the old one, if it is found in the street, will be invalid if another pharmacy takes it. I've put out an email to warn the dispensing chemists in the area. Sadly, you can't be too careful with these drug dependants. As long as you and Anna keep well out of their way when they come in, I'll be happy. I don't like them coming in at all really. It intimidates the other customers. I hope not you though, Sarah?' Fraser held the girl's gaze and then looked down at his feet. 'I was going to ask if you'd be free perhaps for a drink maybe next week, even this evening. I thought a meal out? I had been meaning to ask for a while now, but ...'

Sarah smiled. 'But what? I wish you had asked before. Yes of course. I'd love to.'

The girl blushed and scuttled away; no doubt eager to tell Anna who had been busily stacking shelves.

When Fraser went home that night, despite his swift dealing with the missing prescription incident, he still felt a sense of unease. But he had covered himself as best he could. No-one could accuse him of not doing his utmost to rectify the situation and, as the clinic doctor had said, they could hardly leave Kiean without his three doses over the weekend. Still, though, Fraser had a feeling that Kiean had not been telling the truth. But knowing that no good would come of going over and over the matter, Fraser put the thing to rest and turned to his evening ahead.

Having showered and dressed in something not overly smart, but crisp enough to indicate his interest in her, he arrived at Sarah's door. It was just after seven-thirty and it seemed that she lived with her parents still. It was her mother who answered, much to Sarah's embarrassment obviously, as she tore down the stairs clutching her jacket and bag.

'This is nice,' Fraser said, as they linked arms and walked up the street together to the small Italian bistro. 'I think we're going to have a lovely time together, Sarah.'

Throughout the meal, however, Fraser continued to think distractedly about the Kiean situation. By the end of the main course and with Sarah's eyes shining by the light of the candle on the table, he had a dreadful realisation. What if Kiean had already cashed in the prescription before coming to his pharmacy? Supposing he had gone to another pharmacy in the area? Fraser had contacted the other two establishments and had warned them to look out for the missing prescription if it mysteriously appeared that afternoon, but what if Kiean had been into one of those already? But no, Fraser decided, this was absurd. They would have of course noticed the name and telephoned Fraser back to say that Kiean had been in already and warned Fraser not to dispense any more of the drug.

Fraser smiled across at Sarah who was now considering the dessert menu. No, all was well. He was far too suspicious, that was his problem. All that dreadful hospital business was still affecting him and making him doubtful of everyone around. People could be genuine and good.

Sarah was smiling gently at him. Raising his glass, he toasted his delightful companion for the evening.

'To us, Sarah,' he said. 'To new beginnings.'

Only two days later, on Sunday morning, Fraser was seated at his kitchen table alone. His hand hovered. What had the radio presenter just said? He allowed the spoon to drop. It fell with a clatter in his breakfast cereal, sending a splash of milk and cornflakes onto the table. Fraser didn't notice. He crossed the kitchen and turned up the volume.

'... *in the doorway of a derelict building. Glainkirk Police are appealing for witnesses who might have seen the man: Kiean Watts, on the preceding day. A police spokesperson refused to comment further, but said that the man's death was currently being treated as unexplained.*'

The reporter moved onto another story and Fraser absent-mindedly pressed the button on the radio, silencing it. Dear God, how could it be? He paced the room. The kitchen already been in excellent order when he moved in, and there had been no need to make many changes. His eyes fell to the matching, floral-patterned mugs that hung in a line. He thought of Sarah, and their evening out together. She would surely be hearing the news herself that morning also. What would she think? A sudden, unexplained death in Glainkirk, and one of their own customers.

Fraser thought again of the odd encounter with Kiean on Friday morning. He recalled the man's tale of having lost the prescription for his methadone, and his own sense of unease about the situation. But Kiean's death could hardly be unexpected, and just because Fraser happened to be the man's pharmacist, no blame could lie at his door.

Fraser crossed the room again. 'Lying in a doorway.' He had overdosed, more than likely. Probably, he had been given a bad batch of heroin, or whatever else the foolish man might have been taking that weekend. He had taken too much. Kiean had been treading a very fine line all of these years. Yes, it was a marvel he had lasted this long really. People like that were wholly unpredictable. No doubt the police would give the matter little time. A postmortem would be carried out, as was only fitting in a sudden death of this kind, but it would hardly incite police interest, even if excess methadone was found.

Fraser picked up the half-eaten bowl of cereal and tipped the contents into the sink. The golden flakes heaped and blocked the plughole, but absorbed in his thoughts, Fraser continued to run the tap until the sink was half-filled with murky water.

He was overreacting. No doubt the police would want a quiet word. It was nothing to be concerned over. Indeed, it was to be expected. They would need to talk to him. A drug addict would have to make contact with certain professional people regularly. Himself, Kiean's psychiatrist, even his GP, might be interviewed as a matter of course. He would be quite ready as an expert witness.

But Fraser couldn't settle. All day, he ran over and over that Friday morning in his mind, returning to the interaction with Kiean. He wondering if he had been the cause of the man's death. Why had he been persuaded to give him those extra three doses of methadone? How had the addict pulled the wool over his eyes, despite his attempts to safeguard against it? The only obvious explanation was that the man had somehow cashed in his other prescription before receiving the drug from Fraser.

The anticipated telephone call came that Sunday afternoon. An overdose of methadone, at least that was the preliminary findings on postmortem. He spent the rest of the day in turmoil, but come Monday morning, he had gained enough composure to be ready.

At midday, the policeman arrived, thankfully plain-clothed, as the shop was heaving with customers. Even still, Fraser knew that many eyes might be on him as he led the man through to the consulting room in which he had spoken with unfortunate Kiean only days before. Fraser indicated a seat, and himself, sat across from the visitor. His hands shook and he clasped them tightly in his lap and smiled at the detective.

The policeman thanked Fraser for seeing him at such short notice and commented on the clear demands of the job. Fraser laughed nervously and told him that it had begun as his voca-tion but that he was stuck with it now. The detective smiled and stated that he had fallen into his line of work purely by chance, but it paid the bills right enough. After this preliminary exchange, they moved onto the reason for the detective's appointment.

'I heard of course. Poor Kiean,' Fraser said, shaking his head. 'He was one of our regulars, as you know. We had begun to build up a bit of a rapport. We were all shocked to hear. Even the shop girls. Some of them can be a bit of a bother, you know, to deal with? Kiean though, wasn't like that. I felt quite sorry for the man.'

The detective nodded. 'Been coming to this pharmacy for his prescription three years now, I believe, although you have only been here for the past six months, is that so?'

Fraser nodded.

'We've already spoken to his GP, but in fact, it was his psychiatrist who prescribed the stuff. I have a meeting with him later today.'

Fraser swallowed. 'Of course. I see. You perhaps want to know about Kiean's last visit to us? I have the controlled drug register at hand.'

'I wish everyone we questioned was as organised,' the detective laughed. 'If you don't mind?'

Fraser knew it was going to come out. As he went through the entries over the last few weeks, indicating that really nothing had changed in the drug addict's dose, he knew that the policeman must find out the truth soon enough.

'It's quite commonplace actually,' Fraser said, trying to sound calm but feeling anything but. 'It seems to be the way the psychiatrists are doing things with the regular ones. Especially if they aren't planning on changing the dose any time soon.'

'I see,' said the detective. 'I thought the reason for going on the stuff on the first place was to reduce it down and stop, but maybe that's just me.'

Fraser smiled. 'No, I wholeheartedly agree.' he said. 'Funnily enough, I mentioned it to Kiean and one of my other regulars too. They seemed to think that they'd never get off the stuff, and had no reason for doing so. Kiean, I know for a fact as he told me, was still using heroin to satisfy his needs. I don't think it's unusual for that to go on.'

'So, getting back to the last dispensing of the stuff,' the policeman said.

'Oh yes,' Fraser laughed. 'As you can see it was a Friday. I should have explained that weekends are different.'

The detective looked puzzled. 'How so?'

'Well, of course, we don't open on a Saturday afternoon or a Sunday,' Fraser clarified. 'So, over the weekend, Kiean was given two take-home doses, to self-administer orally on the prescribed days. His psychiatrist had been recommending this for the last eight months and up until this incident, there had never been an issue.'

'I see,' the detective said. 'But surely even if he had taken the two doses together it wouldn't have killed him, having been on the stuff so long?'

Fraser smiled. 'You'd need to speak to a doctor, of course. I do know that if an addict withholds a dose for a time and then takes it, they can quickly become opiate naive and the standard dose that they might usually take quite easily, would become toxic.'

The policeman nodded. 'Yes. I've heard of that too. Surely though, if he had taken his dose in front of you on the Friday as it says in your book here, then a single day of hoarding it for a double-whammy on the Sunday wouldn't be enough to kill.'

Fraser raised his hands in indication of his defeat. 'True enough,' he said. 'I'm not the detective of course. There is a chance he had taken another addict's also, I suppose. You hear from time to time about illicit quantities doing the rounds. I read in the pharmaceutical journal about the problems they have in the US. Apparently, it is ordinary to find 'spit methadone' circulating on the streets.'

The detective looked confused.

'It's quite disgusting really,' Fraser said, warming to the subject and shaking his head, 'but the addicts pretend to take the stuff in front of the chemist. They hide it at the back of their throat or some even actually swallow the liquid, and then on leaving the shop, they regurgitate it, spitting it out again into a container to sell on. Quite awful to imagine, but it's possible I suppose. Not something I would expect around here though and definitely not from Kiean.'

'Different world, isn't it?' the policeman said contemplatively.

'The things people do to get a fix. Well, I really must thank you, Mr Edwards. As far as you were aware, nothing unusual occurred on the Friday when you saw Kiean and there was no odd interaction with the man when you saw him last. He could in fact have obtained the supplementary dose from any source illegally.'

Fraser hesitated and the detective looked at him keenly. 'Mr Edwards?' he asked.

Fraser felt himself go cold and he sat quite still. He ran his tongue over his bottom lip. Oh God. This was it. The policeman looked at him still affably but with a bemused expression. Get a bloody grip, Fraser told himself, and forced a slow smile onto his face. 'A mix-up with the prescriptions, I'm afraid. It seems that Kiean had lost his weekend one. I had to ring through to the psychiatric clinic and get a doctor to check it and fax another. The doctor I spoke with said that there was no funny business going on. Kiean had indeed collected his script that morning at nine-thirty. It was eleven o'clock when he came here. It seems that during that time, he mislaid the thing. He was distracted that morning. Apparently, a friend had died, so he said.'

The detective nodded. 'I see. I'm surprised you didn't mention this at the start. Forgive me for asking, but what if Kiean had cashed in the prescription already, and then come to you with this story of having lost it? That would surely allow him an extra three doses of methadone on top of what he would usually have. His body, I imagine, might well not tolerate that, although of course, I'd need to check with a doctor.'

Fraser shook his head vehemently. 'No, no,' he said. 'I checked; you see? I wouldn't be so trusting as to just go on Kiean's word. We have only three pharmacies in the town including ourselves. I contacted the other two and warned them to look out for Kiean coming in that afternoon. They didn't mention him having already been in with a prescription already.'

'I'll check for myself, of course,' the policeman said. Fraser felt his manner had changed a good deal since he had first come in. 'I'm not casting any doubt over what you've just said, Mr Edwards,' he explained rather coldly. 'I just need to investigate the thing as far as I can. He has to have got more than his usual dose of methadone from somewhere. This little mix-up on Friday certainly seems like the obvious place to start looking.'

'If there's anything else occurs to you ...' Fraser offered, desperately hoping that the man would leave.

'No, I think that's all for now. Thank you for your help. I'll be in touch if anything else occurs.'

At the door, the detective turned. 'And you've been in this position for how long did we say, Mr Edwards. Just for my records, you see?' he said.

Fraser's chin jutted out, but he gave the answer, knowing he had little choice. 'I've been in Glainkirk for a little over six months now.'

'And before that? Was it another pharmacy post in the community, or a hospital?'

Fraser had a slight fit of coughing and efficiently blew his nose. When he answered though, he had himself in hand once more.

'Hospital pharmacy,' he returned, in what he hoped was a normal voice. 'I didn't much enjoy it to be fair. Much happier serving a community than dispensing to faceless numbers.'

'Thank you, sir,' the detective nodded. 'I hope we won't need to bother you again.'

When he was alone, Fraser found himself quite moved. He loosened his tie and rubbed his face with both hands. Oh God, what a horrible experience it had been. That might so easily have been the end of him. Fraser wished he had never set eyes on Kiean Watts. What if they found that he was the cause of the blasted man's death? He had tried to deal with the difficult situation as best he could. He could hardly have sent Kiean away empty-handed after all. Withdrawing from the drug over the weekend would have almost definitely killed him if Fraser had been unsympathetic to the man.

Fraser paced the room. What of the detective's final question? What had he asked that for? Did he plan to go rooting through Fraser's past employment now to check up on him? With rising panic, Fraser allowed his thoughts to move to Jackson, the devious junior doctor who had ensnared him. What if the story of Fraser's past misdemeanour was to come out? What on earth might the detective think if he knew? Illegally procuring and distributing prescription medication was a grave matter indeed and on top of that, Fraser found himself with the blame of a drug addict's death on his hands. Fraser knew that if the Jackson story emerged, he would be undoubtedly ruined.

All afternoon, Fraser attempted to work stolidly. Repeatedly, he reassured himself of his safety. He had most certainly done the right thing that Friday and had nothing to worry about. When all was said and done, he had faced a difficult situation and had dealt with it appropriately. The detective had not blamed him at all.

Despite this, Fraser still found himself far from content. On the contrary, even though he had planned an evening with Sarah, something to which he had been looking forward, the thought of dinner and drinks made him quite queasy. He had been too hasty in doling out the methadone, this he now knew to be true. His intention had been only to do good. He had never meant to cause the death of a man. Oh God, when one considered it in those terms it was too dreadful.

But the only thing for it was to keep his head and to plough on as normal. The police questioning had been a horrible experience. Even though he was still somewhat rattled by the day's events, Fraser continued with his plans to take out his charming assistant, who as the weeks had passed, had grown on him considerably.

The dinner turned out to be a happy distraction and kept him from thinking of his problems. Admittedly, he perhaps drank a little more wine than he might normally have done, especially when young Sarah directed the conversation back to the sad events of the weekend and the loss of one of their customers.

'I suppose it was going to happen one day or another,' she said. 'I know he was unpleasant at times, but you have to wonder what it was that started him on that path in the first place. Something must have made him resort to that. Poor creature.'

Fraser smiled at this rather innocent interpretation of things, but he was somewhat displeased when the girl continued to pursue the topic.

'And the police coming in too,' she said. 'I felt so bad for you, Fraser. You looked quite stressed when the man arrived.'

Fraser shook his head rapidly. 'Not a bit of it. I don't know what made you think it. I'm quite used to dealing with these sorts of things. It was to be expected, them wanting to talk to me. After all, it was methadone that killed him and I dispense the stuff.'

Although they had only been dating one another for a short time, partly to distract himself from the day's events, and perhaps because he was afraid of returning to his immaculate house alone, Fraser touched the girl's arm.

'I think we should head back to mine for a coffee,' he said rather seriously.

The girl must surely have understood what he meant for she blushed as was her habit, and refused to meet his eye.

Fraser mercifully slept well, but he awoke with a dry mouth and heavy head. Sarah had gone an hour before, waking him briefly to kiss him goodbye and to say that she would see him at work later. He had turned over and fallen asleep once more. As he later showered and dressed, he imagined the young girl returning home, perhaps sneaking into her parents' house, hoping that her night-time absence would go unnoticed. He trusted that she wouldn't become too imprudent at work and try to speak to him in indiscrete tones in front of Anna or the customers.

When Fraser himself arrived at the pharmacy that morning, he had managed to push the previous day's unpleasant interview to the back of his mind. He moved through the shop as always, hanging his suit jacket at the back and replacing it with his white coat. Only then, on turning and seeing standing outside the shop, an official-looking gentleman who he had not noticed before, did his panic return. They had come. He had been found out. Oh God, what a fool he had been to think he might get away with it.

7

Cathy's heart sank when she heard a knock on her door after her morning surgery. The door opened and a face appeared.

'Linda,' Cathy said, and paused, hating herself for being so cold.

'Sorry to be a pest,' Linda said, 'I wondered if I might grab you before you went out.'

'It'll have to be quick,' Cathy said, unable to bring herself to look at the girl and instead concentrating on her computer screen. 'I have four house visits to get done before the palliative care meeting and lunch isn't happening today for sure.'

Since returning to work, Cathy had found herself becoming more and more irritated by Linda's tentative approaches. She knew that the girl was trying to be friendly and Cathy was embarrassed by her own inner turmoil. Linda had done nothing wrong, Cathy told herself. It was simply that circumstances had made their professional relationship awkward. Cathy was a very proud person and it had pained her to admit weakness in front of a more junior member of staff, especially one whom she had personally trained. Cathy recalled Linda's faltering words as she left for her three month-long break, her assurances that she would take care of things for Cathy and look after her patients as best she could. At the time, she had been too upset to respond. James and Mark had all but frogmarched her to the door and told her to take the time it took to get well before returning.

The breakdown had come from nowhere it seemed. She had cruised through medical-school without much difficulty. She was far from confident at that stage, but self-assured enough to trust in her knowledge and be able to accept her mistakes when she made them following her studies as a junior doctor. When it had all changed, she didn't know. She had been the life and soul during her hospital days, moving from department to department and enjoying the variety. Even her first year as a GP principle had been smooth.

Since the time off, however, Cathy had painstaking run through the months and years before her mental crash, and had seen that James had protected her to some degree, shielding her from the full-workload in her initial year as a partner. The business side of the practice had been of no interest to Cathy in the beginning. She had trained to be a doctor, not a manager. James presumably saw this, and he and Mark had gradually introduced her to the commercial factors, the staff direction and so on, without expecting too much. Looking back, they had been so thoughtful really.

And then she had begun to take on more. Feeling optimistic about her position, Cathy had agreed to mentoring some of the final-year medical students and then, the year before she became unwell, she had signed up as a retainer-GP trainer, and so had received Linda as her first trainee. The retainer scheme was mainly for returning GPs following time off for pregnancy. Linda had taken a full year away from medicine and had come back somewhat rusty. She had required a good deal of support, her knowledge returning fairly fast with Cathy's supervision, but her self-assurance taking longer. Linda wasn't to blame for the stress in Cathy's life, but she supposed looking back that it hadn't much helped.

At the time, Cathy had been unaware of her own mood alteration. Linda had been one of the first probably to spot it, and this too annoyed Cathy. It had been during a tutorial. Cathy had been teaching the girl about the Implanon contraceptive device, explaining the pros and cons of it, and even going through the insertion technique with diagrams. She must have lost her train of thought though, and only became suddenly very aware of Linda's worried eyes upon her. 'Are you alright, Dr Moreland?' Cathy had stared for how long, she didn't know. Then without a word, she had risen and run from the room to vomit in the staff toilets. This pattern had continued over the coming weeks. Her sleep had been dramatically altered too, with Cathy waking in a cold sweat, panting and terrified. In the morning, having slept fitfully, she had known that it was a simple panic attack, but at the time she thought her world was ending. The lack of sleep took its toll. Her work had admittedly suffered. There had been no reason, that was the upsetting thing. There was no trigger to start it off.

On those days after work, having crawled through a long day, sleep-deprived and emotional, but desperate not to show it, she had found herself counting the hours until she climbed the stairs of her small cottage and forced herself to sleep. The nightmares were appalling. It almost made the act of sleep futile. She craved rest more than anything, but dreaded it too. She had drunk more over the preceding months. She didn't count the units, but it was far in excess.

And then, she had arrived at work on the final morning. Brenda the practice manager, accompanied by James had entered her room and had closed the door. No more, they had said. She was to leave that morning and get help. She had argued and told them that she was fine, that she had patients to see. They were waiting for her. Mark had then come into the room. She could hear his words now.

'You stink of it, Cathy. How you expect us to allow you in front of patients is a bloody joke. You shouldn't have even driven this morning. You must be over the limit. There have been complaints. Your language has been bad, to say the least so God knows what you've said to the patients. Get out before you say anything more and get yourself sorted, for Christ sake. It's a bloody joke, coming in like this.'

She had left immediately, returning the following day sober and full of remorse, but they wouldn't have it. That was when Linda arrived at her door offering to cover her sessions until she was ready to return, presumably having been already primed. James and Mark had given her no option in the end.

And after that day, her life had changed forever. Up until then, she had been able to hide for the most part her inner turmoil. She had concealed the racing thoughts and the music which played constantly in her head, she had masked the erratic moods as best she could. She had failed her patients. Even they must have seen the change in her, the agitation, the lack of patience. It was this that pained her more than anything. When faced with losing it all, she had, of course, gone to speak to someone. The psychiatrist had told her what she already knew herself. But to hear the words 'bipolar disorder' voiced aloud, had all but destroyed her.

She had taken the time out and had rebuilt her strength, although it had been hard to conform to the antipsychotics initially. After a holiday alone up north however, she had come back feeling more like herself. But still, she was terrified of losing what she loved. Her career was everything to her and having nearly lost this, she knew that her fitness to practice was still precariously balanced. Occupational health would continue to assess her, and would do so over the coming months, checking in that she was stable. She was to continue seeing her consultant psychiatrist for the time being, that was one of the stipulations they had made. He was cautiously optimistic about her return to work, given that she had improved so fast, but with this came the caveat that she was to avoid undue excitement or stress. So, she had returned to the practice full of vigour, but gone was any ease of friendship with Linda anyway. The girl stood awkwardly now.

'So,' Cathy said. 'What's up?'

Linda settled herself on a chair and fidgeted with her hands. Cathy waited without speaking. Something was obviously upsetting the girl.

'I know you're not my supervisor anymore. I'm an independent GP. I just thought it should be you I told, though.' Linda paused and shifted again in her seat.

The interview lasted short of five minutes. Following their conversation, Cathy marched through to Brenda's office and without knocking, went in. Brenda looked up in surprise.

'Cathy? Whatever's wrong?'

Cathy paced the small room. 'Brenda you are going to have to do a bit of clearing up. Linda has made an utter mess of something. A major mistake. It will need a good deal of tact from you and the partners.'

'What on earth's happened?' Brenda asked again.

'The flu clinics,' Cathy said. 'We had put her on them to simply crack through the numbers and free up partner time. She was doing them with Irene, but Irene had a leg ulcer to dress so she came in halfway, apparently. I don't even know if Linda's told her yet.'

Brenda continued to look puzzled.

'She's given a child the wrong injection,' Cathy said. 'I've just rung up the mother and explained. I've sent Linda out to the house to check him over. Egg allergy, and she gave him the one containing it. Jesus. If Irene had been in with her it would never have happened, but there's no point in going over that now.'

'I take it he's alright?' Brenda asked.

'The mother, when I phoned, said he had been a little wheezy all morning but she had assumed it was his asthma, ironically the reason for him getting the jag in the first place.'

Brenda leaned back and covered her face with her hands. 'Oh God. It's the last thing we need. How was the mother when you called? Angry?'

'No, not a bit, but that'll come when it sinks in. I've told Linda to admit him for observation to Paeds if she has any doubt whatsoever. I know these things can happen, but what a bloody mess. The worst of it is, that she actually realised her mistake almost as soon as she had done it, it seems, and yet she continued to plough through the clinic hoping it might go unnoticed I assume.'

'But she came and told you?'

'After surgery, yes, but had she acted sooner and admitted her mistake, she might have saved the child further risk. It is just what we were saying upstairs about accepting and owning your mistakes. James gave the talk only days before and yet she seems to have panicked and shirked responsibility. At least she owned up in the end, I suppose.'

'I'll tell her to contact the defence union for advice if we get a complaint. She might be as well contact them, in any case, to run it by them. There have been a few too many incidents recently,' Brenda said.

'Oh? What with Linda?' Cathy asked.

'No, just everyone,' the practice manager said. 'I've just cleared up James's complaint and another has arrived this morning from the pharmacy about Mark and one of his prescriptions.'

'Why that came to you and not Mark I don't know,' Cathy said. 'I meant to speak to you and the other partners about an idea that might kill two birds with one stone, after what you've just said. I've been wondering if it would be worth employing a practice pharmacist for a couple of days a week, perhaps more, to take the pressure off the partners and to tidy up our prescribing.'

Brenda smiled and shook her head. 'You'd need to make a good case for it, Cathy. You know how tight the other two are and presumably, we'd not get many incentives from the Health Board.'

'No, I had thought of that too though,' Cathy went on. 'It won't be a popular suggestion but I had wondered about taking on the methadone prescribing for our patients. You know the drug and alcohol psychiatrists have been asking us to help out for years. If we took on the prescription duties: overseeing the patients and managing their medication, the Health Board would offer us a substantial sum to compensate for the inconvenience. I spent a good deal of my psychiatry job on the addictions ward and was in charge of the alcohol detoxers, and I've done countless locums before coming here at the homeless practice in town. All I did there was write methadone scripts, so it doesn't worry me so much.'

'I worry though, Cathy. You've only just come back.'

Cathy rolled her eyes.

'OK, well I'll leave that to you then, but I don't like your chances,' Brenda said. 'You know how Mark goes on about the addicts lowering the tone of the place, and Cathy, you have to understand that we have a duty of care to all of our other patients, not to mention our staff. Start running methadone clinics weekly, and we'll have people hanging about the place and troubling the staff.'

'Not if we went about it the right way, Brenda. There would

have to be some strict rules. We'd never have them in during normal surgery hours perhaps, so as to avoid other patients being hassled. I'd need to think. It's just an idea. I certainly think we'd do well to look out for an in-house pharmacist though. I'll talk to Mark and James about it at the next meeting. Perhaps I'll not mention the methadone clinic just yet though.'

Brenda laughed. 'You know just how to get around them by now, Cathy. James will take a few days to think things over and to weigh up the risks. Mark might need to believe it was his idea for him to really go for it. I'm sure you'll talk them around if that's what you want to do. I suppose now, we just sit and wait for Linda to return and batten down the hatches for the incoming storm.'

8

It was three months to the day since unfortunate Kiean Watt's had died. Life for the rest of Glainkirk had moved on surprisingly easily. There had of course been an inquest. Fraser was asked to attend as a witness. He had never been present at such a horribly formal meeting before and knowing now that the blame might well rest on his shoulders, he prayed that it might proceed without the result that he feared.

On the morning of the inquest, Sarah had stood before him. 'You know you have nothing to concern yourself over,' she reiterated, touching his neck-tie and moving it slightly to the right. 'There,' she said, stepping back. 'You look wonderful. Authoritative, professional and kind.'

Fraser smiled at the girl. 'I hope you're right but they would be within their rights to recommend I see the pharmaceutical disciplinary body after the inquest. It was due to my gullibility that the man died.'

But Sarah shook her head. 'We don't know anything of the kind, Fraser. I understand that the police found out he did cash in the other 'missing' prescription that morning, but he was horribly devious in the way he managed it. Getting a lift some twenty miles south, to collect it two towns away. How you were meant to alert all the pharmacies in a fifty-mile radius is beyond me. And then he raced back to our shop to put on his act, weeping and wailing about having lost his original prescription, when all the while, the methadone had been in his pocket. No Fraser. I don't think they'd blame you in the least. These people are notoriously manipulative.'

Fraser stepped aside and looked at himself in the hall mirror. 'I hope you're right. Still, I might get a caution or a black mark of some sort. It doesn't look good. Any future employers will be put off.'

'Don't worry about that a bit,' Sarah said. 'Get through today and we'll think about that if it ever happens. I'm sure by this afternoon, you'll be walking taller with the weight of this dreadful business off your shoulders. We'll celebrate when it's all over, you'll see.'

At the time, Fraser didn't appreciate how greatly Sarah had steadied him over those dreadful weeks. It seemed that it was the talk of the town, and wherever he went, he overheard Kiean's name being whispered. Sarah had laughed when he said this and had told him that he was imagining it. When she was out and about anyway, nobody seemed especially interested in the affair anymore. Life had moved on and people were now gossiping about one of the teachers up at the high school who had allegedly been carrying on with a six-form pupil.

As it turned out, Sarah was proved correct. The inquest passed and Fraser, although asked a good number of searching questions, emerged without explicit blame. It was one of those tragic events. Circumstances had meant that the drug user had most likely amassed his own methadone, possibly adding to it, another local addict's, and had accidentally overdosed. Sadly, another young life wasted to drugs, the coroner had said. He made several recommendations to safeguard against another accident of the same kind occurring, and that was an end to the whole sorry business. Despite the horror of it all, Fraser attempted to put it behind him.

Three months on, Fraser sat in the small staff room above the shop. Once again, his life had returned to normal and although he still found himself ruminating on the dreadful Kiean debacle, it troubled him far less. Fraser glanced at his reflection in the glass door of the microwave which sat by the kettle. Things were on the up. His relationship with Sarah had progressed over these past weeks. The girl had all but moved in with him and he rarely had to contemplate an evening alone. He promised himself that the mistakes he had made in the past, he would learn from. Adaptability was the key. It was how all great men developed.

And that lunchtime, it really did seem as if his luck had changed. An answer to his prayers, he thought as he looked at the advert in the pharmaceutical journal. He had initially dismissed it as it was almost too good to be true, but now, rereading the page, something in him stirred. Did he really want to see out his days here in a grotty, little shop? Perhaps this was his ticket to greater things. A more fulfilled life as a practice pharmacist, attached to a doctors' surgery. The opening was right on his doorstep and such an opportunity. He placed the journal down on the table, and rocking back on the hind legs of his chair, he smiled at a stain on the ceiling. Perhaps his fortune had finally changed, after all.

Washing up his mug, he wondered how Sarah might feel about him applying for this job. She must surely know that he was wasted in a shop pharmacy. They had spoken a number of times about his restlessness. Sarah had thought it was to be expected, given that he had come from such a hectic job before and she had said he might take a while to adjust to Glainkirk's slower pace of life. Fraser had, at the time, agreed, but now, with this opportunity before him, he felt compelled to apply. Nothing needed to change between him and Sarah. After all, the doctors' surgery was only on the other side of town. It was perfect.

Over the following few days, Fraser's excitement intensified. He spent the evening in Sarah's company. She quietly read a magazine, while he researched his prospective employers. There was a long paragraph in the British Journal for General Practice about Dr James Longmuir. It seemed that over the years he had been on just about every committee there was going. It concerned Fraser to a degree, for it showed that the man was no fool. Fraser secretly hoped that their paths would rarely cross if he did get the job. As for Dr Mark Hope, he had written a number of dry articles for the publication: Guidelines in Practice, mostly about cardiovascular disease. He had also answered a set of personal questions for Pulse Today, in a tongue-in-cheek manner about his love for skiing and champagne. Fraser shook his head in disgust as he read that Dr Hope's greatest turn-off was arrogance. From what he had heard about the man, he was the very epitome of this.

Moving on, Fraser discovered that Dr Cathy Moreland had indeed taken a particular interest in addictions psychiatry, having a short piece published in Psychiatry UK about 'The Silent Addicts;' people she described as being of an older generation and therefore passing under the radar due to their apparent ability to continue leading stable lives without the disruptive behaviour of many of their younger counterparts. Fraser read the article with interest and moved on to other points of note; her article in GP Guidelines on the psychological impact of cervical cancer, and a few other bits of family planning business. It seemed that none of the GPs were on social media, or if they were, their accounts were private. Finally, he moved on to Linda, the GP retainer, who now seemed to work as a locum of the practice. Linda had published nothing as far as he could see, but her Twitter account was brimming with self-help quotes and messages of endorsement for suicide awareness days and help-lines. Fraser thought it possible that she had either lost someone close to mental health issues, or she herself had suffered from a bout of depression in the past.

This was all food for thought, and when he turned to Sarah who had returned from the kitchen, having made him and herself a cup of tea, he smiled up at the girl.

'It all sounds impressive,' she said after he gave her a precis. 'They're sure to be pleased that you've done your homework. I don't think you should hesitate. Write the application off and send it.'

His cover letter, after much revision, was as professional as he could make it without sounding too stiff. He briefly explained his past employment, his strength in management as demonstrated by his current appointment, and his keen interest in staying in the area due to the strong bonds with staff and clients alike. He made special mention of his interest in the treatment of addictions. His attached CV had not taken as long for he had revised it only the previous year and it required the smallest of amendments to take into account his current employment. As referees, he gave his past two employers, knowing that what they had said before had earned him the job in the shop already, so must surely be good enough to do the same for a GP practice. He had already sent both supervisors a friendly email explaining his situation and excitement at having seen this new job advertised. Hopefully, his efforts would prove enough.

By ten in the evening, the thing was done and Fraser lolled

back in his chair, satisfied. It would be posted in the morning and then it was out of his hands. Once he had the interview date, for which he must surely get shortlisted, he would once again begin his revision and preparation.

To Fraser's astonishment, only four days later, he received a reply in the post; an invitation to interview the following week, on Tuesday at eleven o'clock. Fraser had little time to think, but he telephoned and confirmed that he would be delighted to attend, and then began the work to secure the job he had now become convinced was his alone.

∼

'YOU'VE SPOKEN about your interest in the management of drug misuse patients, Fraser. I wonder if you can tell us a little more?' Dr Longmuir asked.

Fraser shifted in his seat. 'Of course,' he said, spreading his hands wide, and maintaining eye contact with the older man. 'I'm sure you're all too aware that in a town such as Glainkirk, as with many other places, we can hardly avoid the issue of drug abuse. In my experience, in the community, I've built up something of a rapport with these people. We, as a point of contact, see our customers, no matter what their circumstances, as equals. Almost like family, particularly the regular ones.'

The younger male GP called Hope, who had clasped Fraser's hand far too tightly when he initially shook it, snorted. Fraser looked across in surprise, but he hastily returned to the other doctor.

'Yes, I've placed it high on our agenda, to be as community-spirited as possible. No problem should be suffered alone, and many of these people lack the regularity of a stable relationship with someone reliable.'

'We're looking for a pharmacist, not a befriender,' Dr Hope said.

Fraser turned and smiled, but the GP only raised his eyebrows and refolded his arms across his chest. Fraser clasped his hands tightly in his lap. 'Of course. I simply meant to demonstrate my eagerness to act as a reliable member of your team. As it happens, I do have a genuine interest in helping people ...'

'Can I ask about the inquest?'

Fraser's twitching hands froze. His eyes darted around the room and finally settled on the only female GP, Dr Moreland, who, having shot her partner a withering look, smiled encouragingly at Fraser.

Fraser swallowed. 'The inquest?' he asked.

'Yes. Surely you can't have forgotten so soon. The young drug addict who was on your books. I believe some of the blame was placed on your pharmacy?'

Fraser looked at Dr Hope who now smiled at him nastily.

'An innocent question,' the GP continued. 'Of course, if you'd prefer not to ...'

'Oh, I don't mind,' Fraser stammered, and then gathering himself, he took a deep breath and forced his shoulders down. 'Look,' he said, scanning the faces of all the GPs. 'I'll admit that I've been naive in the past, perhaps. The inquest was terribly upsetting to me, as it happens. I felt a good deal of responsibility for the man's death, but the coroner, as you no doubt recall yourself,' Fraser said, beginning to warm to his cause, 'He said that although lessons could indeed be learned, no blame could be attributed to any one agency. Ultimately, although I deeply regret the whole thing, I feel as front-line technicians, we are inevitably going to find ourselves in muddy water at times. Perhaps that's why I was so keen to come and work for you. A team is very important. Team-spirit, and a nurturing, non-judge-mental work environment. That's what I hope to find here, and contribute to, if you're looking for it.'

'Thank you for being so frank, Fraser,' Dr Moreland said, glancing at her colleague before he could interrupt. 'I think we all appreciate your honesty. That's just the sort of ethos we too, hope to achieve.'

9

'There seems little doubt about who we should choose,' Dr Mark Hope said, leaning forward at the large desk in the boardroom.

The three GPs had been seated for the past two hours in a line along the polished table, with Brenda positioned to the side, so that she could pass the candidates paperwork and greet them at the door. They had shortlisted only two from the twelve applications they had received. Cathy and her partners had spent the past few evenings going over the CVs and composing questions. Each partner would ask a total of three questions and Brenda had been told that she might interject any comments throughout the interviews also.

The two candidates had arrived an hour apart, but the initial one had taken longer to interview, so the second had been shown into the library across the corridor to wait. He had shaken up the plans a good deal, however, waiving the initially planned questions with a promise to answer anything they wished but requesting if they accommodate a short presentation that he had prepared. Dr Hope had been a bit haughty about this suggestion, somewhat riled by the audacity of it and had snorted, as was his habit, but it seemed that the young pharmacist had persuaded even him in the end. The presentation had indeed been well-rehearsed and meticulously planned. His questions following this, had been answered with intelligence and humility, in spite of Mark's truculence.

'He was certainly convincing,' Brenda said.

'Perhaps too much,' James said. 'I've seen many like him before. He's intelligent, I'll give you that. Imagine arriving with a PowerPoint presentation on why we should employ him. I've never seen it done before. I wonder if he'll bore quickly though.'

'It was impressive all the same,' Cathy interjected. 'He'd done his homework for sure. When he mentioned his interest in cardiovascular disease management, Mark, and then quoted the paper you had had a hand in writing, I nearly spat my coffee out. Very clever, and he had done his research on all of us. I know what you mean though, James. You're worried about the butterfly factor, aren't you?'

James nodded. 'It never looks good, does it? How many years and how many changes?'

Brenda ran her finger down the candidate's CV. 'Over the last five years, he's been in three positions. Granted, it looks like he has shifted around, but he did explain that too, didn't he?'

'I suppose so,' James assented. 'He wanted to gain experience in all areas of pharmacology. The referees might be of some interest if we're really tipping in his favour. Brenda, would it be yourself that would ring?'

Brenda nodded. 'If that's what you're wanting, I'll do it,' she said. 'I wondered myself about the young girl. I know that she doesn't have half the experience but she would fit in with the team far better. I'm just trying to picture him day-in-day-out, I suppose and I can't quite see it. The other concern is hours. He wasn't keen on the proposed number we had suggested and wanted more. I guess we could adjust as needs be.'

Mark shook his head. 'The girl was too airy-fairy,' he said shortly. 'You saw how she interviewed. Granted she knew her stuff but she'll be pregnant within two years and mugging us for maternity pay. No, I'm not having her.'

'You're essentially ruling out half the candidates then,' Cathy said. 'Forgive me, Mark but it is totally sexist and as it happens, fundamentally in contradiction to employment law to rule someone out in case they might have a baby.'

Mark snorted. 'Getting twitchy, Cathy? I hope you're not planning on it anytime soon. We could well do without the hassle of finding a bloody locum.'

Cathy's face burned. She glanced at James, who was shaking his head. 'I find that really offensive, Mark,' she said. 'What sort of a way is that to speak to someone?'

'Just joking. Don't get on your high horse. I'm only saying what everyone else is afraid to,' he smiled.

James raised a hand. 'Don't rise to it,' he said quietly to her. 'Back to this Fraser chap. I rather liked the way he responded to Mark's question about the death of that young heroin addict earlier in the year. He didn't make excuses or get defensive about the thing. He admitted that he had been too naive. I thought that was quite telling about his character. Are we in agreement then, that his references are at least worth checking now? Depending on what comes from it, we'll make a further decision. Does that sound reasonable? I know we only shortlisted the two candidates, but we can always go back a step and look through the other CVs if he's not right.'

'I'll ask around a bit and see if I can hear anything about him, although, my decision is already made,' Mark said.

'I think that's a good plan,' Cathy said. 'You are both still happy with the idea in principle? I really think it's the only way forward. You heard what both the applicants said about their expertise in tidying up prescription patterns and taking the weight of the chronic disease prescribing from us. The number of hours saved would make the appointment pay for itself in freed up man-hours within no time. There have been too many mistakes recently. Simple prescribing errors and other things that indicate we're too stretched.'

James smiled. 'Yes, I do agree,' he said. 'I know I was the most reticent about the whole idea but I think we need to move with the times. Many other practices are taking on in-house specialists. It saddens me that we're becoming supervisors, merely consultants in undifferentiated care, triaging our patients and directing them elsewhere. Thirty years ago, I would have been the person to ask about chronic disease management. Now we have nurses to do that, and they do it very well. They see our patients and follow them through their journey, altering medication and we simply sign the prescriptions. I suppose the pharmacist is much the same.'

'You're getting old,' Mark said. 'Cathy's right. It had to be done. We're a bloody mess at the moment. We're never going to meet our targets this year, what with Cathy being off those months. That silly girl Linda hasn't coded a single significant illness since she's been here. God knows why she's still with us, other than the fact that we can't get anyone else. Even the nurses aren't faultless. Irene, although I know is very good, failed to bring to my attention a post CABG the other week. It's a sure way to drop revenue if we balls up that sort of thing.'

'Good grief, Mark,' Brenda said forcibly. 'It seems you've shot down just about everyone in the practice in one fell swoop today. Can we stick to the matter in hand for now instead of going off at a tangent again?'

Mark chuckled. 'You're for it next, Brenda. Have you been through the running costs and overheads yet? I need to meet with you at some point and discuss things?'

'Not now, Mark,' Brenda said, like a mother might to her wearisome child.

Mark turned to Cathy. 'I know it's not your area of expertise, all this money talk. You're too busy with your sexual health nonsense and your alcoholics, which to be fair are a small proportion of the practice's income.'

Cathy grimaced. 'Mark, I see the hypertensives and diabetics just as you do. I do that on top of the coils and contraceptive implants. If you're intimating that I haven't pulled my weight in the past, then I think it's a bit unfair. I seem to remember when you took me on, that you were overjoyed to have a female to do all of the women's health, and as for the addiction psychiatry, you were one of the first to hand over your heart-sinks when I arrived. You know I see the majority of the drug addicts and alcoholics now?'

'I thought we agreed that Cathy was taking a step back from all of this anyway,' James said. 'We're trying to support one another and Cathy's just returned to work. Have a bit of tact, Mark, for goodness sake.'

Cathy smiled. 'I don't mind in the least, James. I won't use my ill-health as an excuse and like Mark has mentioned before, so crudely, if I am deemed fit to practice, then I should be allowed to do so. If you want to know, I did have another idea about practice revenue, seeing as we're discussing it now. I think you're putting all your attention onto the wrong side of things as it happens. All this talk about the cardiovascular patients, but we have another subset right in front of us and they might provide us with far more lucrative business and set the practice apart from many of the others in the area.'

Mark snorted. 'My God, Cathy. What have the psychiatrist done with the old you? You used to balk at the talk of money when you first started and here you are now, coming up with a masterplan to save us from ruin.'

Cathy's face burned.

'Oh, don't look embarrassed. I like the new side to you. It's much more engaging. Go on then, what's your idea?'

'Well hear me out and don't jump down my throat before I explain,' Cathy said and glanced across at Brenda. The practice manager raised her eyebrows. 'Methadone prescriptions,' Cathy said and let it hang.

James was already shaking his head and Mark didn't look that keen either but at least Mark, with the promise of revenue, would give her a chance.

'Go on,' he said.

'It seems the right time,' Cathy began. 'I know we've discussed it briefly before in the past and rejected the idea, but the psychiatrists have been emailing me again since I've come back, making the request that we at least sit in on their clinics and see how things are done. My thought was that we could do that; the new pharmacist and perhaps myself. Then, if we were still in agreement, we might take on just a handful of the methadones, with the psychiatrists' support, of course. I would have to come up with a plan, I know, to avoid practice disruption. I don't want our staff, or our other patients, to feel uncomfortable either.' Cathy looked across at James. 'It was just an idea. The money, you see? We might make a good deal from taking on the service as it's high-risk.'

James nodded but still didn't look happy.

'You're conveniently forgetting your own little indiscretion, Cathy,' Mark said quietly. 'It hardly seems appropriate that you of all people should be dealing with this kind of thing.'

Cathy felt herself go cold. 'No, no, it's alright,' she said to James, who had raised a hand. 'No, he's only speaking the truth. I agree, Mark, that I have a good deal to prove. I hope that as time goes on, you'll trust me more and more.'

Brenda met her gaze and nodded.

'I've seen the drug store,' Cathy went on. 'The new procedures in place. The locks on the drawers. I think you were right to do it. But I can promise you that I do not intend on slipping up. It was due to the hypomanic state I was in, that it happened at all. I didn't want to discuss my own health at a practice meeting. It's excruciating enough talking about it at all, but I can promise you this. I will be taking my psychiatrist's advice from now on. Forget about the methadone prescribing. Forget all of that. I just want things to go back to the way they were. Please, Mark. James? If we're going to continue working as a practice, you have to trust me.'

There was a long pause. Cathy looked from one partner to the other.

'That's where you're wrong though, Cathy,' Mark said quietly. 'We don't 'have to trust you' at all. You have to earn our trust. Don't for a minute think that I don't sympathise, because I do, but you stole. You took co-codamol from the store for your own use. You came into work drunk and you swore at one of the patients. I know you were unwell. Nobody is questioning that fact. I'm sorry, you've been ill. But it will take me a good deal of time to come to terms with what happened, even if James can waive it.'

Cathy looked at James. 'We'll chat about it later, Cathy,' he said sadly.

Brenda, looking pensive, spoke. 'Right, is everyone happy for me to bring the meeting to an end?' she asked. 'I'll ring round this afternoon and do a bit of digging on this Fraser chap?'

The three GPs murmured their agreement.

Cathy felt utterly beaten. The conversation took its toll on her and that night, despite her racing thoughts, going over and over what Mark had said, she collapsed from sheer weariness and fell asleep.

10

'Time for a quick confab?' Brenda asked, looking into Cathy's room. 'I'll grab James and we might go through to Mark?'

Cathy, who had just finished dealing with a rather complicated patient, sighed and stretched, raising her arms high up above her head. 'Yup,' she yawned. 'I'll come. Is it about the pharmacist?'

But Brenda had already moved on to James's room.

Cathy got up. She felt refreshed having slept so soundly the night before. Perhaps the meeting yesterday had cleared the air. She had said what she needed to say and she felt lighter for it. She could only do what she could, she decided. The rest was up to Mark and James. They must make their own decision about her, themselves. She couldn't continue begging for their forgiveness forever.

'Mark, we're having an impromptu meeting,' Brenda said, looking around the edge of the door.

Brenda went into the room ahead, and James and Cathy followed. Mark, clearly not expecting the visit, walked to the sink in the corner of his room, and spat something out. Licking his lips, he then smiled at the three of them. 'Well, what is it? We've got a visit each and we need to be getting on.'

Cathy looked around her. She rarely came into Mark's room, but it didn't surprise her to see that it was the very picture of order. Minimal, with desk, two chairs and examination couch, but on the wall, he had chosen a seascape. Stormy waves leapt up, tossing a lone boat towards jagged rocks. A rather odd choice, Cathy thought, but knowing Mark it would be by some famous, local painter or be something suitably ostentatious.

The room was the reverse of hers being on the other side of the corridor. There was a sink by the window, just as she had. Beside it, Cathy saw, sat a neat line of universal containers, what looked like a bottle of mouthwash, and a hand sanitiser. He liked things to be just so. That was Mark all over. The desk in front of him was arranged with careful thought too. The computer screen and keyboard were positioned at the corner and his most frequently required clinical equipment lined up in a neat row: stethoscope, digital thermometer and diagnostic set.

Brenda had closed the door behind them now and finding herself without a chair, she leaned on the examination couch at the side of the room. 'I've been digging, as requested,' she said. 'Fraser Edwards is apparently well respected in pharmaceutical circles.'

James sat with his arms folded across his chest. 'Any negatives?' he asked. 'There must be something.'

'Bit of a loner,' Brenda said. 'I had a good long chat with his first referee. He used to supervise Fraser in the hospital and he intimated that as a young pharmacist, Fraser was a bit aloof with the other staff.'

'He'll fit in fine here then,' Mark said. 'As long as he keeps his head down and works, I don't care if he's stand-offish. Do we really want some jolly buffoon working for us? We're hiring him for his expertise, not his razer-sharp wit.'

'What about you, Mark? Weren't you going to dig a bit?' Brenda asked.

'Not had a minute to myself.'

Cathy had seen him and Tracy leaving the practice together arm in arm the night before. She assumed that the young nurse was keeping Mark occupied.

'I can still ask around if we're really that afraid of making a decision,' he went on, 'but I don't think we'll find better than this fellow, and bear in mind, he's actually from the area too. No,' Mark continued. 'Cathy was right. I wish I had thought of it myself before. I've already got a long list of things for him to get started on. The first thing is sorting out the pigs-ear the rest of the team have made of the computer coding.'

Cathy rolled her eyes.

'Why does it have to be like this?' James said, shaking his head. 'Can't we finish on a good note without passing judgement? Time and again you turn it around and make a dig at someone.'

Mark snorted and turned disdainfully from his partner.

'No, really Mark,' James continued, stepping forward and growing in animation. 'While it's the four of us here now, I'm telling you that this has to stop. This bullish behaviour has gone on long enough. I had Bert in my room this morning. Poor man was beside himself.' James turned to Cathy to explain. 'Apparently, Mark took it upon himself to give the old boy an informal warning. And without speaking to us first,' James said angrily turning once again to his other partner.

Mark shrugged and smiled. 'He's not fit for employment chaps, and that's the honest truth. He's meant to be the practice handyman. Why we're paying him a wage still, is beyond me. We're not a bloody charity, Brenda. I know we all pity the old man because his wife's ill, but he's next to useless. He's still not cleaned the graffiti on that bloody sign out the front. It's hardly much to ask. We've been carrying deadweight for far too long in this place. Time to fell the old, dry wood and allow the young saplings a chance to thrive, wouldn't you say, James?'

Brenda quickly spoke. 'I'll see the sign gets fixed. In future, I'd rather things of this kind came through me.'

Mark snorted again.

'That's not all,' James continued and Cathy turned in disbelief. 'I thought long and hard about what was said yesterday at the meeting,' James continued. 'The way you spoke to Cathy was indefensible. As a senior partner of this practice, Mark, I have to warn you that you are on very shaky ground. Some of yesterday's tirade might have amounted to intimidation. Cathy would be within her right to put in a formal complaint to the GMC. We're meant to be behaving in a supportive manner, not tearing each other to shreds.'

Cathy looked sideways. James's mouth was set in a hard line and his eyes were filled with an emotion that Cathy had not seen before.

Nobody spoke.

'Quite,' Brenda said hurriedly. 'As far as this Fraser's character is concerned, I think myself that it is a minor point. The hospital employment that mentioned it was a good three years ago and he has since worked elsewhere. The more recent referee had no issues at all. Apparently, he is very well-liked by his staff. The area manager described him as humble, and good with his staff, which might show that he has matured.'

'Well?' Mark said, looking up at the wall clock behind them. 'Are we offering him the job then? I need to get on, Brenda. I've got a visit out in the bloody sticks and it's my afternoon off.'

'Everyone?' Brenda asked.

'I'm happy enough,' Cathy said.

James nodded too, but refused to look at Mark.

When they dispersed, Cathy walked past James's room

before heading out on her house visit. Entering, as the door was ajar, she found him rummaging in his doctor's bag.

'James?' she said. 'I just wanted to check that you really were alright with all of this stuff with the pharmacist. I know initially, you were the least keen on the idea.'

James, who had now straightened up, smiled at Cathy. 'I've missed having you around these last few months,' he said. 'I'm fine, Cathy. But I appreciate the sentiment really, I do. Let's see how this pharmacy chap gets on. His contract can be terminated at any time if it doesn't feel right. How are you feeling yourself, by the way? We never do seem to get a chance to talk. I hope Mark hasn't upset you in saying what he did?'

Cathy smiled. 'I'm alright, James. Really. It's good to be back. This place is like a bit of a leveller. I'm just relieved to get another chance.'

Cathy headed out on her visit. The constant battle between her partners concerned her deeply. Mark had been offensive and out-right rude these last few weeks. He seemed to be doing his utmost to antagonised James. She wondered if he was actually trying to goad the man. Her thoughts moved to her gentle, senior partner and she recalled the odd expression he had when he looked at Mark. The set mouth and cold stare were quite frightening. Cathy disliked being sensational but without a doubt, she knew that she had seen pure hatred in James's eyes at that moment.

11

Shortly after eight in the morning, Fraser left his smart little house and drove the five minutes to his new place of work. The doctors' surgery was not quite central to the town, but on the western outskirts. Opposite, however, a small line of rundown shops had been established to serve the residents living this far out. The local high school, an expansive eyesore of boxed subunits, joined by supposedly-modern, glass walkways, dwarfed the doctors' surgery in the foreground. Fraser had in the past, rarely required to drive this way. His own house was on the Langholm Road and it was in this direction that he tended to travel for any of the larger retailers or amenities.

As he indicated and turned in, Fraser felt a sense of excitement rise within him. The GP surgery was newer than many of the buildings in the area. Newer and more promising. It's red, low-pitched sloping roofs could be picked out from afar, now that he knew to look for them. Its walls, pebble-dashed white, represented a clean sheet to the optimistic pharmacist. A clean sheet and a new beginning.

Fraser parked his car carefully on the far side of the carpark so that he might enjoy the approach to his new adventure slowly. Crossing the tarmac, softened by borders of rose bushes, he swung his leather briefcase. He had bought it the previous week and although it contained very little, he thought it gave him the right air of authority. He noticed that a couple of the ground-floor windows facing out onto the carpark were ajar. Through one of the blinds he caught a glimpse of a face watching him, and he raised a hand and smiled. The face, who he thought belonged to a woman, disappeared. Undeterred, Fraser continued.

At the doorway, his passage was momentarily obstructed by a grey-haired man dressed in dark, rather dusty overalls. The man stood over a bucket of soapy water and was poised with a dripping cloth, in front of a gold plaque on the side of the building. Fraser assumed that he was simply polishing the sign, for as he drew closer, he saw that it was a list of the doctors who worked there. The man, only hearing him when he was almost upon him, shuffled slowly out of his way. Continuing on through, Fraser entered the front reception.

The building was bright and airy, with the waiting room ahead offering its occupants a high, glass ceiling. The area was partially concealed by a line of enormous house plants, the sort that grew like indoor trees within their terracotta pots. As Fraser looked further, from between the leaves, he saw a door along the opposite wall in the distance, open and one of the doctors he had met at his interview, emerge and call a name. The patient who had been summoned, got up slowly and crossed the waiting area with a limp. Fraser watched until the door closed behind them. He turned then and smiled at one of the girls behind the reception desk.

'Fraser Edwards,' he said.

She misunderstood and peering at her computer screen, asked what time his appointment was and with who.

'No, no. I'm the new pharmacist,' he began to explain, but at that moment, the practice manager, Brenda, who he had already met several times before, emerged from a door at the side of the reception area and led him through to his new office, which was at the back of the building in a different wing to the consulting rooms.

'I hope you'll be comfortable here,' she said. 'It's all new to us too, you know. We've never had a pharmacist so we weren't quite sure what you'd need to get started.'

Fraser looked around. It was sparsely furnished with a desk, phone, computer and chair. There was a large filing cabinet in the corner and bookshelves on the wall above the desk also. Fraser crossed the room and picked up a large ring-binder and read the title: 'Chronic Disease Management. Coding and Quality Guidelines.'

'Dry, I know,' Brenda laughed. 'That'll have been Mark. He said he was leaving it out for you. I think he's keen to see what you can do with the cardiovascular patients. Don't worry about that now though. There's plenty more things to see to, to get you up to speed before jumping to Mark's tune. I've allocated this morning to go through the computer system, if it suits? Can I get you a coffee before though, and I'll let you settle yourself in?'

Fraser turned and smiled. 'Coffee would be perfect.'

When he was alone, he looked around his office and grinned. He was sure he would be happy here. Already he felt greatly at home. The doctors wouldn't know what had hit them when he got started on things.

Over those first few weeks in his new job, there was little to mar Fraser's happiness. With his finances in good order, and his relationship with Sarah going from strength to strength, he felt on top of the world. He had made the right decision; of that, he was certain and how proud his late father would have been if he had here to see it. The more time he spent in his new office, slowly reading over the documents that he must commit to memory, and preparing suggestions to assist the doctors in their work, he felt he had finally found his calling. This was where he was meant to be. He wasn't some shop pharmacist at all. He saw this now. What kind of a life would that have been? Feigning interest in the concerns of the worried young mothers who brought in their children for him to see. Explaining, and then re-explaining how the old dears should apply their ointments. It seemed a lifetime ago now and a miracle that he had stuck it as long as he had.

As well as enjoying his new employment a good deal, Fraser began to become slowly better acquainted with a few of his colleagues. He was a little reticent at first and rather shy of going up to the coffee room at busy times, but soon his nervousness left him and he felt more at ease.

'So, you're permanent then?' the nurse asked conspiratorially. She had sidled up beside him in the coffee room and Fraser was momentarily taken aback.

He looked at the girl and smiled. 'For now, anyway,' he answered and placing his coffee cup down, stretched out a hand. 'Fraser. New practice pharmacist,' he explained.

The nurse took his hand and shook it. 'Tracy. Exhausted practice nurse,' she said, and did a charming little curtsey.

Fraser laughed.

'So, how are you finding it then? Have you had to deal with the ogre yet?' Tracy teased, as she moved around him, preparing herself a cup of coffee.

'I take it you mean Dr Hope? I heard he can be a bit tricky.' Fraser laughed.

The nurse giggled. 'Oh, Mark would just love to hear that. He's not really an ogre but he likes to test people. Especially new people. He did that with me at the start, took me in his room and absolutely grilled me, and look at us now.' The girl raised her left hand and the diamond twinkled in the strip light above. 'His divorce isn't through, but he's informally asked. I'll have a word if you like, before he tries to maul you?'

Fraser blushed beetroot red. 'I had no idea,' he said hurriedly. 'I must apologise. Please don't bother saying a thing. I'd not want that at all. I'm sure he's not as bad as you make out.'

'Well, Fraser, was it? Perhaps I'll catch you later then,' Tracy said as she moved to the door with her coffee. 'Unlike Mark, I don't like to upset the newbies. I'm really quite friendly as it happens. Some people say I'm far too friendly,' she confided.

Fraser smiled and looked at the ground. He was rather taken aback by the girl's unashamed flirtation, but Tracy was playing it cool once more, and sliding the end of her ponytail over her shoulder, she went, leaving Fraser in the coffee room alone.

During the second week of employment, Fraser suffered his first blow. It had, up until then, been plain sailing. He had found the work quite quick to pick up once he had managed to nego- tiate the passwords and intricacies of the computer system. When he was confident doing this, he found that he had all the information he required to begin auditing all of the areas that the GPs had allowed to slip. Their cardiovascular patients had been thus far managed appallingly, and he had barely a chance to look at the type-two diabetics. It was following a preliminary run-through of the figures that he felt assured enough to approach the dreaded Dr Mark Hope, who he had only spoken to briefly as with the other GPs. He had thought a good deal about what Tracy had said to him and the previous night he had sat up late trying to memorise all of the facts and figures that might impress the infamous GP.

Tapping on the consulting room door, having checked with Brenda that the doctor might be free, he entered at Mark's request. He was sitting at his desk and although Mark knew Fraser was there, he did not look up.

'So sorry to interrupt you when you're busy. I had wanted ...'

The doctor raised a hand and continued to read whatever had his attention.

Fraser stood stupidly for some minutes, growing ever impatient and cursing the cheek of the man. When Mark finally looked up, he smiled rather cruelly.

'Settled in, Brenda tells me. Good. Sit then,' and the doctor indicated a chair.

'I just wanted to say before anything else that I've been so impressed at how well the GPs have documented ...'

But Mark raised his hand again and Fraser tailed off. Not used to being dealt with in such a manner, the young pharmacist sat open-mouthed.

'Cut the crap,' Mark said curtly. 'We both know that's what it is, after all. We're up to our necks in it. Half the hypertensives haven't been coded correctly. It's been a bloody battle for me, trying to teach both new and old doctors how to do it. Save going through the lot myself, I couldn't do much more. Ah. I am speaking,' he continued when Fraser went to interrupt.

Fraser's face reddened. He sat as if turned to stone, but all the while his mind was seething.

'Anyway,' Dr Hope continued, leaning back in his chair. 'We don't need to worry ourselves any further. Along with the rest of the prescribing errors, you're going to sort it, I hear.'

Fraser swallowed and when it seemed clear that the doctor was allowing him to speak, he did so. 'We seem to have got off on the wrong foot,' Fraser said, disarmingly. 'I came in here to discuss the cardiovascular patients and to say that I had been impressed with your attempts to deal with a difficult clinical area. I appreciate that it's been tough, but you're right. I am here to help sort things out. I hope we can do it together, as a team. That's ultimately what I want.'

The doctor snorted. 'How much are we paying you, Fraser?'

Fraser didn't answer.

'Too much if you think I'm wading through all of the diabetics with you. Together as a team? I heard you weren't much of a team player in the past anyway in your previous appointments.'

Fraser gulped audibly and felt for his tie.

'Don't look so horrified, man. We do perform background checks on our prospective staff, you know. You run along and get started on the type-twos. I'll be delighted to discuss the results of your reviews just as soon as you've done them.'

Fraser got up stiffly. His legs felt shaky and he wasn't sure what on earth he should say. He had no idea what Mark had discovered about him. He didn't dare ask.

'Oh, and Fraser,' Mark said, now returning to his reading. 'If you think I'm a fool, you've another thing coming. Keep your hands-off Tracy, there's a good lad. She's cute but she's well out of your league.'

Fraser wanted to reply, but the doctor waved a hand to dismiss him.

Making his way back to his office, Fraser's mind was frantic. How horribly unfair to accuse him of carrying on with Tracy. Goodness knows what the man had heard, but had he been given the chance, he might have explained that he had done nothing wrong. He had a girlfriend after all and had no interest in Tracy. He ran over his conversation with the nurse and wondered how the girl must have warped his words and relayed them back to her lover. Fraser shook his head bitterly at the unfairness of it all. Oh God, what a mess. And what had Dr Hope meant about him not being a team player? What did that even mean? Was it something to do with Kiean Watts? But surely that had been cleared up. Fraser considered the man's words and the menacing emphasis he had put on them. Was it simply all bluff and hot air? He recalled what Tracy had said, although he would no longer trust that girl or allow himself to be seen alone with her now. But hadn't she said that it was Mark's way, to grill new people when they arrived?

Throughout the rest of the day, Fraser repeatedly tried to dismiss the conversation as nonsense. All that week, in fact, the pharmacist, who had been so joyful in his new employment, and so full of ideas and vigour, became more suspicious of those around him, seeing enemies everywhere.

12

As far as Cathy was aware, the GPs were in agreement that they had made the right choice in employing the new pharmacist. So far, she had already seen an improvement in many of the repeat prescriptions. Fraser had taken the time to go through the more expensive medications, and most commonly prescribed ones, and where appropriate had changed the prescription over to the cheaper generic brand. This must surely have had a massive impact on their budget already, Cathy thought. It was such a simple thing too, but none of them had had the time or energy to attend to it before now. Cathy had also seen that Fraser was drawing up guidelines for their chronic disease management registers. This would mean that all the doctors would be singing from the same hymn sheet, so to speak. It was astute of the pharmacist and Cathy recognised that the effort to get things in such good order so quickly, must not have come easily.

'Are you coming up?' James asked, popping his head around her door. 'I heard the nurses heading already.'

Cathy leaned back in her chair. She had been looking over plans for the methadone clinic. These past few weeks, she had drawn up a number of suggestions but had not thus far, felt it wise to discuss them with the team. Mark's argument that he was unable to trust her with such a project weighed heavy on her mind, but driven on by a real desire to do good, she quietly looked into the matter. She discussed it briefly with the new pharmacist to test the water. He had seemed keen to help her, but even he had agreed that perhaps now wasn't the time, given that he had so much to get in order first.

'Coming,' she replied to James. 'Is Mark back yet? I saw he had a late call.'

James shrugged.

Things still weren't good between the two partners. James had all but ignored his other partner following his outburst that day. Whenever their paths crossed, there was an awkwardness. Mark seemed oblivious to the matter but James would make any attempt to excuse himself from the conversation and retreat to his room. Cathy knew that things couldn't go on like this. She had endeavoured to speak to James about it, but he was obviously still too annoyed.

Pushing back her chair, Cathy got up and together they climbed the stairs to the meeting room. Brenda and the nurses, along with Linda were all there. Cathy and James took their usual seats and then Mark came in looking slightly wind-swept.

'Late call,' he explained breathlessly. One of yours, Cathy I'm afraid. Not good. Mrs Davidson on the Jedburgh Road. I'll give you a rundown after the meeting. She'll need a follow-up visit first thing in the morning.'

Cathy nodded. 'Put it in the book, Mark. I'm doing house visits tomorrow anyway.'

It had taken the other two GPs a full month to allow her to take on-call sessions again. Cathy, although exhausted at times, felt that she was really getting back to full speed once more. Her appointments were now the same length as Mark's and James's.

The only difference since before she had gone off sick now, was that she had to see her psychiatrist six-weekly as a requirement by occupational health. Cathy had no qualms about doing this if it meant she could continue to practice medicine. The last meeting with her doctor had gone well. He had been surprised at how swiftly she had returned to full-time work, and had warned her that this might in the future have to change if the stress began to build up once more. The antipsychotic medication seemed to be working well and as she had had no relapses despite the pressure of returning to work, he had been hopeful about her prognosis.

'Before Fraser arrives,' Brenda said, 'I just wanted to give folks a quick head-up. We have an add-on coming tomorrow I believe. A GP trainee who Mark will be supervising for the period of a month. It's out of the ordinary circumstances but if he gets on well, he might come back as a registrar with us next year.'

'Where's he come from, Brenda? Why wasn't he with the rest of the trainees when they came for their induction days earlier?' Cathy asked.

Brenda turned to Mark.

'I'm doing a favour for an old medical-school friend of mine,' Mark said with a smile. 'His son, that's the lad coming, has had a bit of a change of heart. He was all for renal medicine and I think my pal said he had got his part-one of the MRCP, but I think he's crashed out and is looking to change to general practice. Quite smart, so I believe. I don't think he'll be any trouble. We'll do the usual with him. I'll have him shadowing me and then he'll perhaps sit in with the other GPs to see their consulting styles also, if that's alright. Brenda's going to draw up a timetable for him and he'll be in with the nurses one day. I'll speak to the district nurses and the pharmacist also, just so he can see how things work around here.'

'Where's he going to go, Brenda? We're short on rooms,' Cathy asked.

'He'll not need one for now Cathy. It's really just an introductory thing. He'll share Mark's room. Everyone alright with that?'

The GPs and nurses nodded.

Fraser was the last to arrive. He smiled around the group and apologised for keeping them waiting.

'No, we're indebted to you really, Fraser,' Brenda said. 'You've taken on a lot as it is, without this also.' Brenda turned and addressed the room. 'Folks, Fraser has prepared a little presentation for us, as we agreed. I think this is a good opportunity to get everyone together on a regular basis so we'll try to make it the norm, perhaps a monthly educational slot. I don't expect Fraser to do all the work. Maybe the GPs can take it in turns to present a case or a topic of personal interest.'

At this, Mark rolled his eyes. 'Jesus, Brenda. I thought it was just a one-off. As if we haven't got enough to do,' he said, but Brenda chose to ignore the comment and smiling brightly, she turned again to Fraser.

'Now, are we ready?'

Fraser looked around the room, his eyes unable to settle on one individual. While they had been talking, he had gone to the computer at the far end of the table, quickly slotted a memory stick into the machine and found what he was after. Now that all eyes were on him, the pharmacist clicked the mouse with a flourish. He looked up from the screen over which he had been bent and for the first time since entering the room, beamed around at them all.

'Overdoses: Accidental and Deliberate, and Common Poisons,' he said with satisfaction. 'I chose a fun topic to start off with, because I know the chronic disease management stuff is a little heavy.'

Fraser was an amiable person and very boyish in manner. If

he had noticed Mark's rudeness, he was too professional to show it. Cathy had already got the impression that Mark disliked the pharmacist. She watched Mark as Fraser spoke and saw the GP frowning. She had no idea why. Fraser was clearly an asset to the practice and since he had arrived, he had probably saved them a lot of money. Cathy had been impressed when he had also enthusiastically suggested 'educational slots' during practice meetings.

The presentation lasted approximately fifteen minutes. Fraser had prepared a variety of slides with plenty of illustrations and not too much text. Cathy, who sometimes found herself wearied by the number of educational talks she had to attend, found the presentation both entertaining and informative. He had obviously gone to great trouble to go through the past records and summarise all of the attempted overdoses that the practice had seen during the last five years. He then presented a couple of slides on domestic and agricultural poisons and the potential risks of each of these too. Even Brenda asked a couple of questions at the end, which was something she rarely did.

'Well Fraser, on behalf of everyone, thank you very much. Really informative,' Brenda concluded. 'We can have a chat later in the week about the next meeting's topic. Everyone happy?'

The three GPs smiled their thanks and Fraser promised to distribute print-outs that he had produced, detailing the presentation, to the clinical team in the morning.

The following day, Brenda introduced Cathy to their new temporary team member, the son of Mark's friend from university. Although Cathy hated to label people, she found herself taking an instant dislike to the man, thinking that he came across as slightly too blasé.

'This is Tom,' Brenda said to Cathy.

The man who was carrying a rucksack shifted the bag further up his shoulder and went to shake Cathy's hand.

'Alright?' he said.

His handshake was clammy and slightly loose.

'Dr Moreland,' Cathy introduced herself. 'Nice to meet you.'

Cathy watched as he relaxed back again, slouching his weight on one leg. Tom glanced around her room.

'So, you're with us for a month or so? I believe Brenda's drawn up an itinerary for you. You'll get what you put in, of course. If you're interested in a career in general practice, then show that to us, and we'll give you every opportunity to get stuck in.'

The man smirked but didn't reply.

'Right, on to Dr Longmuir next,' Brenda said, leading Tom from the room.

As he left, the young doctor looked at the sign on her door. He turned. His eyes were mocking and Cathy couldn't understand why.

'Oh Tom?' Cathy said before the door closed. 'What did you say your second name was?'

'Jackson,' he smiled. 'I'm Thomas Jackson. I'm so looking forward to working with you Cathy. I think general practice is looking more appealing by the minute.'

Cathy had always been rather intuitive and as he left, she felt slightly sick, but she dismissed the feeling hurriedly. No doubt she was quite mistaken. Jackson would turn out to be just like all the other trainees they had mentored.

13

Come Wednesday evening, Fraser had riled himself into a frenzy. He was jumpy and on edge all the time. He had sent Sarah home to her parents that night following a dreadful evening meal together, telling the confused girl he had a headache. In truth, he needed space to think.

Dear God, what a day it had been. Fraser ran over the events repeatedly as he strode up and down in his living room. How on earth had it happened? What were the chances of them meeting again? Jackson; his nemesis. The man he despised above all others. And after all this time, when he was settled and just beginning to make a go of things in his new job too. He had even thought that he had begun to win over Dr Hope with his last presentation. Things had been looking up.

He pictured Jackson's look of delight when they met. Fraser had been up in the coffee room having a friendly joke with Irene, the older practice nurse, who he found himself liking more and more for her almost-maternal kindness. Fraser had turned around on hearing Brenda enter the room.

'More people to meet,' she said. 'Irene, Fraser. This is Tom, our new trainee for the next month. He'll be shadowing Mark mostly, but no doubt you'll bump into him also.'

'Welcome, Tom,' Irene had said. 'Don't be put off general practice by Dr Hope. He sees the world through different eyes to the rest of us.'

Fraser had found himself standing in stupefied silence, staring open-mouthed at the man.

Jackson composed himself far quicker. 'Nice to meet you Irene, Fraser,' he had said with a smirk.

Thankfully, Brenda had led him away to show him the library and meeting rooms, but Fraser's legs shook so much he was barely able to make it down the stairs to his room. There he had sat, unable to work for the entire afternoon. Repeatedly, he tried to distract himself from thoughts of Jackson, by looking at the chronic obstructive airways register, but it was so hard to concentrate.

Fraser tried to soothe himself. They were both older now. Jackson had perhaps matured. He might also be ashamed of his juvenile exploits in the hospital. But when Fraser ran through their meeting up in the coffee room and the young doctor's triumphant smile, he knew that it was not the case.

In the end, Fraser closed his computer and sat hunched at his desk until four o'clock came and he was safe to creep from the doctors' building. How could he ever work in the place now, knowing that that man was under the same roof?

Fraser knew that Jackson would find a way to twist the unfortunate coincidence of their meeting to his own benefit. And now, without question, Fraser felt he was like a sitting duck, awaiting his fate. His position was impossible. He had done wrong as a young pharmacist, but my, how he had paid the price for his mistake, and ten times over.

Back home, and as the evening wore on, Fraser allowed his

thoughts to take hold. He wondered if the chance meeting had really been just that. Had Jackson been following his career? Fraser wouldn't put it past him. How simple to key into a computer Fraser's name and to track him to the pharmacy in which he previously worked. Fraser remembered that his details had of course been quoted in the local press when that appalling drug addict had died. Had Jackson seen the papers? Did he know about Fraser's error in dispensing the methadone? Had he read the report on the inquest?

It was all too easy to research a person if one wanted to. Fraser thought of the practice website and how he himself had done just this before applying for the job. And now, having had his photograph taken, he was there, along with the rest of the medical team, a brief synopsis of his career and interests for anyone to read. Did the vindictive rat know all about him?

Fraser, having distractedly paced the room a good twenty times, re-seated himself in his armchair with a whisky to take stock of his position. If his past misdemeanours came out, it would undoubtedly be the end of his job at the practice. It would be the end of his career as a whole, he would be essentially unemployable with such a black mark against his name. He did not know for sure, but if the story came out, he thought Sarah's love for him would be tested to its limit. She had supported him through the methadone mix-up, but the past mistake in the hospital had been more than just a blunder. His prolonged criminality showed he was capable of devious planning. Fraser couldn't blame poor, innocent Sarah, if she did decide to bail out, not knowing this side to him.

Irritably, Fraser pulled himself out of this line of thought. It would do no good to continue with this melancholy nonsense. Regrets were utterly useless now. Fraser must face whatever was coming, but when he thought about his life, the one he had built from nothing. the hours of work he had put into his current position, he knew that he could not give it up for anything.

The more Fraser considered things, the more convinced he was that if Jackson was out of the way, he might continue to lead a happy life free from worry and doing the job he loved and at which, he was actually very talented. Fraser compared the difference that he had personally made to the practice in the short time he had been there, with the spiteful existence Jackson had clearly led. Admittedly, the man was a doctor, but what kind of a clinician might he be, injecting poison into people's wounds and twisting a scalpel in their injuries? From his time in the hospital, Fraser had heard that he was disliked by many. The nurses found him condescending and the colleagues who weren't part of his inner circle said that he was dangerous and spiteful.

Fraser wished that the man would disappear. If only he would return to wherever he had come from. He imagined Jackson having a car accident and needing to go back home to recuperate. And then, despite his better nature, he imagined Jackson dying in the accident. Fraser wasn't a bad person but with so much to lose, it might clear many of his worries. If Jackson survived an accident, he might return to Glainkirk and take up again where he left off, but death would free Fraser from this torment forever.

Horrified by this idea, Fraser fleetingly thought that perhaps the only answer was his own death. If only he had the courage to commit suicide. As he considered the possible methods, Fraser doubted that he had it in him.

No, suicide wasn't the answer, but whichever way he turned, Fraser saw that Jackson's existence would only lead to his own ruin. When he realised what he was really contemplating, Fraser felt physically sick. He, Fraser Edwards, a murderer? But no, it was a shocking and horrifying thought. He must banish it from his mind immediately.

But for the remainder of the evening, as Fraser sat alone in his front room brooding, the idea would not leave him. The shadows around him grew gradually longer until the place was quite dark.

14

D
r Suzalinna Bhat cursed under her breath. Turning to
the rest of her team, she smiled sadly. Their faces
were expectant. Presumably hoping for some guidance on how best to proceed. But she had no more answers to
give them. It was over.

'Well done everyone,' she said. 'I think we'll call it there.
Time of death: 13.45.'

The anaesthetist next to her snapped off his gloves before
the others. He'd seen it all before but it didn't make it any more
palatable. The monitor above them continued to wail plain-
tively. Dr Bhat reached up and flicked the switch.

'Thanks, folks. We'll talk later.'

It had been going like a bloody circus all morning in A&E.
Resus hadn't stopped. Suzalinna, the consultant in charge of the
department that day, tried, as all the experienced doctors did, to
shield her juniors from the more traumatic cases. This time,
however, she had not managed. They had even had three of the
anaesthetists down. This was far from routine, but when the
crew bringing him in had radioed ahead, she had called the

crash team immediately. They pulled out all the stops that day, knowing that he was one of their own. But it had all been in vain. Losing a doctor was about as bad as it got, Suzalinna thought.

Slowly, she walked to the wash-hand basin and peeling off her own gloves, tossed them into the bin. Suzalinna turned the tap and welcomed the icy shock of cold water on her fingers. Pumping the hand-sanitiser three times, she scrubbed. She inhaled the sharp scent of antiseptic and it caught at the back of her throat. Here she stood for a full minute, working the lather between her fingers and watching the pink foam circle at the plug and then disappear. It was as if by washing her hands, she might also wash away the failure she felt.

It was a side to the job she hated. She had, of course, seen countless traumatic cases. At the start of her career, she had been thrilled by the excitement of an arrest or trauma. These days, however, having seen so many families wrecked, and having had to break the news to them that their husband, father, sister, or worse still, child, hadn't made it, her enthusiasm had ebbed. And of course, when it was one of your own, another doctor, well, that only amplified the feeling of defeat.

Suzalinna hadn't failed to notice the effect the death had had on the rest of the team. That too was now part of her job; to ensure the safety and wellbeing of her staff. Two of her juniors had left the resuscitation room in tears that afternoon. She would have to speak with them and de-brief when she had sorted out the paperwork and tied up all of the loose ends. Anne, a staff-nurse she favoured above all others for her straight-talking, no-nonsense approach, was fortunately on that day. Suzalinna knew that she would steer the team back on track admirably, until she was able to go through and take charge. And anyway, she had seen that the waiting room was full when she passed earlier. Her junior staff would have no choice but to get on with the job, and perhaps that wasn't such a bad thing.

The telephone on the wall sounded, interrupting her thoughts. Reaching up to the receiver without raising her eyes from the notes she was recording, she waited for the voice. 'Doctor Bhat? I have a GP on the line, can you take the call?'

'Sure,' Suzalinna said and waited for the telephone to splinter and crack as it always did when they connected an outside line. Within moments she heard a voice she knew only too well.

'Suz? Is that you? Have you any news? They brought him into you. Did you deal with it? We've all been waiting to hear.'

'Hang on, hang on. Cath, is that you?'

Suzalinna and Cathy Moreland had attended medical-school together and had formed a firm friendship since their first day of meeting, too many years ago to recall. They had been together on several placements as undergraduates and Cathy had looked up to her highly intelligent, if not mildly-arrogant comrade, whilst Suzalinna envied Cathy's patience and gentle bedside manner. Somehow, they had negotiated the rigours of medical-school side-by-side, despite their differing personalities. Suzalinna had always been destined for A&E and Cathy was best suited to general practice. One particular attachment saw them travel together the four hours to a small district general hospital just north of Aberdeen. It had been a happy time and following the recent nervous breakdown of her friend, Suzalinna had urged Cathy to return for a holiday, promising to join her. Cathy had returned invigorated and ready to face her life once more with Suzalinna's support and backing. Suzalinna was married, but poor brow-beaten Saj rarely got a look in when the two medics got together for an evening of drinks and conversation. It had been a number of weeks since they had last spoken and Suzalinna felt a pang of guilt at having forgotten to wish her friend well on returning to work. But Cathy was talking again.

Suzalinna moved the phone to her other ear. 'What's that you're saying, Cath? Was a patient of yours sent into us?'

Suzalinna turned to look at the prostrate figure lying on bed three of Resus, now with a hospital sheet over his face. One of the nurses was still clearing the floor of debris; packets from needles and other medical paraphernalia that had been hurriedly discarded in the team's urgent attempts to save the man's life.

The nurse, feeling the consultant's gaze upon her, turned and grimaced. Suzalinna smiled and nodded an understanding. The resuscitation was one thing, but it was the aftermath that was usually trickier.

'He was brought in to you,' Cathy said, her voice now becoming higher with impatience. 'Didn't the paramedics say? He was one of us.'

Only then realising, Suzalinna spoke. 'Bloody hell, no. Oh God, Cathy, I really had no idea. They said he was a medic but it didn't click. Was he from your practice then? I'm sorry, darling. I'm so sorry. We just called it five minutes ago. We were going to try pacing him, but it was hopeless.'

The phone was silent for a moment, and when Cathy spoke, her voice sounded distant. 'I tried to intubate at the practice but I couldn't see a thing and it's been years since I had to do one ...'

Suzalinna laughed grimly.

'Cathy, don't beat yourself up. Even I couldn't tube him and I do them every other week.' Suzalinna turned again and looked across at the covered figure. 'Darling, his mouth and larynx were a bloody mess. We did a trachy but we couldn't get cardiac output. We had Anaesthetics and ENT down but he was gubbed, Cathy.' Suzalinna paused but her friend didn't speak. 'What happened anyway? Did he take something deliberately or was it accidental? I'm just writing up and then I'm about to phone the police.'

'I don't know,' Cathy answered. 'We found him in the consulting room like that. I don't know what he took. I don't know what happened. It was in the middle of our morning surgeries with patients waiting. Listen, I'd better go and sort things out here and tell the rest of the practice. They're all waiting to hear.'

'Cathy? Give me a call at home later and we'll talk, OK?' Suzalinna said.

As she replaced the receiver, she swore under her breath. She saw suicide attempts regularly. Joe Public weren't particularly imaginative in the ways they tried to kill themselves. Paracetamol or antidepressant overdoses were common and usually an ineffective cry-for-help. Then there were the attempted hangings. These were occasional and more common in middle-aged men. Sometimes to add variety, they had an attempted bridge-jumper, or in the farming community, a botched shooting. But medical colleagues were seen far less often. Suzalinna presumed that this was because they were usually more successful at killing themselves discreetly and without mistake. They never made it as far as A&E but headed straight to Police Surgeons for postmortem.

Suzalinna wondered what the man had taken. If a doctor wanted to kill themselves there were far better ways of doing it than the method this GP had chosen. Insulin overdose, diamorphine and diazepam were all reasonably easy to get hold of in general practice. But whatever this man had taken had been seriously caustic, blistering his mouth, and causing his larynx to become so oedematous, that his airway was almost completely occluded. Rather than it being a fast, efficient death, he must have suffered very much indeed.

Picking up the phone again she made the call through to the

police station. The hospital, of course, did their own post-mortems, but if there were any suspicious circumstances, as in this case, the body would have to go to the police mortuary for them to conduct their own.

'Hi, can you put me through to the appropriate department? It's Dr Bhat, A&E. I need to report a suspicious death.'

15

Cathy replaced the receiver and getting up from her desk, she walked quickly to the sink in the corner of her consulting room and vomited. She then perched on the edge of her desk for a minute, staring blankly out of her window. A group of school children passed by, cutting across the playing fields that backed onto their staff carpark, crossing to the shops further down the road. Usually, she would have scoffed at their short skirts and laddish behaviour but today Cathy neither heard nor saw them. She wiped her hands on her trousers, back and forth, trying to compose herself. Instead, she found herself replaying the morning's events. Over and over again she saw his gaping mouth, his oily complexion. She shut her eyes but it was still there.

It had been a normal morning up until then. She had been waiting for her next patient to arrive and had been so up to date, that she had managed to go through all her laboratory results.

After a quick coffee, she had returned to her room and was flicking through the next patient's notes. It was a man she had seen many months before and it looked like he had been in regularly to see the other doctors since. All minor ailments. She had wondered if there was something more underlying his visits. As she scanned through the notes, she had become aware of a commotion outside her door, and then a woman had screamed. Cathy had jumped and slapped the surface of the table accidentally and banged her knee on the corner of it. She had opened her door to see Bert hurtling down the corridor at surprising speed for a man of his age.

Only when the old handyman, shuffled to the side did Cathy see the nurse. Tracy was standing holding onto the door-frame swaying, her beautifully made-up face, a grimace of horror. Bert was just in time to grab Tracy, easing her descent, as she crumpled onto the floor just outside Mark's room.

Cathy had been glad of her training in accident and emergency that awful morning. As a junior doctor, her consultant trainer had allowed her to lead the arrests towards the end of her time there and although it was years ago, she felt the familiar adrenaline kick-in. She found herself thinking of her friend Suzalinna and imagining that this must be her life every day.

Doctors are often said to have a dark sense of humour and Cathy was no different. Back in her old A&E days, she and her colleagues made jokes that would have disgusted non-medics. Sometimes they'd laugh during a really messy resuscitation. But Cathy did not laugh today.

Marching down the corridor, she bypassed Bert and stepped over Tracy to find her practice partner Dr Mark Hope, lying sprawled on the floor, half under his table. From the doorway, she noted the staring eyes and mouth gaping wide. She saw hair plastered damp against his almost yellow face and the froth of pink foam which ran from his mouth ending in a congealed pool that seeped into the carpeted floor. She turned to James who now also stood in the corridor but was unable to see past Tracy and Bert.

'James, get the girls to call nine nine nine, tell them it's an adult male, cardiac arrest. Is Irene back from that meeting?'

Brenda, who had also arrived, clutching a ring-binder to her chest, had come to see what the problem was. She answered for him and said that yes, she was.

'I need Irene in here.' Cathy said. 'Get her to bring the arrest trolley.' Cathy had then turned to her senior partner. 'James, get in here with me and someone move that stupid, bloody girl out of the way.'

Brenda and Bert half-carried, half-walked Tracy back to her own room.

'Brenda?' Cathy called after her. 'Sort out the patients in the waiting room. James and I were consulting still. Get everyone who doesn't need to be in the building, out now.'

In the distance, Cathy could hear Brenda addressing the patients still sitting waiting to be seen. Despite the grave situation, she was surprised and impressed by the woman's presence of mind and resilience.

'Oh, dear God. What's happened?' asked James, then coming into the room.

Not bothering to answer, Cathy had made a quick appraisal of the situation. The area was safe for both of them to approach. Inwardly she recited her A, B, C. Airway, breathing, circulation. Well, if she started with his airway, it was a bloody mess. Cathy grabbed a pair of gloves and snapped them on, and then threw the box to James so he could do the same. She turned Mark over and with James's help, pulled the figure clear of the table. He was heavy, like a dead weight, and as they manoeuvred him, his hair flopped out behind giving him a grotesque, casual look. His face was almost like wax, oily and cold to touch. She knelt by his head and tilted it back, lifted his jaw forward. She felt and listened for any signs of life. None. Scooping her first and middle fingers into his mouth she moved his flaccid tongue and produced a handful of bloodied foam.

'What the hell's happened to his mouth?' James had asked in disbelief.

'Not sure. James do you want to start doing chest compressions? He's not breathing and he has no pulse.'

And then Irene was there to join them, looking shocked, but composed.

'Irene, there you are,' Cathy said. ''Don't freak out, for God sake. Bring the Resus trolley right in here and give us a hand.'

Irene did exactly that.

'Throw me a bag and mask and an oropharyngeal airway. I'll deal with this end,' Cathy said breathlessly.

Without needing to be told, Irene cut through her employer's waistcoat and what remained of his shirt, which had been torn already, and steadily stuck on the chest leads to assess his cardiac rhythm. Cathy looked at the monitor.

'He's in asystole. Shit. Listen James, let Irene take over chest compressions. You need to get a venflon in so we have access. OK with that Irene?'

Irene had been fine with that, James perhaps less so. It was probably years since he had last put in a cannula and his hands wouldn't stop shaking.

'James, breathe. OK?' Cathy said. 'You're no use like that.'

Cathy reached over James and pulled the airway kit from the trolley. God, how long was it since she had to do this? She remembered checking the trolley with the nurses and was glad to know where everything was. She removed the bag, mask and airway that she had been using intermittently to give breaths with, and inserted a laryngoscope, squinting to see if she could manage to intubate. Irene continued to compress his chest rhythmically, puffing a little with the exertion. James was still struggling to get venous access.

Fearing she was leaving him without oxygen for too long, Cathy replaced the airway and mask and gave the bag two more squeezes. Then, she continued to try with the intubation.

'I can't quite see. Too much blood. There are blisters everywhere,' she said, talking to herself.

'Try a laryngeal mask,' puffed Irene.

'Yeah, I'll have to,' said Cathy, abandoning the tracheal tube.

The laryngeal mask slotted in easily just as the paramedics walked in the door. Irene and James looked up relieved that help had arrived and stepped back, allowing the experts to take over. Cathy continued to manage the resuscitation and gave the paramedics a verbal history of how they had found him and what they had done to try and help.

As the ambulance left the practice carpark, its lights flashing and siren starting up, Cathy had stood in her consultation room alone. Please God, let it be her friend Suzalinna meeting them at the other end. But in her heart, Cathy knew it was desperate.

Now, rousing herself from her thoughts, Cathy went to the door, knowing that she must break it to the rest of the team that they had lost their colleague. How would the practice go on?

16

Cathy finally got home at seven. It had been a long day. She kicked off her shoes as she entered the house, allowing them to lie haphazardly on the hallway carpet. She lived alone now so what did it matter? Walking through, she flicked the switch on the table lamp in the hall, which spread warmth up the walls and threw elongated shadows from the stair bannisters. She dropped her car keys on the kitchen unit with a clatter and went straight to the fridge and found the unopened bottle of white wine. She really must eat, but the alcohol had to come first. Oh God, what a day. She wanted to cry but felt too tired to do even that. Wine would help. It always did. She watched the yellow liquid slap the side of the glass, rearing like a wave, and settling at the bottom. The bottle glugged, the air taking up the space where alcohol had been. Cathy took a deep breath and leaning over the counter, sipped the top of the glass awkwardly, she had filled it so high that some splashed on the worktop. Her hand shook. She drank thirstily, without noticing the taste.

They had advised her to not drink on top of the medication, but Cathy had ignored this recommendation right from the very start. She needed some small pleasure in her life, she reasoned, and at times of stress, alcohol could certainly be relied upon to give her the required letup. Doctors, she supposed, always made the worst patients. This thought came to her again, as she refilled the glass, and laughed. The sound echoed around the bare kitchen, bouncing off the shiny cupboard doors, back to her. When had she last cooked in here, she wondered?

Things had been far worse before her enforced break from work though. Back then, she had really struggled. She had not taken enough of the practice's opiates to be physically addicted thank God, but she had been emotionally dependent on the drugs.

Cathy walked through to the living room with her wine and remembered James's reaction on hearing what she had done all those months ago. He had been so disappointed in her; she could see it in his face. Mark had ransacked her consultation room for any remaining drugs, so terrified was he of her concealing them. It had been a truly awful time. Her lowest point, if she was honest. Guilt gnawed at Cathy as she remembered her fury, directed particularly at Mark. He had been forthright as always, storming into her room and accusing her of not only drug abuse but stealing. 'Malpractice,' he had shouted. She had argued that it was no different from him taking antibiotics from the store when he had had a chest infection, but she knew she was on shaky ground. Mark had questioned her fitness to practice ever again, and only James had managed to convince him of her need for support, not anger.

Cathy wondered how much the rest of the practice knew about her disgrace. Sometimes she suspected it when she looked at Irene or Tracy. Nothing had been said, but she supposed that they knew. They certainly knew about her breakdown, everyone knew that. Cathy wondered what Mark had said to Tracy about practice business. She was sure the young nurse knew more about their private affairs than she should.

And what of poor Tracy now? She had been almost inconsolable on hearing of her boyfriend's death. It turned out that she had moved in with Mark only the month before. Cathy recalled the young nurse's reaction up in the coffee room, and then, when Irene had suggested that she come and stay at her house for the next few nights, she had nearly exploded.

'I need to feel near him,' Tracy had sobbed. The rest of the practice members had looked on in embarrassed silence.

But in reality, it would have been ridiculous to return to Mark's house alone. Even Tracy had to admit that she might feel strange. So, Irene had had her way and Tracy had agreed to stay with her, on the understanding that it might just be for the one night.

Cathy recalled watching her practice team waiting their turn up in the coffee room. Huddled together at the far end, some sitting, others standing, looking out of the long windows that ran the length of the room and trying to comprehend what had happened that day.

The only positive, as Brenda had said, was that the young trainee; Tom, had called in sick that day. When Cathy had heard that he was absent after only a week in the post, she had found herself doubting his enthusiasm. She had felt somewhat uneasy in the man's presence since he had come. Now she supposed, he must find a new trainer. She doubted if she or James would feel able to step in after all that had happened.

Cathy thought too of their most recent permanent addition to the team, their practice pharmacist and wondered what on earth he must be thinking about the whole affair. Only a few weeks into the new job and he had found himself embroiled in a sudden death. Cathy had caught his eye and he had quickly turned away, his face pale. What a dreadful day it had been for all of them.

Cathy had backed the young pharmacist when he arrived. He had hit the ground running as far as the work was concerned, taking Mark aside and asking for his advice on auditing the high-risk cardiovasculars. That, Cathy had thought at the time, was rather clever of the man. He must surely have known that Mark would be the hardest nut to crack. Even still, Mark had held him at arm's length and when questioned, he refused to admit that the idea to employ him had been a good one. Over the past few weeks, there had been several concise yet friendly emails sent out suggesting ways in which the GPs might tighten up on their prescribing. 'Quick fixes' that might make a real impact on the budget very rapidly, Fraser had said.

Cathy held her glass of wine to the light now, and watched the liquid slosh dangerously high up the side. How the practice might continue now, was beyond her. Goodness knows how any of them would continue to work there, walking past Mark's door having seen the waxy features and staring eyes. She took another slug of wine.

The living room was too quiet. Cathy shut the curtains and then turned on the television, at least finding some comfort in the chatter of voices in the background. She must phone Suzalinna and speak. Perhaps she would know more. The police had been very vague, reluctant to comment on the cause of death.

As she sat in her armchair, Cathy went over her interview with the detectives that afternoon. It wasn't unusual for the GPs to deal with the police. Often, they came into the practice to take a statement following an accusation of assault, and if one of the GPs had examined the alleged victim, they were asked to detail any of their findings if it didn't breach their confidentiality agreement with the patient. But the circumstances were of course, rather different this time. She had lost a colleague and in the most traumatic of circumstances.

The police had been kind. The more senior of the two, she supposed, had taken the lead. He had introduced himself as DCI Rodgers. He was a middle-aged man, dressed in a navy suit. His hair was prematurely thinning. His colleague was introduced as DS Milne. He was a slightly younger man and less weathered by the rigours of the job.

As she sat there, Cathy wondered if she had always been this cold and detached. She heard herself telling the police that she'd help in any way she could.

'We just need to go through the day's events with you, Doctor, if you don't mind? I know this has been a long and upsetting day for everyone, so the quicker we can get the details sorted, the sooner we can all get home,' said DCI Rodgers.

Cathy nodded. She felt like she was watching herself in a play.

'You arrived at the practice at what time this morning, please?' he asked, and his colleague stood expectantly, his hand poised and ready to write in his notebook.

'Seven forty-five exactly,' Cathy said, trying to focus. 'I'm usually here at about that time. It gives me a chance to get the computer on. Sometimes it takes forever to get logged on and I often like to check some of the lab results before kicking off.' She noticed that she was jogging her leg up and down repeatedly, so stopped this, catching the young policeman's eye.

DCI Rodgers nodded. 'And you were the first in the building, Dr Moreland?'

'Oh God no. seven forty-five is late really. It's usually Brenda that opens, but this morning she was at her meeting. Mark was always in early so he must have done it, or Bert – he practically lives here.'

'Bert?' The detective looked at her questioningly.

'The handyman. Oh God! I forgot about him,' Cathy said, her hand going up to her mouth. 'He wasn't upstairs with us, was he? Has he left, or is he in the cupboard?'

'In the cupboard?' Both policemen now looked incredulous and DS Milne had begun to get up from his chair.

'He has a cupboard,' Cathy explained. 'Well, it's really a small room of his own, but it has no windows so we call it a cupboard.' Cathy knew that she was gabbling and tried to slow herself down. 'He was here,' she continued, considering. 'He got to Tracy before me when she was doing her fainting thing. I don't know where he went.'

The more senior officer turned to his colleague.

'Better go and check,' he said, and DS Milne left the room.

Turning back to her, the detective looked grim. 'Listen, Doctor, let's be frank with one another, shall we? What do you really think has happened here today? You tried to help him, Dr Hope, didn't you? So, what's your professional opinion?'

Cathy felt as if the tone in the room had shifted now the other man had gone. She tried to think.

'His mouth was a mess. It was horrible,' she said, picturing his greasy skin and the gaping hole of a mouth. Shaking herself from this image she continued. 'I assume he must have taken something orally, something caustic, an acid maybe. I don't know why though.'

'Yes, something caustic. Well, the postmortem will hopefully tell us exactly what he took. Was there any reason that you can think of, for him taking anything himself deliberately?'

'Suicide? Oh God no,' Cathy replied with feeling. 'Mark would be the last person; I would have thought. I can't imagine him doing it on purpose. He might have swallowed something accidentally but surely ...'

'Why is it impossible to believe that he could have killed himself?' the detective asked.

'Well, he was in the middle of his morning surgery for one thing. He had patients waiting. Why would anyone choose to do it at that time?'

The detective shook his head, but said nothing.

'And anyway,' Cathy went on, 'he was so meticulous about time-keeping, actually, he was meticulous about everything.' Cathy thought of Mark. His perfect suit and waistcoat combination, his matching tie and slicked-back hair. Even his teeth were even and white and perfect.

Still, the detective didn't speak. She sat in silence, until she could bear it no more.

'Well, he'd at least have left a note,' she continued with exasperation. 'He wouldn't have done it without explanation.'

DCI Rodgers looked at her sharply.

'Oh, you looked then, did you? For a note?' The question hung in the air for a moment or two.

Cathy felt uncomfortable. 'After the paramedics left,' she said. 'In case there was a clue as to what he had taken. So that we could inform the hospital if it was a known poison.'

The detective looked doubtful. 'I see, but you knew he was, and I am sorry to be frank Doctor, but you knew, to all intents and purposes, that he was dead or dying when he left here didn't you, Dr Moreland?'

Cathy felt her face redden. 'It depends what you mean,' she said obstinately. 'Clinically, as long as cardiopulmonary resuscitation is taking place, as it was in his room with us, in the ambulance, and in A&E, he was still classed as living.'

The detective smiled but said nothing.

'He had a non-shockable cardiac rhythm,' Cathy admitted, 'so the chances of revival were slim.'

'As I said, you thought he was essentially dead?' said DCI Rodgers, allowing tiredness to enter his voice.

'Yes.'

DS Milne had come back in at that moment and Cathy forced herself to take a slow, deep breath.

'Found him,' he said. 'The handyman's upstairs with the rest of them now in the coffee room.'

'Right, so back to suicide,' said DCI Rodgers, returning to Cathy. 'You say that Dr Mark Hope would not, under any circumstances, have killed himself during morning surgery. Does that mean that you think it even conceivable for him to have planned to do it at some other time?'

'No, no,' Cathy said. 'That's not what I meant at all. I was just saying that was just one reason for him not killing himself ...'

'That, and the lack of suicide note?'

'Yes. But mainly because he wasn't the type. He was so real, so opinionated about everything.' Cathy looked around exasperatedly, almost appealing now to the other detective. 'He was so full of life,' she explained.

'When you say opinionated, Dr Moreland?'

It wasn't coming out as it should, Cathy thought, and turning to DS Milne again, rather than her interrogator: 'Just that he got wound up about things. He wasn't depressed. He was enthusiastic. A strong character.'

The young detective smiled understandingly but his pen continued to scrawl across the notebook page. She turned back to the other man.

'Just to be clear,' he said. 'You're saying he was a strong character and was stirred up? Have I got that correct?'

Cathy felt wretched. They seemed to twist everything she said. Shaking her head, she sighed. 'No. I didn't mean anything. He did have opinions, like everyone does. He was animated when he disagreed with people. It's who he was.'

'Recently?' the detective asked.

Cathy sighed once more. remembering the practice meeting

just a few nights ago and James's exasperation at his partner's rudeness.

'There has been some disharmony between the partners over recent months,' she said unhappily.

It all came out, well the majority of it anyway. She told them briefly about her own ill-health and without going into too much detail, explained that her absence had undoubtedly put pressure on the other two doctors, despite the help from her locum-cover, Linda. She told them about Mark's new relationship with Tracy, their practice nurse, and the concern it had caused. Finally, when pushed, she found herself telling them about the last impromptu practice meeting, and James's unexpected outburst.

Sitting in her living room now, Cathy felt lightheaded. It must be the exhaustion, and the wine on an empty stomach, she thought ruefully. She wondered what the police had said to James after her. When they had parted, he had said very little on the subject. Getting up unsteadily, Cathy emptied the rest of the bottle into her glass.

17

'Come on then, darling, tell us everything. Have the police been in asking you twenty questions then? It sounds too awful to imagine,' Suzalinna said.

The meal was arranged several weeks before and although Cathy had wanted nothing more than to be alone with her thoughts, her old medical-school friend wouldn't consider it.

'Stuck on all alone at home brooding over it all, darling? No. I'm not having it. You come at seven. Saj has already planned a south Indian curry. It's something he's been going on about making for months now and he needs a guinea pig. Prepare to have your head blown off though.'

So, she had come, and as the conversation flowed and Cathy watched her two friends lovingly bicker over who was dishing up, Cathy smiled. Not many men would tolerate Suzalinna's sharp wit, but Saj, pleasant and kind in his manner, did what he often did, and placed a hand on his wife's shoulder. Suzalinna quietened and glanced sideways and up at her husband. That was enough. Saj saw Cathy watching them with amusement, and grinned across at her. Not for the first time, Cathy found herself envying her friends' companionship. She loved them both dearly, and following the past few months of her own mental illness, they had proved themselves to be loyal and devoted to her also.

Saj threw a sideways glance at his wife, presumably wondering if she was being rather insensitive in her lust for detail, but Cathy laughed, knowing her friend only too well.

'Yes, as you can imagine. I totally put my foot in it from the start though and they ended up twisting everything I said. It must have been the nerves, I suppose. It's not every day, is it, after all?'

Saj nodded, but said nothing, moving to fill both his wife's and Cathy glasses with wine. Suzalinna waved him out of the way, but Cathy grinned up at him and mouthed her thank you.

'So, have they decided if it was an accident or suicide?' Suzalinna asked. 'Seriously, we all got a bit of a shock when he was wheeled into Resus that day. Even the more practiced amongst the team.'

'They mentioned suicide at first, but you know what I think about that scenario,' said Cathy, taking a sip of wine. 'In the middle of his morning surgery? And why? Why would Mark do kill himself?' Cathy asked them both. 'He's cruising along at work; he's living in his immaculate house. He's finished with his ex-wife and had a nubile, young nurse in toe. Seriously,' Cathy said with feeling, 'why would he?'

Saj shook his head but didn't speak.

'Well, you'd know better than anyone I suppose, being his partner, darling,' Suzalinna said. 'What's James saying about it all? Is he in shock?'

'Horrified, of course, as is everyone. We've had to shut up shop this last two days to allow the police to come in. Our phones are being redirected to the out-of-hours hub. Poor Brenda, our practice manager, is having kittens.' Cathy looked around at them both. 'God knows how we'll get over it.'

'What about the girlfriend? Have the police been asking her about it? She was the first to find him, wasn't she?'

'Tracy? Yes, she's taken it very badly, although it all comes over a bit false, if you know what I mean? Oh, don't get me wrong, I'm sure she's upset, but really? They'd only been dating for a few months but the way she's carrying on, you'd think they were soulmates. She keeps showing off a ring he gave her. Says that they were engaged, but I never heard Mark mention anything of the kind. I feel bad saying it, but it is all rather uncomfortable.'

'Well if it wasn't suicide, the alternative is, of course, far worse. And you said that the police thought it was something in the coffee?'

'Well, not exactly. That's what the rest of us are assuming. The police haven't said a thing, as far as I'm aware. But it's the only explanation really.' Cathy placed her glass of wine on the table. 'So, we have a routine every day,' she said, settling into her story. 'After morning surgery, we head upstairs for a quick cup of tea or coffee and then the on-call doctor, it was James that day, either does house visits or sees drop-ins that come to the practice late. Both Mark and I were booked up with another four or five patients after coffee break and we were then due to go out on house calls. Fortunately, it was quiet that day, as it happens,' Cathy continued. 'Anyway, we have this routine of going up and chatting to the office girls and sometimes the nurses come upstairs too. Often, it's the only time we can have an informal conversation during the day. I do my prescriptions upstairs while I chat.'

'OK,' said Suzalinna. 'So, when Mark came up, who made the coffee?'

Cathy turned to her friend. 'No, that's just it. Mark never came upstairs; he always had his coffee brought down to his room. I think it was a bit of an ego trip, having one of the office girls fetch and carry for him. I always found it a bit old-fashioned. Even James made the effort to come up and talk.'

'So,' continued Suzalinna playfully. 'Who's in the frame then? Which girl took him his coffee that morning?'

Cathy grimaced, suddenly realising the horror of what they were implying. 'I feel awful talking like this really,' she said. 'He was my partner and this isn't a game of Cluedo. He died. I know that I didn't like him a great deal at times, but I respected him and now he's dead.'

Suzalinna placed a hand on her friend's arm. 'We'll shut up about it, shall we? I was being insensitive. I'm a bit disconnected, you see? I see trauma every day. You become a bit immune.'

Cathy smiled once more. 'Sorry,' she said. 'I'm all over the place at the moment. Anyway, let's talk about you guys. It's been ages since I saw you both. Saj, tell me about this fabulous curry we're eating.'

When Cathy finally took her leave, Suzalinna held her close.

'I know you're thinking this over, darling. I can see the way your mind works, but leave it to the police, OK? Your own health is too important.'

Cathy had smiled and nodded.

It was only when she was sitting in the taxi, going home that Cathy really thought about her friend's words. It was close to home, admittedly. But the more she considered it, the more she wondered how it could have happened. If Mark hadn't intended on poisoning himself, and still Cathy couldn't understand why he might, had there been some kind of dreadful accident? Cathy found herself imagining Mark unintentionally drinking a cup of cleaning fluid or bleach. But the very idea was ridiculous. One had to face the facts that deliberate poisoning was the only plausible alternative. If that was so, the practice had a killer in their midst. Was that what Suzalinna had meant about leaving it to the police and her own health being too important to risk?

Cathy had thought she meant her mental health, but perhaps she, along with the other members of staff, might be in actual danger.

Arriving home, Cathy found herself jittery. She paid the taxi fare and walked quickly up the path to her front door and fumbled with her keys. It was ridiculous really, to be this way. Cathy moved through her house, turning on all of her lights and calling out to her cat, who would usually greet her when she returned.

A murderer in their midst, she repeated. How appalling. Cathy wondered if the police had made any progress and if they suspected anyone even now. With all of her strength of mind, she braced herself for what was to come.

18

The practice was shut to emergencies, with only a skeleton service in place for the time being. This mopped up the few patients who had already been booked in, and allowed the GPs to deal with urgent paperwork. The neighbouring practices were helping, and the out-of-hours team were staffing the emergency cover. Cathy sat in her room, feeling unsettled.

Outside, a local news-team had begun to set up, keen to get an interview or even a short quote from a member of staff. Bert had ushered them away holding a broom, rather comically, and when Brenda had seen them hanging around still asking patients for their thoughts on the events, she had marched out of the building, and threatened to call the police to have them removed. She shouted that they were breaching patients' right to confidentiality asking questions when they were on the practice doorstep. The news crew had moved respectfully further down the road to appease her. But their cameras were still on the building. Cathy had watched it all from her window and then Brenda in near-hysterics, had come through and recounted the morning's events to her. It seemed that all of the staff were on edge.

The small town was buzzing with the news. It sickened Cathy, that they could delight in the practice's misfortune so readily. It seemed that the handful of shops on the street were doing excellent business because people wanted to be out, and wanted to talk. Michelle said that some of the more elderly residents who had been almost housebound, appeared to have found a new lease of life and were speaking to people they hadn't seen in years. The general mood of the town was of upset of course, and this had led to an outpouring of stories of Dr Hope's heroic rescues, his selfless tending to the ailing members of the community over the years. Most people had a personal story, or had a relative who had one. As often happened, when someone died, the less worthy characteristics of the person were forgotten, although someone in the shop did wonder how the floozy he had hooked up with recently was going to cope. What a disgrace that had been, him carrying on with someone so young. Cathy had overheard the last of these sentiments as she had stood in the queue at the post office. Granted, she had thought much the same when Mark had been alive, but to talk about it so openly after he had just died, seemed somewhat callous.

And now, the so-called floozy sat before her. Cathy watched as the practice nurse settled herself in her chair, folding her leg under her, and smoothing the fabric of her uniform trousers. Cathy noted Tracy's immaculately manicured nails. Tracy shifted, and the cushioned seat sighed beneath her.

Cathy had wanted to have a word. It seemed to her madness that the girl had come into work as it was that day. She had said as much to Brenda, but the practice manager seemed to be having a bit of a time of things rearranging appointments and fielding calls, so Cathy had said she might say something.

Tracy seemed to have established a carefully considered role of grief that would not have looked out of place on a film set. She swept her hair back, and then seemingly unhappy with its arrangement, pulled the tortoiseshell clasp free of the golden strands. Cathy wondered if the girl had any female friends, she doubted it. Tracy leaned back in the chair and scraped her hair quickly back from her face, pulling it high, drawing her forehead taut, and then snapping the clip in place. She probably was bravely getting on with things as best she could, but externally it all came over as a little untrue.

'So, how are you doing, Tracy?' Cathy asked, sitting herself down also, having closed the door. 'I just wanted to have a quick word and to see that you were alright.'

The girl smiled wanly. 'Getting there, Dr Moreland. It'll take me a while, though. Every time I go past his room, it sets me off, and I need to go back to the house and sort some things. That'll be hard.'

Cathy nodded. 'I can imagine.' 'It'll take all of us a while. You know you're entitled to leave of absence? It shouldn't be an issue at all, if it would help.'

Tracy shook her head.

'I thought I would feel useful here,' Tracy said. 'Better than being alone at home.'

'Yes, I can understand you want to keep busy.' Cathy paused, and then taking a deep breath, continued. 'Listen, Tracy, I'm sure the police have quizzed you enough already ...'

'We've all been interrogated,' said Tracy strongly.

'Yes, it seems so,' continued Cathy. 'I suppose I just wanted to ask, as we are in the dark really, the police not having told us much. But was there any reason for Mark to take his own life? You being one of the closest people to him, I thought you might know. Did he confide in you at all? Were there any worries?'

'It could only have been an accident,' the nurse said with

feeling. 'That's what I said to the police too. There's no way Mark would have done it deliberately, he had so much to live for.' The girl leaned in and showed Cathy the ring. 'We were all but ready to set a date if it hadn't been for that bitch of an ex-wife,' Tracy said, and without warning, began to cry most genuinely. 'She dragged it out for all she could get,' she said between sobs. 'He told me not to worry. He said he'd take care of me.'

'Were you actually engaged then?' asked Cathy, barely able to disguise her incredulity.

'Not exactly,' said Tracy. 'That was still to come. But it was a declaration of his commitment. I agreed that marriage was outdated too, and he had already had his fingers burnt, so I couldn't blame him for wanting to go slowly. When I think of him, lying on that carpet ... Oh God, it's too much to even ...'

Cathy got up. 'Tracy, I think you should get yourself home. There's no point in being here right now. We have no patients booked in until tomorrow morning. Why not go home now, and in the morning, you can see how you're feeling? It's been a dreadful shock for you. You're still staying with Irene, aren't you? So, head back and try to get some rest.'

Tracy nodded and said that perhaps she should go. She didn't want to be in the way, and certainly didn't want to make a nuisance of herself. Cathy walked her back to the nurses' room, where Irene was sitting typing at the computer. Beside her was the presentation handout that Fraser must have distributed. Cathy's copy was probably sitting in her pigeonhole, along with a mountain of other work. That evening meeting seemed like a lifetime ago to Cathy now.

'Catching up on my paperwork,' Irene said, smiling. 'Have you told her to go? I don't think she should have come in at all today, should you Tracy?'

Tracy grimaced. 'I need to go back home. To our home, Mark's and mine,' she said.

Cathy and Irene exchanged looks.

'I don't think it's such a good idea,' Cathy started tentatively, but Irene waved her away. 'We'll have a talk, Dr Moreland, won't we Tracy, about things? It's probably not a good idea to go back to someone else's house ...'

Cathy left them to it. As she closed the door, she could hear Tracy's voice rising, and Irene's remaining low and calm. Thank goodness for Irene, Cathy thought. Without her, that silly girl really might make a fool of herself.

Having safely dispatched Tracy, Cathy walked back through reception and slipping behind the desk, found Michelle their junior office-girl, leafing through some files. Michelle had worked for the practice for a comparatively short time. It seemed to be the norm for office staff to come and go. Perhaps the doctors weren't paying them enough. Cathy had raised this concern at a practice meeting months ago, before she had gone off sick herself, but Brenda had been adamant, saying that it was a job with high rewards in other areas, and a greatly sought position. Few young girls coming out of college these days could expect to earn more, and certainly the training and prestige that the job offered could not be denied. Since then, office girls had come and gone. Cathy supposed that it would always be the same.

'Michelle, hi. Quick question. I'm sure you've been asked by the police already anyway, but how was Dr Hope that morning when you took him his coffee? It was you wasn't it, or did Julie do it that day?'

Michelle straightened up. She was probably in her early twenties, and Cathy guessed that she would have been unlikely to have ever encountered death before, certainly not a sudden, violent one. Despite the situation, Michelle seemed to be remarkably composed. 'The police asked that too and I told them,' the girl said simply. 'It was a strange one that day.

Everyone was a bit all over the place with Brenda, Linda and Irene being away at that asthma meeting, oh, and Fraser too. I was late actually. You know he always liked his coffee bang-on ten forty-five?'

Cathy smiled. 'So, he gave you an earful, did he? For being late? That was typical of Mark.'

Michelle smiled. 'No, he would have been mad though I guess, if it had been me, but it wasn't. Like I told the police, it wasn't me or Julie that day.'

Cathy waited for more, but it didn't come. Michelle flicked through the notes she still held, now apparently disinterested.

'Michelle? Who then?' Cathy asked, unable to hide her exasperation. 'Who took Dr Hope his coffee?'

'It was Dr Longmuir,' the girl said, as if Cathy was stupid.

Cathy stared at the receptionist. 'Dr Longmuir? Are you saying James took Mark his coffee the day he died?'

'Yes. That's what I said. The police thought it was a bit funny too. Can I get on?'

Cathy stepped back without speaking, and the girl passed, her heels, ridiculously high for working in a doctor's practice, clipping on the thinly carpeted reception area.

19

Cathy tortured herself that evening, replaying the circumstances over and over. She had seen James several times in passing in the corridor, and had smiled but not spoken. Both of them had been working side-by-side all afternoon, but both had had their doors firmly closed. Cathy wondered what James was thinking in his room. Had he spoken with Mark that dreadful morning, and what had been said when he had taken him his coffee? More importantly, why had James taken the cup from Michelle that day anyway? As far as Cathy knew, he had never done such a thing before.

She tried to keep busy. There were all the laboratory results to go through and now that Mark's patients would have to be redistributed equally between her and James for the time being, Cathy found that she had more than enough work to keep her occupied. Still, despite all of this, she found her thoughts returning to James, who sat just metres from her in the neighbouring room. What must he be thinking? What had he done? She stopped herself from going any further. It was too awful to contemplate James having anything to do with Mark's death. How could the idea even occur to her? She should simply knock on his door and go and see how he was. Perhaps she should admit that she was feeling confused and helpless. Maybe he'd say the same.

But Cathy knew with it being six o'clock, she had left it too late to speak with him that day. She heard the door next to hers open, and the light switch being flicked. Part of her desperately wanted to go out into the corridor and to stop James, knowing that she would be unable to sleep for thinking about him. Her heart rate quickened as she mentally prepared to get up and go to the door. But something stopped her. All she needed to do was to ask about the coffee. James wouldn't be offended and it would be cleared up in seconds. But instead, Cathy sat in her chair and listened as her senior partner walked to the back door and left. From her window, between the blinds, she watched James slowly cross the staff carpark and get into his family car. How different James and Mark had been in many ways, and most definitely in their car choice. Mark had driven a sports car and had always arrived at the surgery with a flourish. James was far less brazen. He had driven the same car for years and showed no interest in such material things, it seemed.

As she watched the car reverse and then turn smoothly, the tyres whispering on the damp tarmacadam, she wondered if James knew she was looking. If he did, he chose to ignore her. He stared straight ahead as he left, his car sweeping out into the main road that headed into town. His home was almost a mile on the other side of the shops; a grand old Victorian mansion that had been divided years before. Cathy had been invited over a couple of times. She had never met Maureen; James's wife, who had died only months after Cathy had herself taken on the GP partnership. Her illness had been swift, Cathy had heard. Mark had mentioned that in the past the partners had often met regularly for evening meetings and James's house had been used. This had changed after the death of his wife, however.

Since then, James had held no dinner parties and there had been no invitations to visit. Cathy wondered how the man could live on where he did still, without his beloved wife, but then perhaps leaving would be even greater torture. Anyway, if ever the partners had needed to meet outside the practice since Maureen's death, Mark's farmhouse had been chosen. But there hadn't been a social occasion in a long time.

She thought once again of Tracy and how odd a situation she must find herself in too. She had been surprised to hear that Mark had asked her to move in. Where did that leave Tracy now? Would she have some entitlement to the house? Cathy thought not. Only a month of living together and Cathy assumed, no financial contribution to the house or bills from Tracy. No, surely the girl would have no rights whatsoever.

For the first time, Cathy considered then who might inherit Mark's money. Perhaps Mark's ex-wife, or maybe even, a distant relative. Cathy knew that his parents had died many years ago, and that he had no siblings. She hoped that he had left some sort of a will. Perhaps he had left everything to the practice. Cathy had snorted out-loud thinking of this. Mark certainly wasn't altruistic in that way.

She had spoken briefly to Brenda before leaving for the night. The practice manager had been unable to help fill in many details of that dreadful morning, now that Cathy found herself attempting to piece things together. Brenda hadn't even arrived at the practice on the day of Mark's death until gone eleven, accompanied by Linda and Irene, and followed closely by Fraser, as the four of them had been at an asthma meeting in the next town. Brenda explained what a horror it had been to walk in and find Mark lying there and Tracy collapsed at the door.

Now home, and having pondered the matter a good deal, Cathy got up from the kitchen stool, and took the near-empty bottle of wine and the glass with her through to the living room. Suzalinna would be furious if she knew how much she was drinking again. It had been a point of contention in the past.

She had an addictive personality. She must have. Since she had returned to work, the temptation was most definitely still there. In the back of her mind, Cathy knew was being watched. Sometimes Brenda hovered a little too long, or even Bert, who she doubted knew about the drug-taking, was present in the corridor for longer periods of time. It was understandable. She had betrayed her partners, and Brenda.

Cathy had noted that some things had changed since returning. The drug procedures had been tightened, and going into the store to restock her doctor's bag, she saw that now two members of staff were required to be present when withdrawing an injectable control drug from the stockpile. The drug logbook had been removed and there was a sign in the drug store saying that it was now kept in Brenda's office and that the keys to the control drugs could be obtained from her. To be fair, and Cathy knew this was dreadful to say, but they hadn't been that rigorous in their measures. Granted, they had protected the abuse of the injectables and the high-dose morphine tablets, but Cathy saw that along with the other emergency medications that the doctors used in the practice and in their work bags, she could still easily remove codeine-based capsules, the weaker form of morphine, without having to sign or check with another practitioner.

Cathy told herself that any non-addict would not have noticed. But she knew that she was one, and always would be, even if another pill never touched her lips. She would forever be tempted. She was surprised though, that Fraser hadn't spotted this flaw in the procedures yet and changed it. He had been so rigorous in so many other areas. It was his remit after all as their pharmacist, to oversee the practice drug sourcing and storage.

Had Cathy been more virtuous, she might have pointed out his error, but something stopped her from alerting her colleagues; the part of her that had already stolen from the practice in the past when she was ill, and that could potentially fall into the same trap again.

Cathy took a swig of wine, barely tasting it now, and remembered sitting in her consulting room all those months ago. The illness had been exhausting. She had struggled to sleep at night because of the racing thoughts. So many ideas, and all of them terrifying. She had eaten less. Food had become of secondary importance. Her boyfriend at the time had been frustrated by her outbursts; her swings in mood, from euphoria to crashing despair and fear. Cathy had become unpredictable. Having managed to conceal her fluctuant moods at work all day, she had come home and, she supposed, her then-boyfriend, had borne the brunt of her temper. Once, she had slapped him and she still remembered the sting as her palm had struck his cheek. Pleading for his forgiveness had done little to repair the damage though. They had drifted apart. Cathy laughed to herself thinking of this now. Such a euphemism if ever there was one. Drifted apart. It had hardly been that. He couldn't stand the sight of her in the end. She had pushed things too far. In many ways, it was a relief not to have to pretend anymore. Cathy could come home and be herself, her true self, without having to hide and pretend anymore. She had felt the bitterness inside her grow.

Her perception of the world had changed though, and she saw things differently now. She had been so happy to be allowed to return to work following her illness, but now this. Mark had died and in such hideous circumstances too. What the hell were they all playing at, getting on with things as if it hadn't happened?

Cathy knew that she was no longer the young, hopeful

general practitioner she had once been. She had been full to the brim with idealism. She smiled at the blank television screen. Oh, how things had changed. Years of relentless work. Most of which had been mediocre. The worried-well wanting advice and support. Sometimes Cathy wondered why she had spent five long years obtaining her medical degree, as most of her day was spent doling out sick-lines and cheap bits of motherly advice. What a bloody joke it all was. And the real stuff, the real reason for becoming a doctor and making a difference? Well, that too disheartened her now. She had seen too many generous, kind, honourable people die lonely, ugly deaths. They had told them at medical-school that they could ease people's suffering and really make a difference, but it had been a lie. Everyone faced the same end. Some, she couldn't forget. Their pleading eyes. She had shut thoughts such as this away for years and years. Why did she torment herself now? And of what help had her training been when her partner had needed her?

Cathy again saw the gaping hole of a mouth, the blistered lips and the beseeching eyes. Oh God Mark, why that way?

When sleep finally came that night, it was not tender and welcoming. Instead, Cathy lay spent on the living room floor, her head at an awkward angle and her body growing cold. In the early hours, she wakened and crept up the stairs to bed, her head throbbing mercilessly. She felt more alone that night than ever.

20

They all made a real effort to get on with work in a positive manner now that the practice was open to patients. It was difficult. The atmosphere was very strange. It felt like picking through the wreckage after an enormous hurricane had blown through. A natural disaster, although of course, it was anything but natural. Cathy knew that Brenda was trying her best to be as visible as possible. It seemed that the practice manager had spent much of her morning out at the reception desk helping the girls. They were on the front-line really and needed her. In truth, Cathy surmised that poor Brenda would have liked nothing more than to stay in her own room and hide.

The practice manager, seeing that Cathy had a gap between patients, had come through to vent. Apparently, the police had called her late the night before, saying that they were locking up the building having been back with forensics again. Brenda had told them that she couldn't imagine what was taking them so long, or indeed what they were doing. Cathy had smiled when she had said this.

'Brenda, they need to investigate thoroughly,' she had said, but the woman was having none of it. It seemed clear to her that it had been a suicide and of course that required some sort of an investigation, but it wasn't as if anything could be done now. Cathy didn't disagree, although of course, she suspected that something more sinister might well have occurred. Brenda admitted that she wished, more than anything, that the police would go away and allow her to get her practice back on track. She confessed to Cathy that she had already begun to worry about how they might replace Dr Hope. Cathy told her it was too soon.

'Anyway, I've told that Jackson boy not to come in this next week,' Brenda said. 'God knows what he must be thinking, and having come here to see how a career in general practice might be.'

'What about the room?' Cathy had asked.

'Mark's room? Oh, that's to stay locked. Not that any of us would want to go in. They've taken the keys and they're welcome to them. Took them off me as soon as they arrived that dreadful day,' Brenda said. 'There's no way any of us could think of using the room for a long time now. Every time I walk past it ...'

Cathy nodded.

'I'll let you get on,' Brenda said. 'I don't suppose you'd take some flowers home tonight? God knows how many bunches have been sent in. I've got them dotted around reception, but it's beginning to look like a shrine.'

Cathy laughed. It was rare to see Brenda so flustered, but then they all were. The receptionists had been so busy and the phones hadn't stopped ringing. Leaving her room mid-morning, Cathy had gone through to get a form and had seen how hectic the place was. It seemed that Brenda had felt compelled to offer further support and was now answering calls, so great was the volume. It was partly because people were keen to get an appointment just to pry, Cathy thought. It was also the logistical nightmare of managing patients who had called before when the practice had been closed and rather than going elsewhere, they had waited to been seen by their regular doctor.

When the surgeries finished and they put the phones over to emergencies only, the girls on the desk were allowed some respite at least. At the usual time, the team found itself filtering upstairs to the coffee room, keen Cathy assumed, to stick to a routine.

'Did you sleep last night?' asked Michelle, turning to her workmate. Usually, there was an opportunity to gossip at the front desk, but what with the place being so busy, and Brenda hanging around, they hadn't yet had a chance.

'No,' replied Julie. 'I kept going through it again and again and was trying to think if we could have done anything else to help. The police made me feel dreadful with all of their questions.'

'What did David have to say about it all?' David was Julie's other half. He was four years her senior, and almost always had an opinion.

'He's the same as the rest of the town, I suppose,' said Julie, biting into a slice of cake that Irene had apparently brought in that day. 'He can't believe it happened, and here too. Didn't want me coming to work this morning though.'

'Why?' asked Michelle, also helping herself to a large slice of cake. She, having been exposed to David's sentiments in the past, held him in high regard. If David said the practice wasn't safe, then perhaps they should listen. 'We can't leave Brenda in the lurch, though,' Michelle went on, 'and anyway, the patients won't stop coming, I suppose.'

Cathy tried hard to look as if she was doing something busily in the kitchenette that jutted out into the coffee room. It wasn't unusual to overhear the staff talking, and a good deal might be gleaned from what they had to say. Julie's voice dropped to almost a whisper, so that Cathy had to stop clattering the mugs, as she removed them from the dishwasher, to hear.

'Haven't you heard what they're saying about Dr Hope? It's all over town. David was full of it.' The girl asked, and then turning, Cathy was just in time to see the girl mouth the word 'murder'.

Just then, Linda walked in, closely followed by Brenda.

'Morning ladies,' Linda said. 'I hear it's been tough out there.'

'Oh, morning Linda,' said Michelle. 'Been going non-stop. Cake?' she asked, and Julie handed across a plate. 'Irene brought it in,' Michelle explained. 'Julie and I were just saying, weren't we Julie? You were very quiet the other day. We were just saying exactly that, weren't we, Julie?'

Julie shifted uncomfortably but didn't speak.

'I'll bet you were glad to be out of the building when all of the commotion with Dr Hope was going on,' Michelle continued cheekily. 'Away at your asthma conference.'

Cathy watched Linda's expression and saw that her colleague looked acutely uncomfortable. 'Yes,' said Linda, her tone flat and serious. 'It was bad enough arriving back when all of the patients were leaving. And then the ambulance arrived.' Linda wiped a stray crumb that had fallen into her lap.

'When did you get back, Linda?' asked Michelle, and Brenda took a step forward, perhaps to prevent the conversation from going any further. But before she could interrupt, Michelle continued. 'Didn't you get back with Brenda and Irene? They were right in there helping, weren't they?'

'Yes, I drove back with them. I just didn't want to get in the way,' Linda said and Cathy, although she had in the past struggled to warm to the woman, saw that she was blushing and felt sorry for her.

Michelle and Julie looked at one another.

'But you're a doctor,' Julie laughed, clearly buoyed by her friend's confidence. 'You'd have been more help to them maybe. I heard that Dr Moreland was calling out for folk to help her, weren't you Dr Moreland?'

Before Cathy spoke though, Linda got up.

'Yes,' said Linda, frostily. 'We all have our skillsets ladies, and cardiac arrests aren't mine, I'm afraid.' Putting down her plate, she smiled acidly at Brenda who was still standing frozen beside them, holding a limp tea-towel in her clenched hand. The young doctor stalked from the room.

'Hiding in her room I reckon. She should've been getting stuck in like the rest of them, and she knows it,' Michelle said.

'Ladies. I think we should have a word,' Brenda said with finality.

21

F raser sat in his office alone and fretted. It had been four days. Four days since Dr Hope's death. Dear God, what a mess it all was. Fraser got up from his seat and crossed to the window. He looked out blindly. He could barely remember what he had done, or how he had got through the hours. Sleep had been elusive these past few nights and it was little wonder after what had occurred.

After he had made his dreadful decision, he had been seized by such an overwhelming feeling of revulsion and self-loathing, that at times he felt that he might physically disgrace himself by vomiting in public. Waves of nausea lapped at him now. It was ghastly, even to contemplate.

And now it had gone so horribly, horribly wrong. Oh God, what a mess. That vindictive animal Jackson would live to see another day. Thank God though, he had been absent since the debacle. Thank God Fraser hadn't had to look into his hateful eyes. Brenda said that she had told the trainee GP not to return to the practice for the time being. It gave Fraser some respite at least.

Fraser had been questioned by the police. He had tried to

stay calm, for he knew that his freedom depended upon it. They had thankfully dismissed him. He had been away all morning with Brenda and Irene at the asthma conference. That at least was a small mercy, for it gave him an alibi of sorts. They would find out of course, though. It was just a matter of time.

The actual endeavour had been dreadful enough, but the aftermath following the mix-up had been far worse. Fraser envisaged his life being like this forever. The slightest oversight, a relaxation of watchfulness, a slip-up of words, and he was done for. If they suspected him in the least, they wouldn't let it drop. Already, having thought that they might assume it was suicide, Fraser had heard the word 'murder' mentioned. It was all around the town. He would spend the rest of his days looking over his shoulder now. This he had done since Jackson had ensnared him, but the rat had done far worse to him now. In calling in sick that morning, Jackson had dodged a bullet and had turned Fraser into the reluctant killer of an innocent man.

Fraser knew that forever his peace of mind was gone. In truth, it had left him the day he encountered Jackson all those years ago in the hospital. From now on, in the background, fear would crouch huddled, waiting to emerge from the shadows at the corner of every room. Fraser knew that in doing what he had done, he had sacrificed his own happiness. He thought of sweet, innocent Sarah, of her look of shock on seeing him that evening. He had returned from work much later than he should have of course, as the police had kept them all back for questioning.

Word had not got out by then and the shock was almost as great to the girl as it was to him.

'Oh Fraser, how awful. But what had happened do you think? An accident? Had he drunk something he shouldn't?'

Fraser had sat with his head in his hands. Finally, he had uncovered his face. 'I don't know,' he said again and again, until

Sarah had gone to him and cradled his head in her arms and sat like that, rocking him for God knows how long.

Sarah assumed that he was susceptible, being a sensitive person, but this, of course, was not the truth. He was a monster. If Sarah found out, she would spurn him, and rightly so.

Even now, four days on, Fraser could not fathom how it had happened. He had had the whole thing planned so meticulously. It had taken some nerve and he had backed out of it a dozen times, but then he saw how it might be done and while he was away also. This gave him some courage at least.

He knew that Dr Hope and Jackson would be consulting together, as they had done all week. Fraser had even gone to the trouble of double-checking that it would be so on the morning in question. He had no access to such information on his own computer, but he had gone behind the front desk surreptitiously the day before and had seen that Dr Hope's surgery was blocked out with longer appointments. Fraser had noted the previous few days in fact that Dr Hope, trusting the odious devil, Jackson's clinical skills more and more apparently, often took the time to get on with paperwork. The previous day, in fact, Dr Hope had come through to talk to Fraser himself, leaving Jackson to see his patients, and he had then gone back later probably to check that Jackson had made the correct diagnosis and treatment plan.

Come coffee time, for the past few days, Jackson had left Dr Hope in his room and had gone upstairs to get his own, which he took to the back door with him to have a cigarette. Fraser had passed him the day before and the vindictive beast had tried to engage him in conversation. He had continued upstairs seething as he listened to Jackson's laughter following him up the echoing stairwell.

Fraser knew that Jackson was the only one in the practice who smoked. He did this alone, taking with him one of those large, thermal mugs, to keep his coffee warm. The mug was, of course, the key to Fraser's plan, for it was only Jackson who used the damn thing. Fraser had never seen it before the man arrived, so he assumed it actually belonged to Jackson, but Fraser had noted that he chose to leave it at the practice overnight to go in the dishwasher along with the rest of the mugs and plates.

The night before, Fraser had waited until he thought most of the practice had gone home. Creeping upstairs, he had finally found the mug at the back of the dishwasher. He had cleaned and dried it as efficiently as he dared. If anyone had walked in, the entire thing would have to be abandoned.

Fraser had been carrying the universal container in his pocket all day. As he had gone about his business, he imagined all those he spoke to must know he concealed a fatal concoction, just waiting for his chance to deploy it. He was tense and on edge as he spoke to Dr Hope about the diabetic register. When he saw Brenda later, he imagined that she looked at him in a suspicious manner too. Goodness knows how he had made it through that day without spilling the damn stuff all over himself. As he sat waiting for the rest of the practice to go home so that he could tip the contents into Jackson's mug, swilling the oily liquid around the sides to avoid easy detection, he had momentarily considered downing the lot himself.

Suicide had most certainly been on Fraser's mind that day. Even as he replaced Jackson's mug by the kettle, knowing that the following day, diluted with coffee, it might end his enemy's life, he still considered taking the other choice. Death might come painfully, Fraser knew. He had looked up the symptoms of hydrocarbon poisoning and they weren't pleasant. Contact burns, eventual coma and respiratory arrest. Fraser held the cup to his own lips for only a second, and then replaced it hurriedly on the kitchen counter. What was he thinking? He had made his choice and he would stick to it now.

How then, had it gone so disastrously wrong, Fraser asked

himself. Oh, the horror of returning from the asthma meeting the following day. He had gone straight to his room assuming that the commotion was the other doctors attempting to resuscitate Jackson. Above anything else, Fraser did not want to see or hear that. It was only when the ambulance had gone, its blue lights illuminating Fraser's room fleetingly as they passed, accelerating out onto the main road, that he had felt safe to emerge.

The shock, the utter horror, he had felt on hearing that it was, in fact, Dr Hope who had taken the drink. He had killed an innocent man. And still, Jackson walked free. Not only had he survived his assassination attempt, but he lived guilt and blame-free, unlike poor, tortured Fraser.

22

C athy had been consulting and had missed the commotion, until as a patient had left, Brenda had come unexpectedly into her room, slamming the door behind her.

'Brenda, what on earth?' Cathy had asked as she looked up at the woman's flushed countenance.

It seemed that Brenda had been in her own room. She had dealt with the police earlier on, when they had been asking about the CCTV and the emergency buzzer system. Cathy had made the practice manager pause.

'Was the CCTV on then?' she interrupted, and Brenda had looked uncomfortable. It turned out that Brenda had decided to use it only as a visual deterrent, as they were trying to cut costs. 'I doubt there would have been anything to see anyway,' Cathy reassured her. 'What about the buzzer system? That's always on, isn't it?'

The practice, as with most GP surgeries had a system in place with hidden emergency buzzers below the desks in all the consulting rooms. This was for the doctors' or nurses' safety, so that if they had a difficult or abusive patient, help could be summoned without drawing attention to the fact. Cathy had already wondered why Mark hadn't activated the system if he was in trouble.

Brenda nodded impatiently. 'The detective asked about that and I told him it was on. You know yourself; it can be switched off at the front desk, but the staff won't touch it without my permission.'

'Sorry Brenda, go on. After they spoke with you, what happened?' Cathy asked.

'I thought they'd left. They said they were taking some things from the coffee room to analyse. I wasn't really paying attention because I had a phone call, you see?'

Cathy nodded and waited.

'So, imagine my horror,' Brenda said, pausing for effect. 'I was just tidying up and I heard the back door not ten minutes ago. You know what a din it makes, clanging? The three of them came out. I watched it all from my room. The two detectives and him. I could barely believe my eyes.'

'Who, Brenda?' Cathy had asked.

'James. Dr Longmuir. They led him to the police car and drove away.'

Cathy had been forced to continue her afternoon surgery, with the weight of this news on her shoulders. Having got through, but not having done a particularly good job for her patients, she found herself, at the end of the long day, considering what this latest development meant for them.

Brenda stood at her doorway once more, clearly having had time to think. 'I'm heading home, Cathy. No good will come of brooding on it. We'll know more in the morning and like I say, he'll be back in and making light of the situation, no doubt.'

Cathy wondered if she said this as much to comfort herself, as anything. Brenda looked tired. Her eyes were serious despite her smile. Cathy supposed that it had been probably more of a strain on her than the rest of them.

'None of it's right though, Brenda,' Cathy said, rubbing her temple trying to clear her mind 'I don't know what to believe anymore. I know it was James apparently, who took down Mark's coffee that day, but they must have something more. Surely they must know something we don't?'

Brenda shrugged and moved her handbag to her other arm. 'I asked about the postmortem results this afternoon and they said they still hadn't heard. The grumpy one told me that it sometimes took weeks to get a result back.'

'Well there has to be something,' Cathy said and sighing, she let her pen fall on her desk with a clatter.

'Go home, Cathy,' Brenda warned. 'No good will from of sitting around here moping. You need to look after yourself.'

Cathy glanced up at Brenda, who caught her eye.

'This morning,' she said. 'I could smell it on you, the alcohol.'

Cathy felt her face redden but she didn't speak, and Brenda continued.

'A glass is fine, but just watch, that's all I'm saying. I'm not one to judge and really, it's none of my business, but we need you more than ever Cathy. I'm relying on you to hold this practice together with me. Don't let things get like last time, please.'

Cathy watched Brenda go, having promised the practice manager that she would turn off all the lights and computers when she herself left. She listened as Brenda's heels sounded on the carpeted corridor outside. She heard the back door open, and then slam shut.

Cathy had promised to lock up also. Usually, it was Brenda or Bert who saw to this, but she knew what to do. She watched as the practice manager walked to her car and then saw the headlights as they caught the building, momentarily illuminating her own room, and then turning out onto the main road, to join the others heading home. Cathy sat, unaware of time. Her room grew darker, and the orange glow from the streetlights outside gave the place an air of abandonment. Cathy shivered. The radiator by her desk clunked twice, making her jump. The heating must be going off now, Cathy assumed.

She turned the day's events over and over in her mind. The police had got this all wrong. She knew James better than most. He was gentle and kind. He was vulnerable. For all she knew, the man might even be depressed. Cathy wondered if he had spoken to anyone after losing his wife. There was surely no way he could have had anything to do with Mark. She pressed her forehead trying somehow to make her thoughts clarify, smoothing her fingers across her eyebrows.

One partner dead and another a suspect. And Brenda was right. It now fell to her. The weight of the practice's future was on her shoulders.

Cathy spun herself around in her chair and getting up, left her room, walking down the corridor and back towards reception. As she came level with James's door, she paused, and then continued, following the ground-level lighting that lit the building in the evening.

James had been very good to her over the years and she couldn't bear to see his reputation shattered over a misunderstanding. She supposed that patients would soon start to lose trust in him as a doctor if the police kept him in for any length of time. 'No smoke without fire' would be the uneducated gossip's viewpoint. She wondered if that bloody news crew had got a photograph of him sitting in the back of the police car as they had driven away. They had continued to sit outside the place that morning, hoping for a story. She hoped that James had had the presence of mind to turn the other way and avoid the flash of the camera if they had caught him.

Standing in the empty waiting room now, Cathy considered. She wasn't a fool. If Mark had been murdered, and the word still jarred, even without it being voiced. But if he had been killed, then she knew that James had a motive. She recalled the last practice meeting and the sneering manner with which Mark had addressed his senior partner. Not only that, Cathy thought, but he had done it so often in front of the rest of the team. That would have been dreadful for James, and who knew what had been going on in her absence? Perhaps James had suffered a great deal while she had been away. He and Mark had always had a brittle relationship, but she could just imagine Mark getting more and more bullish, while James became more and more withdrawn.

Cathy left the waiting room and continued along the corridor to the nurses' rooms. All the doors were shut of course. If the police had been told that James had brought Mark his last drink before dying, then yes, she could understand why they suspected him. Motive and opportunity. It did make sense. However, the police didn't understand. James took his duty as a professional more seriously than most. Cathy felt sure that he must have gone to Mark's room with the coffee, to try and make peace, not to murder the man. She could just imagine James psyching himself up for the conversation in his room all that morning. What had passed between them, ultimately only James now knew. Poor James, he must feel very alone and afraid. Cathy supposed that he might think she suspected him too, and that was why she hadn't been into his room to speak since the tragedy. What a mess it had all become.

Cathy didn't know what they were going to do, or how the practice could function without him, even if he was only away for a short time. She turned in the corridor and began to walk back, retracing her steps, not thinking as she did so. She paused by the drugs store and without considering what she was doing, opened the door and went in, flicking on the light switch with a nonchalance that suggested that what she was doing, was entirely routine.

She knew that they were labelled alphabetically, and it would be on the top. Oh God, what a horrible day it had been. The handle felt cold to her touch and she startled slightly as she slid out the drawer and it creaked. The boxes and bottles were aligned neatly. She deserved this. Things had been tough. Cathy knew that Irene, as with all of her jobs, took hers of keeping the storerooms neat, very seriously indeed. She touched the cardboard box, stroking the top, allowing her fingers to hover over the braille print that labelled every drug available these days. Inside, she felt the weight of the bottle, and then the capsules shift within, tinkling against the side. So easy. It would be just so easy.

She felt the familiar longing and a voice in her head pleaded that it would only be one. Just tonight, to help her sleep. Imagine how good it would feel to sleep, in blissful ignorance of the previous day's events, to be oblivious and lost to it all, to float and to tumble on the codeine-based cloud. It would work faster and better than wine, and come morning, Brenda wouldn't smell the tell-tale signs of alcohol. She would awaken refreshed and able to cope. No-one would know.

As she pulled the door shut to the store and walked back to her room, Cathy realised how close she had come. It was only as she began to set the alarm at the rear of the building that she heard a noise and froze. But surely it must have been her imagination. Momentarily, she wondered if she might not have been alone. She stood listening, but no further sound came. Shaking her head ruefully, she closed the door to the practice. Guilty conscience, she thought to herself.

23

'Brenda, is there any news?' Cathy asked the next day.

She had come in especially early that morning having awoken with a new urgency and drive to clear James's name, and when she knocked on Brenda's door having seen two minor injuries that had walked in before morning surgeries had started, she felt her spirits rise further.

Brenda turned and beamed at her. 'He's just called. Thank goodness Cathy, he's home. Got home late last night and sounds exhausted. I told him to leave coming in, but he's insisting on doing on-calls this afternoon and he's told me to open up his morning surgery tomorrow.' Brenda exhaled. 'Oh God, what a relief. I'd been phoning around the locums already and they're all booked up. I hardly slept thinking about him.'

Cathy smiled. 'We'll manage whatever, like you said before. Linda and both nurses are in today. We can only do what we can do.'

Brenda nodded. 'Yes, that's fine. I got myself in a bit of a state about things.'

As Cathy returned to her room, she considered all they knew about the dreadful event so far. Already, Cathy had thought a good deal about the problem. It seemed to her now most unlikely that Mark had taken his own life. She thought also, if the police had taken James in for questioning, they too had their doubts. Assuming then that circumstances made suicide highly improbable; Mark's character for one, and the fact that he was in the middle of morning surgery, it appeared that only accident or murder were the alternatives. Whatever Mark had drunk, and Cathy assumed that it was a liquid he had consumed given the mess of his airway, it must have been administered in such a way that he was unaware that he was taking it. Something clear perhaps, and of not such strong taste or smell that he might realise. Cathy knew very little about toxins really. As GPs, they saw accidental poisonings so infrequently and the majority ended up in A&E, but in Mark's case, whatever had caused such damage had been caustic to the extreme. Cathy doubted very much that it could have been completely odourless. Without cutting corners, she then arrived at the same conclusion that she assumed the police had: that the poison had been administered in Mark's coffee. The coffee, strong and bitter in taste, might well prove an excellent disguise for a noxious substance.

Cathy thought of the ways in which a poison might have been added to the cup. There was a chance that it had been mixed in with the coffee granules, the water or the milk. Cathy knew that Mark did not take sugar, so she could rule this out at least. Then there was the cup itself. If someone had swilled the poison around the sides beforehand. But all these things troubled her. How might one guarantee that Mark alone took the drink and nobody else inadvertently? As far as Cathy was aware, no-one in the practice had their own special mugs, and the coffee granules, milk and obviously boiled water, would have been shared by all.

The only conclusion was that the poison had been added after the drink was made and declared ready for Dr Hope. Cathy herself had been in her room still of course, when the coffee making had been taking place. She knew how on a usual day, things worked, however. She was still to find out why James had taken the mug of drink down to Mark instead of one of the receptionists, but while James was absent, she thought that she might still investigate this line of inquiry.

By coffee time and after a hectic morning consulting, Cathy realised that she would have to be quick if she was going to afford this luxury before heading out to begin the ever-lengthening list of house visits. She knew though that this morning, her coffee break was far more important than usual. She had made her decision during morning consultations and it seemed to her the only way forward. She must test out her theory. She recognised that James was not the person responsible for Mark's death, but fearing the police's continued interest in him, she felt compelled to try and prove it herself. If she could just verify that it was possible for the coffee to have been poisoned by not just James as he carried it downstairs, but anyone in the room before James took the cup, she might have something to go on.

Having first washed her hands, Cathy slipped a five-millilitre syringe from the drawer in her room. She removed the cellophane. She took a polystyrene cup by the sink and filled it with water from the tap She drew back the syringe plunger and submerged the tip, she pushed the plunger down and then drew back again, watching as the water sucked up to the mark. Perfect. She might get a slightly soggy pocket, but she was ready to see if the poison could have been administered this way without notice.

Michelle and Julie were already upstairs in the kitchenette. Julie had found the remnants of the ginger cake and was wondering if the police had looked at this too.

'Not much left anyway, do you want a bit? Dr Moreland, you look like you need cake.'

Cathy leaned over the girl's shoulder. The cake looked like a crumbled brick, but the strong ginger smelled good and she was hungry.

'Yes, please. No icing for me though.'

Cathy's heart began to beat faster. She slipped her hand in her pocket and toyed with the plastic syringe. Turning it over and over. She was close enough to both to try out her little experiment, but she felt too exposed, they were both too attentive. At that moment, Brenda came in.

'Morning Brenda,' Cathy said too brightly. 'How's it been for you then?'

'Morning. Busy,' Brenda said, moving to the cupboards to take a cup for herself. 'Has this water heater been on all night? How many times do I have to say to switch things off? If you could see the bills I have to deal with.' Brenda turned, only then realising that all eyes were on her and looked suddenly embarrassed. 'I've been trying to ring round and get locum-cover all this morning,' she said more evenly.

'And? Any luck?' Cathy asked.

Brenda was now shaking the sugar bowl and knocking the side to dislodge the remaining granules. 'No, I haven't managed yet. Half of them say they won't do house visits, and some are only free to do a handful of odd days here and there.'

'Brenda, have you thought about asking Linda to take on an extra session, at least until we're able to find permanent cover? I'm sure she'd be delighted to be asked.'

Cathy had still to speak with Linda about her error in giving the wrong flu vaccination to a child. As far as she was aware the mother had decided to let the matter drop. The partners had written a letter of apology, promising that they had already made changes to the way things were being done to avoid such a mistake occurring again. Definitely not partnership material, Cathy thought of Linda, but she would mop up some of the empty shifts at least, giving her and James a chance to trouble-shoot over the coming weeks when he returned also.

'I've already asked Linda,' said Brenda sighing. 'She's committed to another locum job and can only do four sessions for us until mid-October. Anyway, I don't have time to keep ringing around,' Brenda said. 'I need to go out later, but I'll be back mid-afternoon and take up the hunt again then.'

Cathy shook her head. 'Sorry Brenda, but James and I can only see so many people. You'll need to sort something, and fast. I've barely had a chance to look at lab results this morning and you'll have seen the house calls mounting up.'

'Here you are Dr Moreland,' Michelle said, interrupting and handing her a plate. 'Take a bite of that first before you head out on your visits.'

'Thanks,' said Cathy, taking the plate and placing her own cup of coffee down. As she did so, she finally found the courage required and slipped the syringe from her pocket. While Brenda's back was turned, and apparently unnoticed, she injected the full contents into Julie's mug of coffee next to her own. It was only five-millilitres of tap water and it probably wouldn't even cool the coffee that much.

Cathy smiled. She then took a bite from the cake. It was dry and stuck to the roof of her mouth.

It proved that it could be done though. James was surely not the only person in the frame, no matter what the police thought. Cathy headed out on her visits with a spring in her step, knowing that she was on track to clearing James's name.

24

C ome mid-afternoon and with a lull in activity, Cathy walked to the front reception and slipped behind the desk. Julie and Michelle were occupied printing out repeat prescriptions, but Michelle looked up and smiled.

'Calmed down a bit now, Dr Moreland,' she said.

Cathy nodded. 'Thank goodness. Listen, girls, I wanted to ask a couple of questions about that morning. Have you got a minute? I'm trying to find out what on earth happened that day, especially if the police are taking it upon themselves to pull us in for questioning now. Who knows, they might drag me off next.'

Since her experiment that morning, Cathy had thought a good deal. She had at least proved that the coffee might have been tampered with upstairs without necessarily drawing attention to the fact. Not happy to make assumptions too hastily though, Cathy considered when other than this, the coffee might have been poisoned. James had taken the cup from Michelle; it seemed, and had walked down the stairs to Mark's room. Had he met anyone in the stairwell? This was a point that needed clearing up.

Cathy also wondered for the first time, if Mark had left his room unattended at any point following James's visit with the coffee. If the mug had been left on Mark's desk, this too, might prove a potential opportunity to add a lethal dose of whatever it was that killed him. As the reception desk looked out almost directly onto the doctors' corridor, Michelle and Julie were the most likely to have noticed any unusual activity that day.

Michelle snorted. 'Well, Dr Moreland, what do you want to know? We're next to useless and totally unobservant, aren't we Julie? I'm sure that's what the police thought when they questioned us.'

Cathy grinned. 'I just wondered if you remember Dr Hope leaving his room after Dr Longmuir had brought down the coffee? Perhaps he went to the toilet or into another room, and left his own door ajar?'

'You're forgetting,' Julie said. 'We'd put the phones over by then. We were upstairs for some of that time taking our own coffee break.'

'Of course,' Cathy nodded. 'But when the whole drama kicked off, you were on reception again, weren't you? I know it was quiet, because it was only the last few patients left, but can you remember seeing anything unusual?'

Michelle shook her head. 'I wish I could think of something,' she said apologetically.

'Not to worry. It was just an idea,' Cathy said. 'Now, I need another bit of help.'

It had bothered Cathy that Mark could have drank poison and apparently called in a patient afterwards. How he continued consulting while feeling unwell, she didn't know. Perhaps there was something he had written in the notes, something to indicate his mood or his demeanour, that might help?

Michelle rolled her eyes.

'I know,' Cathy said, 'but bear with me. Dr Hope's list, the morning he died. I wondered if he'd written anything in the notes that might give me a clue as to how he was. He had his coffee, and then assuming he didn't leave his room, and we have no evidence he did, he continued consulting. I just wonder how he was feeling.'

Michelle got up and followed Cathy back through to her own consulting room.

'Are you doing a bit of proper digging?' the receptionist asked, and Cathy smiled.

'Hardly that, but I feel we can't just sit around waiting for the police to come back and arrest another one of us.'

Michelle nodded. 'I can get Dr Hope's patients up on your screen if you can wait a minute or two.'

Cathy gestured for her to sit, and the young receptionist typed her username and password into Cathy's computer with impossible speed, and then began scrolling through the previous days' patient lists. Finally, she came to the right day, and moved the viewfinder along the screen, bypassing both Cathy's column, and James's lists, before she came to Dr Hope.

'There,' Michelle said. 'That's his morning surgery. Brenda said that the police took a print-out too, but they didn't ask to look at any of the patient files. I think Brenda was glad. She wasn't sure about patient confidentiality.'

'I think we'd have to waive that right, given that someone died,' Cathy said.

Michelle got up. 'Obviously, he had less booked in than you and Dr Longmuir,' she said.

'Oh?' Cathy asked. 'How so?'

'He was supervising, remember? Well, he was meant to be, but that boy Tom, didn't turn up. Don't think he's as keen as he made out at the start.'

'Of course,' Cathy said thoughtfully. For the first time, it occurred to her that Mark might not have been the intended victim.

'Well, I hope that you can come up with something,' the receptionist said.

She walked to the door and Cathy had already seated herself and was scrutinising Mark's list. Some names she knew, and others she'd not come across before.

'Can I access this like I would a normal surgery, Michelle?' she asked without looking up.

'Yes of course. Just click on it as you would usually, and the notes should appear. The view is a bit different because it's in my account and not a doctor's view.' Michelle re-crossed the room and bent over the keyboard. 'Look here, these are the early morning ones. He saw, wait a minute, he saw five before he'd blocked himself out for coffee. See that's like you all do on your screens. Now, here are the ones after coffee break.' Michelle scrolled down the screen. 'There you are. All the late morning's appointments. See the ones in red? Those are the ones he never got to and I had to reallocate. All the white ones were patients he saw.'

'Michelle, thank you, that's perfect,' Cathy said.

Cathy returned to the screen and began to scroll through Mark's last morning. It felt strange. Cathy's thoughts returned to that fateful day and the dreadful hours after Mark had seen these people. Surely only he could have been the recipient of the poison that day, even if the trainee Tom, had been there. Cathy considered how the surgery might have run, with Tom perhaps taking it in turns with the GP to see the patients. Their coffee break would not have been affected though, she thought. Mark always remained in his room, and as far as Cathy was aware, the trainee had always gone upstairs and taken his mug of coffee to drink by the back door. Cathy wasn't hugely impressed to find that the boy was a smoker. Hardly a good example to set his patients, she had thought when she saw. No, it seemed that had Tom come in that day, the only difference might have been that Mark could have been able to alert the boy that he was unwell. Cathy doubted that even this would have made a difference. Once he had swallowed the poison, he was beyond any heroics.

She peered at the screen, her hand hovering over the computer. She clicked the mouse twice and then opened up a patient file, but this soon had to be halted because her phone rang and Michelle told her that her first two patients were in the waiting room and one had already complained that she hadn't been seen. Reluctantly, Cathy closed the window that she had been looking at and opened up her patient list for the day. She strode out into the corridor determined to catch up and to get through the morning's patients as quickly as possible in order to return to her investigation.

She was all apologies and politeness, smiling at her first disgruntled customer, and by the time her patient left the room, they were pacified and marched out through the front door clutching the prescription that they had wanted.

Cathy rattled through her list, and if she was brutally honest, she didn't give her customers her full attention. She kept thinking about Mark's final day and the last few people he must have spoken to. Could there be something in the notes; a message, or an indication as to why he had died?

By the time her allotted break came, Cathy had caught up. She did not, however, go upstairs as she normally would, but instead closed her door and went back to the computer. There were only three patients highlighted in white. They were the ones that she was interested in. Maybe Mark had written something, or perhaps, if she spoke with them, they might tell her if he had been acting strangely after his coffee break.

Cathy opened the first patient's records and scanned down to Mark's summary for that morning's consultation. As she read, she could almost hear her partner's voice. Pouring over Mark's words, she tried to feel how he might have felt as he typed.

'Dysuria and frequency for 24 hours. Simple, uncomplicated UTI. Discussed risk factors, prescription: Trimethoprim. Discussed wasted appointment – THIS COULD HAVE BEEN DEALT WITH OVER THE PHONE!'

Cathy smiled. Well, Mark had clearly been his usual self for that consultation at least. She had to say she agreed with his sentiment regarding the urinary tract infection, but it was a little unprofessional to actually record the final line in the notes. Cathy decided that there was nothing to be gained, and closed the file. Moving on, she opened the next, and knowing the patient's name, scanned the text.

'TATT, postmenopausal, overweight. TFTs and FBC checked last time - normal. Breathlessness on exertion?? Nil on PE. ECG and CXR and RV by me or Dr M with results. ??Psychosomatic – husband died last month.'

Cathy hadn't heard that the patient's husband had died. She paused a moment and thought of her. They had been a lovely couple. She would give her a call later and see how she was doing. Still, there was nothing unusual in what Mark had said, so she continued.

She opened the final patient's file and found that her hands were trembling. Ridiculous, she said to herself. But in reality, she knew that this had to be it; her last chance to see what Mark had been thinking that morning. His last written words. She followed the records down the page, to the final line and paused. In some ways, she was disappointed not to find more. She had perhaps expected too much. Mark had recorded just two words during his final consultation. Cathy read and reread them.

'*DRUG SEEKER.*'

She closed the patient's file and rested back in her chair, closing her eyes. There was really nothing for it, she had to dig further.

25

Cathy had the address scrawled on a torn corner from her prescription pad and, having let Michelle know she was going out on a house visit, she set off. She had shut the computer files down in her room earlier, knowing that what Mark had recorded that day wasn't right. To just type two words seemed so out of character for the meticulous man she knew. Everything about him had been perfect; his appearance, his record-keeping. Cathy smiled remembering how she had walked into his room one day and had found him brushing his teeth at the sink.

'What are you doing?' she had asked.

'They expect us to be flawless,' he had told her, 'and I don't like to disappoint.' He had pushed past her then and then rudely looked her up and down. That was Mark all over though.

Before leaving the practice, Cathy had sat in her room for some time, wondering what she should do, but the answer was obvious. She must visit the patient, the last person Mark had spoken to, and see what he could tell her. Cathy wondered what she might find. Mark would have had his coffee by the time he had seen this man. He would have seen two patients before him, and should have seen more after, but following the 'drug seeker's' consultation, as Mark had worded it, the doctor had been unable to continue and had been taken unwell. Cathy supposed that this put the patient in the frame as much as anyone in the practice. What if the poison, or whatever it had been, had not been administered in the coffee? Cathy thought about this, and regretfully decided that this was perhaps wishful thinking. It would be a great relief to find that none of the practice staff had been implicated in the accidental, or even, as it seemed to look now, deliberate death, but it did seem improbable.

Whatever, she must see what this man had to say. Even if he could confirm that Mark was looking unwell, or perturbed, that might indicate his mood at the very least. She wondered if the police had done, or were doing the same. They had the same list of patients as she did, after all. She hoped they were doing something, anything to move the investigation on further.

Cathy knew the practice catchment area very well. It was a reasonably affluent place overall but had some pockets of poverty that were quite startling in contrast. Of the six-thousand patients they had registered, probably around twenty had a serious drug problem. It seemed that heroin was most commonly misused. Ironically, it had been what had attracted Cathy to the practice originally. She had taken an interest in drug misuse during a psychiatric attachment as a junior doctor and felt that with her knowledge in this area, she might offer the practice fresh eyes on the problem.

She knew that such patients were draining on resources, time, and on staff morale often. Both she and her partners had discussed it at length before her extended leave of absence. Cathy knew that few made it off the drug and few integrated successfully back into society to hold down employment. It was something she was frustrated by as a doctor but something with which she was still keen to assist. But that would have to wait for now.

Cathy glanced down at her prescription pad, which lay on the passenger seat beside her. She recognised the address and knew it was in one of the less salubrious areas, which was hardly surprising, given Mark's comment in the notes.

It felt good to have a purpose. Cathy depressed the button by her door and her window slid down. The wind on her face felt good. Her hair had only been roughly tied and loose strands flicked back and whipped against her face. She opened her mouth wide and swallowed the cold air, something she had done as a child. She knew James hadn't killed Mark. She was going to prove it and she was going to be the one to sort out this mess. Mark's death had been awful, but life would go on and the practice would recover. She could see her and James enjoying interviewing potential candidates together and choosing a well-rounded replacement. Someone who would truly fit in. The team would be tight, and after all of the trauma, they would stick together. After an obligatory settling period, she and Fraser might after all, set up that much-needed methadone clinic and the practice would thrive.

As it turned out, the flat wasn't easy to find. It was in a council estate and most of the house numbers weren't visible, either worn away, or they had never been there in the first place. Cathy drove up the street, her enthusiasm waning with every frustrating minute. Eventually, she asked someone walking their dog, and was pointed in the right direction. She turned the car awkwardly. Cathy hated these narrow streets. Finding a number close to the one she was looking for, she pulled in to the side and got out to continue on foot. She found the flat, but only because the number was painted on a bin sitting at the side of the pavement.

Feeling that she should look official, she got her doctor's

bag from the car and pushed the flimsy iron gate. She climbed the concrete stairs looking at the doors for the number. The stairwell had been used for a multitude of purposes, an improvised toilet by the smell of it. A child's buggy sat outside one door and some crushed beer cans and a split bin bag was outside another. She heard a dog barking and realised it was coming from the house she was looking for. Sighing, she rang the bell.

Cathy met the dog first. She shielded herself partially with her bag.

'Oh hello, I'm Dr Moreland. I'm looking for ...' She looked at her scrap of paper. 'A Euan Saunders?'

'Come in, Doctor,' said the woman, as she grabbed the still barking animal by the neck. 'So sorry about the dog. He's all noise, but he'd never hurt you. Come through.' The woman turned and called through to who, Cathy presumed was her partner.

Euan was sitting on an oversized leather sofa, watching the television. The room itself was tidy but smelt strongly of nicotine. Euan struggled to get up and holding his back, he gasped. He was a clean-shaven man of about forty years, but cigarettes and possibly other addictions had not done him any favours. Cathy noted the yellow, stained fingers and the slight tremor. She guessed his weight must be only around nine stone, making his BMI dangerously low.

'Sit down, Doctor,' said the woman, following her in, and closing the door. The dog could still be heard barking, but the sound was now muffled. 'We've not seen you before, have we, Euan? What did you say your name was?'

'Dr Moreland,' Cathy said, and sat down. The leather sofa hissed.

'So, what can we do for you, Doctor?' the woman asked. 'We heard about the little problem at the surgery the other day.'

Turning to Euan, her tone changed. 'Well, tell her what he said, then.'

'Shut up Lorraine,' the man replied. 'Let her say what she has to say. But if it's some sort of an apology, you can forget it. I'm writing a complaint even if the bastard's dead.'

Cathy grimaced. 'You heard then,' she said.

'All over the bloody town, and even on the news this morning, wasn't it? They're all saying what a great man he was, just in the shop down the road they were saying it. Maybe I should speak to a few of the newspaper folk and tell them what he was really like.' Euan crossed his arms tightly over his chest.

Cathy sighed. She could see how things had escalated that dreadful morning, and could understand if Mark had fallen out with this man. 'Dr Hope died. It was a tragedy,' she said simply, pausing and almost goading him to contradict her. The man before her rolled his eyes but didn't speak. 'And I've come because I think that you were his last patient. Possibly the very last person to see him alive.'

Euan looked sulky. 'Well I didn't have anything to do with it,' he said. 'How was I meant to know he was going to die?'

'The police...' Cathy began, but she was interrupted.

'Police? I'm not talking to the police,' Euan said.

Cathy clenched her hand around the handle of her doctors' bag. Her nails dug into the stitching, leaving a line. 'The police,' she went on, trying to control her voice, 'seem to think that he might have swallowed something. It might have been accidental, or perhaps deliberate.'

'What, and you think I did it because we fell out? Is that why you've come here? To accuse me?'

Cathy shifted and the sofa creaked in protest. 'No. I'm here because you were the last patient he saw, and I wanted to know ...'

The man's voice was now raised, and his partner shook her

head as if she had seen it all before. 'I didn't kill the bast–' he started to say, but Cathy couldn't stand this anymore.

'Listen to me and shut up!' she shouted angrily.

She felt a cold sweat between her shoulder blades and tucked a strand of hair behind her ear.

'Jesus,' she said under her breath.

Deliberately slowing her words, she continued. 'I need to know what he was like and what he said during that consultation. It might be extremely important.'

It seemed that her rudeness had shocked Euan into talking civilly, at least for now.

'I couldn't get an appointment with that young doctor, the girl I usually see. She always deals with my back. So, I had to get one with him. The other doctor knows me. She knows about all my problems. I haven't been able to work for months now. She's the first one who's listened. Tried me with a different painkiller, di-hypro-something.'

'Dihydrocodeine,' Cathy said. 'It's a highly addictive opiate-based drug.'

'Yes, yes we talked about that,' said the man, now warming to his cause. 'Me and the girl doctor, we spoke about it and I said no, I would only use it as and when I needed it, and just when things got really bad.' He looked at her self-indulgently. 'And things have been bad recently. I've maybe allowed them to run a bit low.' His breath was unpleasant and sour, even from this distance.

'And you've been on them for how long now?' Cathy asked.

'Six.'

'Months?' Cathy asked, barely about to hide her incredulity. Surely Linda couldn't have been so stupid. It was practice policy not to continue someone on an opiate-based drug for this amount of time, and especially for something like chronic back pain.

'So, the appointment that day?' Cathy asked, but she already knew the answer.

'Well, I finished the tablets a bit early and needed some more.'

Cathy sighed. Drug seeker was a fair description then, but the only person to blame for it was Linda. Deciding to ignore this for now, Cathy continued. She still needed answers and she'd have to deal with Linda later. 'OK, so how did Dr Hope seem when you were in?'

The man leaned across the sofa to her, as if he was going to confide something of great importance. Cathy saw the pock-marked skin now close-up, and his yellowed teeth smirked at her through thin lips. 'A bloody jumped-up bastard,' he said slowly and deliberately, letting the words fall heavily.

Cathy got up sharply, but he kept on talking, and rose too, following her to the door. The dog began to bark again.

'Listen, Doctor, I'm happy to tell you everything I know, but how about you give me an apology for the way your friend behaved and then write me a nice prescription for my pain killers?'

She slammed the door behind her, and as she ran down the steps, she heard laughter drifting down the disgusting stairway.

26

W hen Cathy returned to the practice following her house visit, she found it was twelve-thirty already and most of the staff had either drifted upstairs or home for lunch. By now, the carpark looked nearly empty, and there was no sign of the news reporters, thank goodness. She hesitated a moment outside the practice to look at the brass sign, with all the doctor's names listed on it. Dr J. Longmuir, Dr M. A. Hope, Dr C. Moreland. The graffiti that had been scrawled next to Dr Hope's name had been removed, presumably by Bert. Glancing around her, she ran her fingers across the engraving. They would need a new sign now. She had to get to the bottom of this. The practice waiting room was deserted. The glass automatic doors closed behind her. The whole place felt abandoned.

'That you back then?' said Michelle, suddenly appearing from behind the reception desk. 'They've all packed up for lunch and left me to it. Police have been in again though.'

'Oh?' Cathy transferred the doctor's bag to her other hand and crossed the hall, her heels clipping on the polished floor, sending echoes like ricocheting bullets.

'Spent an age with Brenda and then Bert again,' said

Michelle conspiratorially. 'No idea what they were asking him, but Brenda ... Oh, well she can tell you herself.'

Brenda had obviously heard voices and had come through from the doctors' corridor.

'Bit quiet Brenda,' Cathy said. 'It's not usually like this at lunchtime. Did you let them all off early?'

Brenda laughed. 'Hardly. No, we do have normal surgeries this afternoon, but it was Linda's idea really. They've gone to the new café down the street. Linda said she was buying cake to cheer them all up, and Irene and Tracy, oh and Julie, went along. Bert's still skulking about. I think he's taken this business very badly.'

'I think we all have,' replied Cathy shortly.

'How was the house visit?' Brenda asked.

'Fine. Listen, Brenda, Michelle was saying that the police had been back. What were they wanting this time? It wasn't anything to do with James, was it?'

'That was the strange bit,' the practice manager said. 'They were asking about Maureen, his poor wife. Goodness knows why. I couldn't tell them a thing. Anyway, he's just phoned to say he'll be in later.'

'So, do they know the cause of death yet?'

'Yes. Although I felt I had to drag it out of them. They came in and asked me about cleaning products and paint stripper for the practice. Of course, I didn't know a thing about that and pointed them in Bert's direction, but that's what they think it was, something called hydrocarbon? Fraser mentioned them in his talk.'

'Hydrocarbon?' Cathy asked, feeling sick.

'Yes, I'm afraid. They seem to think it wasn't an accident either. Cathy, it's too dreadful to even imagine.'

Michelle leaned in.

'Patients have all been talking today. Apparently, the newspapers got a photograph of poor Dr Longmuir getting into a police car.'

'Oh God,' sighed Cathy.

'But I thought you were onto something earlier? You chased out of here with a bee in your bonnet about something. Did you get anywhere?' asked Michelle.

Cathy blushed. True enough, she had marched out of the place, only calling to the girls at the desk that she had her mobile on her but not to call unless it was an emergency.

'Not really,' she said, rather embarrassed. 'I thought Mark's last patient might have been able to tell me something, but it turns out that he was behaving quite normally before he died and didn't show any sign of being unwell. His last few patients all seemed pretty standard.'

Cathy thought it likely that Mark had not felt so good during his final consultation. As she had driven back to the practice, she had considered that this was probably the reason for him only recording two words to describe the patient. If it had been a hydrocarbon poison, Cathy wondered if he had starting to feel tingling in his mouth, or pain when he typed in the notes. Perhaps he had done well to even manage those two words.

Cathy went to her room. Leaning back in her chair, she sighed and rubbed the back of her neck, trying to make sense of it all. Hydrocarbon. It couldn't have been worse. She had seen a case once before, a long time ago. The man had left a note and had downed a bottle of furniture polish. Cathy still remembered going into the side room to tell his wife after they had failed to revive him. It had been her first time at breaking bad news to someone, and she felt afterwards that she could have done the job better. She had been too matter-of-fact. She supposed that it had been because of the nerves. Cathy still didn't know why her consultant had asked her to do that one. She watched a woman crumple, almost dispassionately. Time seemed to stop. Cathy had spoken briefly. 'If there was anything they could do ...' but the words were empty. She had left a nurse with the woman. It still plagued her, that one encounter with hydrocarbon poisoning. She had even mentioned it at the practice meeting the other night, when Fraser had given his talk. At the time, he had asked if anyone had come across any commonly-used poisons. In fact, Fraser had said that accidental poisonings were rarely found nowadays other than in children.

Cathy logged onto her computer and began to type in the notes. She sat wondering what to say about the encounter and finally recorded: *HV – nil of note. Drug-seeking for DHC. DO NOT PRESCRIBE DHC FOR THIS PATIENT* *** She would have to discuss it with Linda later.

Having done this, she leaned back in her chair. She thought that she was getting another headache. Perhaps if she ran upstairs for a quick coffee before starting her afternoon surgery, it might settle her. Opening the door, she came face to face with Bert and jumped.

'You scared the life out of me Bert,' she said, clutching her throat.

'Just checking the buzzer system, Dr Moreland, no need to concern yourself,' the old man said.

'I was just getting a coffee,' she said, not sure why she had felt the need to explain.

'Sorry to make you jump. We're all a bit that way inclined at the moment though.'

'We are,' said Cathy considering. 'Bert, Brenda said you had the police in asking you questions today.'

The handyman smiled, and his face wrinkled into a thousand creases. 'Ah,' he chuckled, 'they were indeed and a whole lot of daft questions at that.'

'Bert,' said Cathy, her headache now forgotten. 'Did they ask if you heard anything from his room?'

'No,' he said simply, and then as an afterthought: 'Thought I was deaf most likely, though.'

Cathy smiled. 'So, did you, then? Did you hear anything? You came out of your cupboard didn't you when Tracy screamed? I saw that bit. Did you hear anything earlier in the morning though?'

The old man's brow crumpled like linen. 'Maybe a shout,' he said thoughtfully, 'but not so as I knew it was from his room. Could have easily been from your room, or Dr Longmuir's, for that matter.'

Cathy felt confused now. 'So that was about when, Bert?'

But the old man shook his head scornfully. 'No, I've no idea on time. I was busy. Not sitting looking at my watch all day.'

'But it was after the coffee break, am I right?'

'Perhaps,' he said non-committedly.

The old handyman shrugged and turned slowly 'Need to get on,' he said and began to walk leisurely down the corridor away from her.

27

Cathy had never attended an inquest and wasn't quite sure what was expected of her. She did remember one of her colleagues, a GP at a practice she had locumed for years ago, who had been called as a witness following a patient suicide. A young girl had jumped in front of a train and the GP had only seen her the day before and judged her as being mentally stable. Her colleague had been very upset by the whole business and had felt guilty for not spotting how desperate the girl must have been.

Cathy had done a fair amount of psychiatric training, and recalled the words of one of the consultant psychiatrists when she had first started working for him. He had said that unfortunately, in this line of medicine, you would meet some very disturbed people, some of whom would make repeated attempts to kill themselves. He warned her that a 'cry-for-help' with a seemingly poorly planned, failed-attempt at suicide should never been taken lightly. Eventually, the more 'cries-for-help,' the more likely a disturbed patient would be to go through with it, and ultimately succeed. He did follow this up with one important reminder though. Never feel the need to take on the guilt and responsibility for someone else's death. As a doctor, you clearly try to assist people, you offer them support, you refer them to get the help they need, but at the end of the day, it was impossible to watch over people twenty-four hours a day. Ultimately, he said that if a person was determined enough to commit suicide, then they would find a way. Cathy had felt uncomfortable when he had said this, and seeing her unease, he had continued. 'Never take it as a personal failing, if you have done your best for them,' he had said. She could still hear his voice now. Cathy had repeated those words, saying it to her distressed colleague at the time, but she never did hear what happened at that inquest.

The room wasn't as Cathy had imagined it would be. For some reason, she assumed that it would be like the courtrooms you see on television. But it was more like a boardroom, informal with a large circular table in the middle and along the sides of the room, rows of chairs. It was all very modern and soft compared with her expectations. Brenda and Cathy had driven together to the court. Brenda apparently knew this area of the city and had offered. There was no reason to come separately. Irene and Tracy had arrived shortly after them, and Cathy saw at the far side of the room, an elderly couple who she assumed were distant relatives.

'Where's James?' whispered Cathy to Brenda.

'Coming. He had a late call and said it was going to be tight.'

James walked in then and looking around, saw them. Cathy waved.

'Here he is,' she said.

He sat down next to her, awkwardly shuffling his arms free of his jacket. Glancing over his shoulder, Cathy turned to see DCI Rodgers and DS Milne, who were in the doorway talking.

'James, how are you?' asked Cathy, touching his sleeve. They still hadn't spoken properly since he had returned to the practice the previous day following his encounter with the police. Cathy had hoped to catch him before, but both had been run off their feet.

'Worn out,' James replied. 'This is an awful business,' he went on. 'They've found out it was some toxic household cleaner. Did they tell you? Hydrocarbon showed up on the post-mortem. Can't believe this is happening.'

'We heard. They told Brenda. James, you look dreadful,' Cathy stated.

The police came into the room and sat at the table along with another man they didn't know. Then the coroner walked in, accompanied by another woman. The police stood up, and they all followed suit, as the woman walked to the front of the room and sat at the other side of the large table with presumably her assistant next to her.

'Good morning everyone. Thank you for coming. Please sit,' the coroner said. 'I believe we are missing the usher today, so I'll go through a few minor preliminaries on courtroom etiquette.' She smiled around the table. 'We understand that most relatives and witnesses have no experience in court so please don't worry about finding the right words. Any respectful comments or questions are welcome. I also have some practical requests. Please switch off mobile phones, do not eat, drink or chew gum.'

James reached into his pocket and fishing for his mobile, switched it off. The coroner waited and then went on.

'Right, initially, I will explain why, in general terms, this inquest is being held and I will then discuss the issues we will cover today. If anyone has any hearing difficulties, we have a loop hearing aid system and as you can see, the courtroom is designed for those with mobility issues. Today I will not ask anyone to stand as they give evidence or statements.'

Cathy was surprised at the informality of the situation. The coroner was very reassuring. She explained that everyone who spoke that day would be asked to take a non-religious affirmation rather than swearing on the bible. She then told them that the reason the inquest was being held was not to attribute blame to anyone, but as in the case of Dr Mark Alexander Hope's death, the police had informed the court that there was reasonable cause to suspect that a death was unnatural, due to violence, neglect, or that it may have occurred in suspicious circumstances.

The coroner read out each witness statement in turn, and allowed each of them to add to, change or confirm what they had said to the police. She read out the postmortem statement, and as it turned out, the unidentified man who had come in just before the coroner was in fact, the police pathologist. He had clearly attended many inquests before and sounded both eloquent and succinct. Mark had died of respiratory arrest due to pulmonary oedema, but was going into multi-organ failure with liver and kidneys also affected. It seemed that coffee had been found in the stomach, along with a very small trace of a hydrocarbon-based oil-like substance.

'And the small amount of hydrocarbon that you describe as being found in the stomach; would this have been enough to result in death?' the coroner asked.

The expert witness bowed. 'Indeed. Merely a tablespoon would have been ample,' he replied.

'May we move onto timing, doctor?'

The pathologist consulted his notes. 'Of course. There is a range of variability in what might be possible, but within an hour of ingestion, would seem likely,' he said. 'I would add, that although not inconsistent with my experience, the oral mucosa in this case, was quite extensively damaged in comparison with the stomach lining. I only say this as a matter of note.'

'Would this be caused by any particular circumstance in

your opinion? Would the timing of ingestion alter because of this finding?' the coroner asked.

'I can only be clear that the time from ingestion to death was within one hour,' he reiterated, and the coroner thanked him.

Tracy was then asked to confirm that it was she who had found Mark. She was unable to say much more than that though and disturbed the proceedings considerably by repeatedly blowing her nose.

It was then Cathy who was asked to speak. She had been fine up until that point but now found that her legs were shaking slightly. A fine cover of perspiration had formed across her forehead and she licked her lips repeatedly. Saliva pooled in her mouth and she thought she might be sick. She was very glad that she didn't have to get up and stand. She was asked about the resuscitation attempt and a little about Mark's behaviour that morning. It was all over and done with very quickly. When she finished speaking, she felt exhausted.

Irene and James were asked briefly about the resuscitation attempt, and then the coroner asked DCI Rodgers to make a short request to the court as how he would like them to advance. The detective stated that he would like to be given more time to investigate the circumstances of the as yet, unexplained death.

The coroner finally summed up. 'This preliminary inquest has been to establish the answers to four questions,' she said. 'Who the deceased was, where they died, when they died, and how.' She paused as she looked around the room. 'As yet, we are unable to establish fully how Dr Mark Alexander Hope died and I must, therefore, give an open verdict and allow the police to investigate the matter further.'

'Cathy?' Brenda asked, as having been dismissed by the coroner, they got up to leave. The practice manager had begun to slip her arms into her jacket, but instead came around the table to her. 'You've gone pale, hang on.' She took Cathy's elbow. 'Don't start fainting on us. That's all we need.'

Brenda gestured for James to come over, but Cathy shook her head and smiled. 'Overthinking and not enough sleep,' she said. 'I'm fine, honestly. I'm fine.'

Although she couldn't see it in herself, it was clear for everyone around her that she was anything but fine. Having it spoken of so plainly was enough to shock anyone. Cathy knew that very grave reality of the matter was that there must be a deliberate poisoner in their practice.

28

That evening following the inquest, Cathy had the kind of uncomfortable inkling that something wasn't right. The sort of instinct that only comes when one has forgotten something of both great importance and urgency. The nausea had lessened somewhat since the afternoon, but she still felt off-kilter, as if her head wasn't quite up to speed. Trying to think, she filled the kettle and made a mug of tea. Something had been said to her, or in her presence and it was vital she remembered.

Slowly, she walked back through to the living room. The curtains were drawn shut, and the TV was blaring. She had been half-watching a programme about some animal rescue centre and it had just finished. She didn't usually watch sentimental rubbish on TV. Tonight though, she had put it on for company more than anything else. A background noise, to drown out her own thoughts, but now she needed to think.

As she sipped her tea, the something-that-had-niggled-her began to resurface. As it happened, it was a TV advert that must have jolted her mind. It had been a request for donations to a cancer charity. And then it hit her like a slap to the face. She scalded her mouth as she accidentally gulped on her hot tea. Why had the police been asking about James's dead wife? Wasn't that what Brenda had said to her earlier in the practice? Cathy had only been a doctor at the practice a short time when James's wife Maureen, had died. Cathy recollected that it had been an aggressive form of ovarian cancer. James's children had briefly come back to be with their mother, but they were abroad now. The illness had been short. The disease, Cathy assumed, had been diagnosed late, and must have been too advanced for surgical treatment. Cathy wondered if James had much contact with his children now that his wife was gone. He didn't really speak about his home life or family, but then, he was a private sort of person anyway. Did his children know that their father had been questioned by the police, Cathy wondered?

As she sat cradling her mug of hot tea, Cathy considered the police's apparent new line of inquiry. Was it possible that they were beginning to suspect that the death of James's wife was suspicious now too? What on earth had James been saying to them? She couldn't remember any talk within the practice, or gossip for that matter, after poor Maureen had died. But Cathy had been new to the scene then and perhaps still trying to find her feet. Was it possible that she had missed something? Brenda had been there though.

The streetlights had long since come on and it was the kind of half-light that made driving quite difficult. Cathy pulled down the visor to shield her eyes from the glare of oncoming car lights. The early evening was tinged auburn and above, the clouds drifted restlessly on a quickening wind. Brenda's house was only ten minutes' drive away, but to Cathy, it felt like an eternity. What on earth was she going to say? Turning onto the high street, Cathy saw that the town was fairly quiet. A few adolescents still hung around on street corners and she saw a harassed mother cajoling her screaming toddler. Cathy's route took her past the front of the practice, and she noted that all the lights were out.

When Cathy arrived at the house, she felt an increasing sense of unease. Getting out of the car, she awkwardly climbed the stone steps. On either side of the front path, despite the poor lighting, Cathy could see that the borders had been tended to with care. Cathy wondered if it was Brenda or her husband who was the keen gardener. She had only been to Brenda's once before to drop the practice manager off after a practice night out, but Cathy had not been invited in. Stealing herself, Cathy knocked on the door and hoped that nine o'clock wouldn't be too unreasonable an hour for visitors. A light in the hallway came on and then, a pale-faced Brenda appeared. Cathy considered how differently the woman looked without make-up or her usual smart, floral attire.

'Brenda,' she said apologetically, 'I am so sorry. I know it's late. I couldn't settle though for thinking about things.'

Brenda hurriedly adjusted her face from shock to passivity and stepped back. Cathy continued to talk as she accepted the woman's unspoken invitation, and walked in.

'I just wanted to run something by you. Have you got five minutes?' Cathy said, pausing in the hallway, unsure through which door she should go.

'Come on through,' Brenda said and led Cathy into the living room. 'We don't usually get visitors at this time of night. I thought it might be kids messing around and ringing doorbells. Frank's just gone up,' and then to Cathy's look of anguish: 'Oh don't be daft, I wasn't ready to turn in just yet. He likes to go up and watch the television in bed sometimes. His leg's been bothering him all day.'

'I'm sorry,' Cathy said, realising that she knew nothing about Brenda at all and feeling that she had been impulsive. 'Maybe I should have waited.'

'No,' Brenda said firmly, seating herself and indicating that Cathy should do the same. 'No. I couldn't stop thinking about it all either. Do you want a cup of something? I was about to have myself. I was worried about you earlier at the inquest anyway. You looked so pale.' Brenda got up again.

Cathy had just had a cup of tea and didn't really want anything, but agreed to another tea to ease the awkwardness of the situation. While Brenda was through to the kitchen Cathy was left alone. Getting up, she wandered around the room, looking at some of the photographs propped up on the sideboard, a painting on the wall. She noticed a book face-down on the coffee table, its spine stretched. She picked it up to see what her visit had interrupted.

Coming back through with two cups, Brenda laughed. 'Oh goodness, don't look at that,' she said.

'Didn't have you down as a romance fiction reader Brenda,' said Cathy putting the book back.

The other woman laughed 'Not normally, I fancied a change. I'm usually not a big reader at all. No time for it. I forgot the biscuits,' Brenda said, and before Cathy could stop her, she had gone through the house once again.

The room was small, but clearly well-loved. Brenda had obviously taken care to choose pleasant, neutral soft furnishings. She evidently had a passion for cushions. The sofa was fit to burst, and Cathy had already moved three to inch herself down. She was surprised to see no TV, just a computer on a desk. The room was lit by only a lamp behind the chair that Brenda had obviously been reading in before she had arrived.

Brenda came back with the biscuits and fussed around trying to find a placemat to protect the coffee table surface from the hot cups.

'It's fine. I'll hang on to it Brenda,' Cathy said. 'I need to warm my hands. Chilly out there this evening.'

Brenda finally found the placemats and pushed one across the table to Cathy anyway.

'Cheers,' said Cathy and tasted the tea. The cup smelled strongly of washing up liquid and she felt slightly sick.

Cathy started her query slowly. She didn't want simply to jump in and make something of nothing. And she didn't want to scare Brenda. Since she had arrived, Cathy realised that the unexpected visit had possibly done just that. She watched the other woman, clearly unpracticed at hosting visitors in her own home. Usually so self-assured at work, Brenda now came across as quite the opposite.

'So, you've been worrying too?' Cathy said, smiling across at Brenda who was now settled opposite. 'What are you thinking about it all then? I've not been able to relax since the inquest.'

Brenda nodded in apparent understanding. 'Oh, I just don't know. It's like a nightmare. I can't believe they still might have James in mind. I've tried to play it down to the reception staff, but it looks awful. I've already had to have sharp words with Michelle for talking out of turn.'

Cathy winced involuntarily on hearing this. 'Brenda,' she said, her determination renewed. 'The reason I came out tonight was because of something you said to me actually. It was something today and I only just got my head around what it was you were telling me.'

Brenda looked quizzically at her and Cathy felt herself blush.

'You said the police were asking about James's wife,' Cathy said with resolve. 'Can you tell me what it was the police were asking about? If you remember, I had only just arrived at the practice as a new doctor when poor Maureen died, so I don't really know much about it. But there wasn't anything strange, was there? Maureen had cancer, am I right?'

Brenda seemed to stiffen as Cathy spoke and the older

woman set down her cup on the table in front of her, as if unable to take another sip. 'Poor Maureen,' Brenda said. 'Yes. It was tragic really.' She paused as if recalling something and then went on. 'Cancer, yes, but there really wasn't anything to tell the police when they asked.' Brenda looked directly at Cathy now. 'When Maureen was dying, and goodness what a terrible time it was, James insisted on nursing her at home himself. The district nurses and the Macmillan nurses, or whoever it was, were going in and out to do her medications from what I can recall. It went on for weeks rather than months though. It was only at the end that there was something slightly odd.'

Cathy leaned forward in her chair as Brenda continued.

'From what I remember, there was some query from the district nurses at the end. I can't quite remember. It was so long ago now. Some discrepancy though, and I know for a fact that James was quite hurt. I think he was quite annoyed with the nurses. It didn't sit too well, if you see what I mean? Left a bit of an after-taste.'

'What were the nurses questioning? Can you remember anything, Brenda?'

But Brenda looked embarrassed. 'Something and nothing,' she said, shaking her head. 'It was a mix-up to do with the painkillers from what I recall. James wasn't too happy about it though.'

'What? Had they given her the wrong dose or something?' Cathy asked.

Brenda shook her head. 'A vial of something went missing, if you really want to know. I don't know what the stuff was. It didn't matter anyway, but it never turned up. I think it was emergency pain-relief for poor Maureen. It wasn't accounted for after she died. Nothing more came of it. I think at the time; James was adamant that there had been some silly mistake and that the medicine hadn't actually been in the house at all. I suppose it must have been a controlled drug because they had to notify the pharmacy about it, I think.'

'Were the police involved, Brenda?'

'Oh, my goodness, no! Whatever for? No. Dr Frobisher calmed James down and sorted the business out.' Brenda said half-laughing, and then in explanation: 'Your predecessor, Dr Frobisher. James's hero really, in many ways. Although I never thought of it before, I suppose it was his final act of support to James before retirement. And of course, then you arrived and took Dr Frobisher's place.'

Cathy smiled grimly. She knew only too well that what Brenda had spoken of was of significance. The police must think so also, it seemed inevitable. If a vial of a controlled drug like an opiate given to someone dying, went missing, usually a protocol was swiftly kicked into action. A drug such as morphine or diamorphine might quite easily get into the wrong hands. To an addict, a drug such as this might have a very high street value indeed. Diamorphine, after all, was simply another name for heroin. As Cathy drove home having apologised once again for disturbing Brenda, she considered why this apparently unexplained and serious incident had been brushed under the carpet so hastily. Could it possibly have a bearing on the inexplicable death of her colleague, and was her other practice partner, further implicated now that this new piece of information had come to light?

29

'James? The girls at reception have just told me that you've had the police at your door again?'

He looked up from his desk, and sighing, relaxed back in his chair. 'Talk of the town?' he asked, with the intonation of exhausted sarcasm.

Cathy shrugged. 'Seems so. Well? What's going on? Did they come to your house then? I've not seen them here today anyway.'

It was the following day and James's predicament still concerned her a good deal. After leaving Brenda's house, she had struggled to sleep and that morning awoke with a dreadful sinking feeling when she recalled Brenda's words.

James rubbed his forehead. 'Oh Cathy,' he said, and then glanced up at her.

She didn't speak.

'They were rooting around,' he finally said. 'I suppose it's par for the course, in an investigation of this sort.'

'Rooting around where, James? I wish you'd just say.'

'The house. The shed.'

'They've been in your garden shed? Whatever for?'

'What do you think, Cathy?' he asked. He blinked slowly and she saw defeat in his eyes.

'James?' She was now gravely concerned. 'But they didn't find anything, did they?'

'They found what they would find in anyone's shed. A whole host of potential poisons. Weedkiller, creosote ...'

'Oh James,' she said in horror. 'But they'll send them for analysis and it'll be alright. They'll be forced to move onto someone else.'

James shrugged. 'We've both got patients waiting, Cathy.'

He'd given up already, she thought. It was as if he knew that the police would find something with which to incriminate him and he had given up even trying to argue. But it made her task all the more imperative. If the police really were trying to prove James's guilt, she must keep one step ahead. Firstly, she must first find out if there was any truth in what Brenda had told her about the death of his wife, and the missing vial of diamorphine. Undoubtedly, the police would be looking into James's past now, and this would show up as a glaring red flag.

She waited until her last patient left the room. It wasn't that difficult to find out the details really. James had mentioned his previous practice partners many times before. Cathy knew that her predecessors had been held in high esteem by not only the patients who still talked of them even now on occasion, but by James himself, who must have been fresh out of medical-school all those years before, when the two doctors had taken him on. From what Cathy had gleaned from the various mentions of them in the past, the partnership had been at that time, a very happy one. And so, whilst scrolling through the computer records, it hadn't taken her that long to discover that poor, old Dr Frobisher had died three years ago. Cathy paused and read the man's obituary. 'An excellent doctor, being both hardworking and methodical,' the author had said, but added that more than this, 'he was caring and empathic, a man who was loved by his patients and peers alike.' Cathy wondered what on earth could be said in Dr Hope's memorial. Empathic and caring could be most definitely dropped.

Having made this discovery, Cathy instead focused her attention on Dr Clark, the other retired partner. He turned out to be rather trickier to trace. She eventually found that he had moved to a nursing home some time in the last year. Closing the computer screen, her hand slightly shaking, she sighed, now knowing what she must do.

∾

CATHY HADN'T ANTICIPATED how busy her morning's visits might be. She arrived for her appointment far later than she had intended. It was clearly a rather up-market nursing home. It seemed that it had been a mansion house of some sort in the past and had now been sold off and tastefully converted. The driveway leading up to the front door was lined by trees and there were wooden garden chairs positioned at the sides of the entrance. The stone steps had been made wheelchair friendly with a small ramp and a handrail ran up to the door. On the manicured front lawns, bird tables had been placed, presumably so that residents could watch the wildlife from the comfort of their rooms.

Cathy stood in the foyer leading to a grand staircase spoiled only by the ugly chairlift attached to the bannister.

Soon enough, someone came. A woman in green uniform carrying a huge pile of white sheets. She knew who Cathy was immediately, presumably having been warned by the matron.

'I'll just put these away,' said the woman, indicating the sheets, 'and then I'll find Jennifer. She's Dr Clark's keyworker and she'll take you up. Have a seat.'

Before long, the aforementioned Jennifer appeared, all smiles and politely batting away Cathy's apologies at being so late. Together they walked through the hall to a further set of stairs at the back of the house.

'And you're a doctor yourself, the matron said?' Jennifer asked, walking ahead now.

'That's right,' Cathy said, following her up the stairs. 'I work at the practice that Dr Clark used to be a partner with, and thought I'd come and meet him. Some of the patients still speak very fondly of him.'

'I can imagine,' Jennifer said, turning on the landing. 'He doesn't get many visitors, so he was delighted to hear someone was coming today. He's quite a character as you'll see. Keeps us all on our toes.'

'So mentally, he's still quite ...?'

'He's brighter than most of the staff. Nothing wrong with his brain at all. That's the shame of it, I suppose. He does get so frustrated at times. His body's not holding up so well now,' she said in explanation.

Cathy didn't want to ask but was told anyway.

'Prostate problems and osteoarthritis,' the other woman said. 'He's had a bad chest infection recently too, so he might get a bit out of breath talking.'

Having divulged this piece of information, Jennifer then turned and they headed along a wide, carpeted corridor. There were doors on either side of the passageway. Cathy glanced sideways as they went. Each door displayed the name of its resident. 'Alice Booth's' door was slightly ajar and Cathy could see that the lady was sitting by the window. Beside her was a birdcage, and something chirruped from within.

'Pets are allowed then?' Cathy asked the back of Jennifer's head.

'Oh, the budgie? Yes, we encourage them to have pets actually, within reason of course. We have a cat going around somewhere downstairs and a few others have birds in their rooms. No dogs though. The staff end up having to do too much.'

They finally arrived at the door marked 'Dr Reginald Clark.'

Jennifer knocked. 'Dr Clark can we come in?' she asked, and not waiting for an answer, she opened it.

He was seated at a writing bureau and rose slowly to come and greet her, completely ignoring Jennifer. His outstretched hand was cold and all knuckles, but his grasp was firm, and he met her with a steady gaze. His blue eyes, clouded by cataracts, hinted at a touch of humour behind the glasses. Although stooping with osteoarthritis of his spine, he still had an air of formality and correctness. The immediate impression he gave was that of confidence. She wondered if it had always been so, or if it was something that had developed with age.

'You come from my old practice; I believe, Doctor?' He turned to Jennifer who stood in the doorway and gestured for her to go.

Cathy turned to thank the woman who had brought her to the room, but she was already leaving.

'Nurses!' the old man said with feeling. 'Like to boss you around but some have hardly a qualification, and assume you know nothing. Come and sit down so I can look at you better. My eyes are going. Cataracts in both but an anaesthetist wouldn't touch me because of my neck, so I just make do with the glasses and live in a cloudy haze.'

Cathy sat down in a matching leather chair. The room was flooded with sunlight and she could see that he had an excellent view from his desk of the garden and drive leading up to the house. He followed her gaze.

'It does me fine. I tolerate the staff as best I can. I have my work to keep me busy and privacy from the rest of them in here. They used to try and get me down for all the social gatherings but they don't bother anymore,' he said, settling himself now in his own chair.

'What are you working on?' Cathy asked, leaning to look at the writing desk, piled high with ancient-looking medical textbooks. She could barely read the scrawl of writing on the A4 page. It looked like a spider had dipped in the ink and had run across it.

'Something and nothing,' he said dismissively. 'It's an article for the *British Journal of the History of Science* on phrenology. I have done a few for them over the years and have been researching this small lead for a number of months.' He smiled at her obvious surprise. 'I might be eighty,' he said, 'but no signs of dementia as yet. Thank God.'

Cathy laughed nervously. 'I'm glad you agreed to see me today,' she said, knowing that what she was going to ask would be awkward at the very least. 'You know, I suppose, that I'm the newest partner at the practice. I've been there for four years now?'

'Oh, I know,' the old man said 'I get the local paper every week and I saw the announcement. Dr Longmuir's told me a little about you when he's visited in the past. It's been a while, of course. He's a busy man. I don't expect him to come often.'

'I had hoped that he might still be in contact with you,' Cathy said, 'I assume if you get the local paper, that you've heard about the death of Dr Hope?'

'Suicide? Yes. I'm afraid I had read about it. All the staff were gossiping about it too. Not that it's any of their concern.'

'You say suicide,' Cathy said slowly, 'but the police don't think it was. They think that Dr Hope may have been poisoned deliberately.'

The old man didn't appear to be shocked but merely raised his white eyebrows and shook his head.

Cathy continued. 'I'm sorry to say that the police have been concentrating their efforts on Dr Longmuir.'

Still, the elderly man showed no sign of surprise.

'The police have been asking questions about his wife and how she died.'

He sighed and shook his head once more. Cathy heard his chest wheeze and tinkle as he exhaled.

'I know,' Cathy said in response. 'But I was only at the practice for a few months when Maureen passed away, and I wondered if you could shed some light on the matter. I want to clear James's name more than anyone.'

Eventually, he spoke, and when he did, his voice had a distant quality. 'Maureen had an aggressive ovarian carcinoma,' he said. 'It was a grade four when she was diagnosed. Terrible. She was offered palliative radiotherapy but declined it, I believe. Dr Longmuir and she agreed that it would impede her quality of life being driven back and forward to the hospital when it would only prolong things by a few months at the most.'

'I see,' Cathy said. 'And Dr Longmuir nursed her at home, I believe? Presumably, she was on a syringe-driver for analgesia nearing the end?'

'Yes. It was over very quickly, and she died with her husband and children around her.'

'Thank you, yes,' Cathy went on, knowing that she was possibly going to offend the man by asking further. 'I'm sorry to ask this,' she said, 'but a suggestion was made to me, and it may well be idle gossip, but a vial of diamorphine went missing around the time of her death. I just wondered ...'

Dr Clark turned and looked at her. His eyes, if it was possible, seemed to fog over even more.

'Dr Moreland,' he said heavily. 'What is it that you want me to say?'

Cathy uncrossed her legs and leaned in towards the man. 'I

know that Dr Longmuir still holds you in very high regard,' she said with feeling. 'He speaks of you and Dr Frobisher often, as do many of our patients. I don't know James as well as I should do having worked with him for four years, but he is a potential murder suspect now. I need to know if he was capable. I have just lost one partner and I don't want to lose another one.'

'You want to know if he assisted in Maureen's death, I take it?' the man asked after a long pause.

Cathy didn't speak and the old doctor's eyes seemed to somehow brighten.

'May I ask, Dr Moreland, how many years you have yourself been a GP?'

'I qualified in 2001 and did my house jobs and then went straight in. Nearly ten years now. Four as a partner at this practice,' Cathy said.

He shook his head and again turned his gaze out of the window. 'Can you tell me,' he went on, 'in those ten years of practice if you have ever assisted a death?'

Cathy didn't know what to say.

'Let me put it another way, then,' he went on. 'Can you tell me, hand on heart, that you haven't helped someone nearing the end of their life? Maybe not intentionally, but might you have known that by increasing the pain-relief that you had been using to ease their discomfort, you might also possibly compromise their breathing?'

Cathy met his gaze but did not need to answer.

30

Fraser looked unhappily out of his office window. He had come in to work really to avoid suspicion, but he knew that it was hypocrisy, given that he was unable to settle to anything. Since Dr Hope's death, he had been all but useless to the practice in his capacity as in-house pharmacist. It seemed that the police were concentrating all their efforts in quite the wrong direction. He had heard that Dr Longmuir had been asked into the police station for questioning. It was he who had carried down the mug Fraser had poisoned to Dr Hope that day. Goodness knows why the man had made the coffee in that ugly, thermal mug. If only he had used one of the normal ones. Fraser couldn't comprehend how the thing had happened.

He had turned the dreadful chain of events over and over in his mind. He thought with despair of the minor incidents that must have led up to the calamity. Jackson calling in sick that morning, Dr Longmuir making the coffee that day and taking it down instead of one of the receptionists. If only Julie or Michelle had made the coffee, the poisoned mug might still have been sitting unused in the kitchen. Fraser wondered how different it might have been. If the whole thing hadn't happened, how might he have felt on returning that morning to find that Jackson hadn't come in at all and the tragedy hadn't taken place? He had barely concentrated during the asthma meeting for worrying about how he should react on hearing the news of Jackson's death returning to the practice. Fraser considered if after further thought, he might have run upstairs and washed the mug out, abandoning any plans of murder. Had it been such a good idea in the first place really? Fraser certainly doubted it now. All in all, he had suffered a dreadful run of misfortune.

Although the past few days had been filled with abject terror for Fraser, he clung onto one small hope: that the police, with no evidence to charge Dr Longmuir, would abandon this line of inquiry. With this optimism though, came the inevitable question of who they might turn their attentions to next. Fraser of course, prayed it would not be him. True enough, he and Dr Hope hadn't got on particularly well, but towards the end, they had begun collaborating to improve the cardiovascular disease register and things had been more settled. Of course, Fraser had been out of the building when the incident occurred, so he hoped that this might protect him to some degree also.

Who might the police focus on next though? Fraser had already looked around the practice and had begun to size people up as having had motives to kill Dr Hope. It seemed that just about all of them did, as the man, despite apparently having been a respected and liked clinician, was undoubtedly rude and abrasive with his staff. Fraser had started to study with interest, the rest of the team's reactions to the tragedy. Brenda had been quite off-kilter. Fraser had never seen the woman in such disorder. He knew that Dr Hope had caused the practice manager a good deal of grief while he was alive, perhaps more than most given the demands he made upon her, but certainly his death had benefited Brenda little. She was, after all, a full-time doctor down and the last time Fraser had seen her, she was close to tears trying to pin down a locum.

Fraser then moved on to the receptionists. Neither Julie or Michelle, he decided, despite disliking the doctor, and seemingly much enjoying the gossip and intrigue of a real-life drama, had any real motive, so he thought that they might well escape police interest.

Fraser considered the remaining doctors. Linda, the long-term locum, was a little disorganised and careless, he had found. He knew that she disliked Dr Hope and apparently, she had been vocal about this in conversation before the man had died. If hearsay was to be believed, she had complained to Brenda that she found his manner intimidating. This had since been relayed to him by Michelle, over coffee one morning. Dr Moreland was quite a different matter. Fraser still hadn't quite worked her out. He had heard that she had been unwell, and reading between the lines, it seemed that she had had some sort of a nervous breakdown recently. He got the impression that the other GPs had been trying to protect her. He found himself rather drawn to Dr Moreland. She had a fragility that the others did not and of all the doctors, he felt that if he had a problem, he might go to her first. She had spoken about setting up a methadone prescribing clinic with him. He wondered if she would have the mental strength to deal with such individuals and he knew that Dr Longmuir and Dr Hope hadn't been keen. The police surely wouldn't suspect her though. He certainly hoped not.

The nurses though, were a different matter. Irene might easily be crossed off. She hadn't a bad word to say about anyone and Fraser found himself smiling when he thought of how the elderly nurse had pulled the team together, insisting on bringing in traybakes to cheer the staff up. No, Irene was unquestionably safe. What of Tracy then? Dr Hope's girlfriend and possible inheritor of his fortune. Having witnessed the girl's callous flirtations first-hand, and then suffered the repercussions of her insinuations later, he thought that she might well warrant a police investigation.

Fraser closed the computer file that he had been looking at and glancing at the clock, decided to go upstairs. It was late afternoon and although he didn't want a hot drink, he needed to get out of his room. He hated his own company and even the chatter of the receptionists was preferable to sitting alone with his thoughts. Gradually, as he walked through reception and along the corridor, passing Dr Hope's room, and turning his head in aversion, he felt his panic begin to lessen. It was alright. He would be fine. Perhaps in some ways, he had done the practice a favour given that Dr Hope was so universally disliked. Maybe the police would give the thing up. Put it down as suicide. Dr Hope might have had some hidden financial worries, and then there was his divorce settlement. Maybe the police would think that this was reason enough to end his own life. He continued to the bottom of the stairwell and climbed the steps. Yes. Certainly, there was no call for panic just yet. He had behaved naturally and of course, there was the alibi.

With the thought of his alibi, Fraser's confidence returned. The police had taken away the coffee granules for analysis. They were clueless as to the real route of ingestion of poison. And then, Fraser for the first time considered the mug and what had happened to it. He assumed that it must have been washed up by Dr Hope in his own room and then taken for analysis by the police. Had they found any trace of poison within? He assumed that they had checked it for fingerprints also, but having been sat in the communal kitchen for days, it seemed likely that the thing might have picked up a good number of innocuous prints. His own would be amongst them. That did not bother him in the least. He wasn't criminally minded, but he knew that had he wore gloves, the patches of no-prints might well have led to more questions. Better to plead that they had all used the damn thermal thing and be done with it.

Fraser found himself now running up the stairs. He was safe for surely the police might have asked to speak to him further if he was truly a suspect. Hopefully, Tracy might get a good grilling at some point. Yes. She deserved to be shaken up at least.

He pushed the heavy door to the room and entered. The kitchen area was around the corner and at first, he thought he was alone. He moved rapidly with a jauntiness to his step but to his shock, came face to face with the last person he expected to see.

A slow smile crept across Jackson's face. 'In a hurry, Fraser? Finally, a chance for a good catch up.'

Fraser stood stock-still and watched as Jackson shifted casually around the kitchen. In his hand, he held the thermal mug. Fraser couldn't take his eyes off the thing. How could Jackson possibly have it? Surely the police must have taken it away?

'I thought they'd told you not to come back,' Fraser finally said. 'You've no supervisor.' All the while, his eyes didn't leave the cup.

Jackson laughed. 'Is that what you thought, Fraser? Or rather hoped. No, well I'm ever so keen,' Jackson said as he walked across the room towards Fraser. 'I gave Brenda a call the other day and asked if I could be of any help. She was falling over herself to take me back. I'm a qualified doctor, you see? I can deal with the day-to-day dross that these simpletons see without thinking. As long as the beautiful Dr Moreland keeps an eye on what I'm up to, it's fine. Nice set-up too, no? I knew I'd like general practice and what a treat to work amongst old friends. I've even been thinking about going the whole hog and completing my training here. Lovely, lonesome Tracy looks to be in need of some cheer, and I heard that Dr Moreland was looking for a hand setting up a methadone clinic. Sounds fun, don't you think?'

Fraser shook his head.

'No?' Jackson laughed. 'I thought it was right up your street, Fraser. From what I recall, you're very sympathetic to the needs of drug takers.'

Fraser flashed him a look of anger, which only caused Jackson to laugh.

'If looks could kill, eh Fraser? Forgive me for being melodramatic, but given that I was meant to be consulting on the day that Dr Hope was killed, I find myself a little twitchy. If the coffee that Dr Hope received had been meant for me ... Well, anyway, cheers.'

Jackson raised the mug to his lips and Fraser watched in horror. He didn't understand. Had there been two mugs, both filled with poison? But before the man could take a sip, Fraser darted forward and without thinking, he snatched the mug from Jackson, downing the hot, bitter liquid himself.

31

Tracy had it seemed, settled into a new role. Cathy thought that in many ways the situation could not have been better for the young nurse, who looked incredibly comfortable now as the grieving widow. Cathy had overheard the suggestion that Tracy might be expected to inherit at least some of her lover's fortune. She did not know if there was any truth in this rumour, but one thing that had struck her as distinctly odd, was the fact that Tracy had apparently moved into Dr Hope's farmhouse since her brief time at Irene's, rather than returning to her own flat. Michelle had been particularly vocal on the matter, behind the nurse's back of course. It could not have been a more scandalous arrangement in many of the patients' eyes either. The only thing Cathy could do was remain tight-lipped. It wasn't any of her business and as long as Tracy continued to arrive for work and attend to her patients with care and respect, there was nothing much else to be done.

Since Cathy's visit to the nursing home, things at the practice had become more complicated. Although Brenda had tried to dull down any concern on her part, Cathy could see all too easily that the practice manager was unsettled.

'It's not really a problem if they do talk to him,' Brenda had said, having just relayed the news to Cathy that James had been taken in once again for questioning, apparently this time to further discuss the police's discovery of a very old bottle of paint stripper in his shed at home. 'We know he's innocent and the police will find that out too,' she went on. 'It's unfortunate that he has to go in and explain himself but at least I've found a locum who can cover for now. Oh, and that young lad, Tom Jackson has asked to come back today. Although I thought he was a bit of a know-it-all at the beginning, he seems genuinely keen to help us out. If you don't mind keeping half an eye on him?'

'No, that's fine,' Cathy replied, automatically, but she wasn't listening. She felt sick at the thought of poor James sitting alone in a police station again trying to talk his way out of the ghastly situation. Had the police checked any one of their sheds, surely, they might have found weedkiller, paint-thinner and a whole host of potentially lethal concoctions. Cathy said this to Brenda and the practice manager grimaced.

'Maybe,' Brenda had said, 'but typical of Dr Longmuir, he had the old-fashioned stuff. It isn't even sold nowadays because it's too dangerous.'

Cathy sighed. The situation seemed to get more and more impossible.

Brenda had promised to phone the police later that morning to try to find out what was going on and Cathy set about her morning surgery with a heavy heart, but renewed determination to clear her partner's name. She saw Jackson in passing and told him to pop in if he had any queries. Perhaps she had misjudged the young doctor after all.

She returned from house visits that morning, having taken the majority of calls to spare the locum who was unfamiliar with the area. Having asked Brenda who said that there was still no news, she set about some much-needed tidying up. The pile of insurance company doctor reports had been growing larger and larger.

She still thought hard about what Dr Clark had said the previous day as she went about clearing the insurance claims. She felt humbled but a bit of a hypocrite in truth. She found that rather than confirming his guilt, the suggestion that James had assisted the death of his wife, had made her, if anything, more sympathetic towards him. She was sure that if the police found out, however, they would be unlikely to take a similar view.

She was coming to the halfway point, having already quickly run through the most straight-forward insurance claims. When she came across Irene's name, Cathy did a double-take. It was true that usually, they encouraged their staff to seek an alternative practice as treating a colleague was often fraught with difficulties. Brenda had allowed this policy to waver over the years however, and Cathy knew that they were doctors to Bert and his family, and both Julie and Michelle on the reception desk also. This was the first time that Cathy had come across Irene's notes.

She scanned the claim quickly. It seemed that Irene had been in a minor car accident some months before. When Cathy thought about it, she seemed to remember the nurse referring to something of the kind, but having been off sick herself at the time, Cathy must have missed the incident itself. Irene appeared to be challenging a refusal of payout for whiplash injury. Cathy logged onto her computer and keyed in Irene's date of birth as stated on the insurance form. The company had asked for a second doctor's opinion. Cathy read briefly through the most recent entries. It seemed that having initially seen Linda with the first presentation of neck pain following the accident, she had then seen Mark. Cathy's heart sank as she read what her colleague had said about Irene. '*Untenable claim*,' he had typed. '*Vague symptoms and little evidence of distress to individual or ability to undertake day-to-day tasks.*' It put Cathy in a difficult position. She could hardly ignore Mark's appraisal of the situation, and why on earth was Irene making such a claim in the first place? Were things so tight, that she was forced to, even when ethically it seemed she had no right to do so? Cathy knew she would have to have a quiet word with Irene and explain her position.

But quite apart from this new and worrying issue, by late afternoon, Cathy was growing more and more concerned to hear news of James. She had been through to Brenda's office and had asked her several times if the police had been in touch. Brenda's act, if that was what it was, was wearing a little thin.

'Well, shall I call them?' Cathy had asked in exasperation, having met Brenda at the front reception after finishing a number of telephone consultations.

Brenda had rolled her eyes. 'By all means, but you'll get the same snooty call-operator who'll tell you nothing. Honestly, it's bad enough as it is without you hounding me every second of the day as well.'

Standing in reception, a sudden peel of laughter echoed through the hall. Michelle, who had been sitting at the front desk, tutted.

'Not grieving that much is she?' she said.

Brenda looked uncomfortable. 'Michelle, be careful,' the practice manager said.

'I know, I know,' the young girl went on, 'but really Brenda, how can you laugh like that and then be in floods of tears the next minute? One of our doctors, her boyfriend, is dead, and another of our doctors is suspected of killing him. Honestly, how can anyone laugh?'

'Everyone deals with grief in their own way,' Brenda said stiffly. 'I think we have to be understanding of one another at the moment. We're all clearly struggling,' she said looking at Cathy. 'The worst thing we can do is start bickering amongst ourselves. Stressful times make people act out of character.'

'Well that's just it,' said Julie, now coming through from the filing-room and joining Michelle at the front desk. 'It's not out of character, is it? She's always been superficial. I overheard that young trainee doctor asking her out or offering to go over to her place to keep her company earlier. You know, that new Dr Jackson? Disgusting. Poor Dr Hope's only just died and she's flirting with the first man to come along.'

'And I know for a fact that she thinks Dr Hope's left her the house,' Michelle said.

'You can't go around saying that!' Brenda seemed genuinely horrified.

'It's true,' Michelle said, twirling a pen between her fingertips. 'I heard her on the phone the day before to some pal of hers. Chatting away, she was. Not a care in the world.'

'I wouldn't put it past her to have poisoned him,' Julie snorted.

Cathy watched as Julie's face fell, and turning along with the rest of the gathering, she saw Tracy standing only ten feet away. She had come out of her room and was holding a pile of patient records. Her face was cold and frightening.

'Well, at least I now know where we all stand,' the young practice nurse said, inching closer to the group.

'Let me just say that I did not murder Mark, if that's what you've all been thinking. You must think I'm a fool, but I know more than you could ever imagine about what happened.' Tracy turned and looked from Cathy to Brenda, and then back again. Her cheeks were ugly, red blotches. 'I saw what was missing from his room, you know? Someone in this practice had better be very careful about what they are saying. When Dr Longmuir is released, the police will be looking for the real murderer and I might just have a name for them.'

With that, she spun on her heel and retraced her steps back to her room. They all winced as they heard the door slam.

ll that afternoon, Cathy went over and over the silly girl's words. She found herself pacing her room long after her patients and many of the practice staff had left, trying to make sense of it all. Several times she thumped her head with the heel of her hand in utter desperation. 'Think,' she told herself. 'For God's sake, think.'

She was still to hear any word from James. She had left easily a dozen messages on his answer machine, asking him to return her calls as soon as he was out of police custody, no matter what hour. Cathy wondered how Brenda was. She hadn't come in to say goodbye for the evening. The practice manager had seemed mortified by Michelle's words, and by Tracy's reaction on overhearing them. Even Irene, who had appeared at the desk seemingly simultaneously with Tracy, had gone white as a sheet. Cathy wondered if there was any truth in what the office girls had said about Tom and Tracy. Cathy felt that she knew so little about either one of them. She had been so caught up in her own day-to-day routine that she had missed any signs of warmth between them. Tom had only been here for a week or so before

Dr Hope had died. None of it really made any sense to her, and what had Tracy meant by what she said?

Cathy eventually gave up and slowly began to tidy her room, logging out of the computer system and turning off her light. She collected her doctor's bag and jacket, but seeing that by her sink were three cups that she had amassed over the course of the day, she decided to nip upstairs to the kitchen with them before leaving. The building felt quite deserted, although Cathy knew that there must still be someone there, or the corridor lights would be switched off. It was one of Brenda's bugbears, leaving the lights on. She had scolded the doctors about it a dozen times before and had told them that they should look at the running costs of such a large building as this. As she moved towards the stairs, Cathy thought she heard a bang and then a noise from outside, perhaps in the carpark. She stood for a moment listening and then dismissed it as simply her overactive imagination. She was jumpy and overreactive. It made sense that she would be after everything that had happened.

Cathy didn't notice anything when she first walked into the half-darkened coffee room carrying her three mugs to the sink. But as she turned, she froze. For a split second, she had a sense that something was very wrong.

It was then that she saw. The figure was huddled; partially concealed by the table in the corner. Cathy moved stiffly across the room, but without needing to touch her, it was clear that she was dead. Steeling herself and turning the body gently over, Cathy gasped as she looked at the once-beautiful face of their practice nurse, Tracy. She had been stabbed. What looked like the handle of a kitchen knife, was sticking out from her chest. A pool of blood spread out from the wound, across her nurses' tunic and onto the coffee room carpet.

Cathy stayed crouched beside the girl and in horrified disbelief, she studied Tracy's face, as if for the first time. The heavy powder of make-up to the girl's cheeks contrasted with the twisted grimace of lipstick gave the body a grotesque clown-like state. Tracy's eyes were wide, but the creases in her face, that must surely have been present as the pain and realisation of the attack dawned upon her, were all but gone.

Cathy wasn't quite sure what happened after that. Discovering Tracy's body was very different to finding Mark. On that terrible day, she had a job to do, and thought that she could potentially save a life. This time, she could see there was nothing to be done and almost as a self-protective mechanism, she shut down.

She remembered hearing herself scream. And then Bert had suddenly been there with her, hauling her up and guiding her out of the room and downstairs to her own consulting room once more. He had disappeared for a moment and inexplicably returned with something for her to drink. She did so without thinking and gagged at the strong, unexpected taste of whisky.

'Best medicine for a shock,' Bert said and disappeared, presumably to call the police. They had then waited together.

'No need to go up there again,' Bert had said several times. 'Better to stay put and wait.'

Cathy hadn't spoken. She sat hunched and unable to move. She had no idea how long it had taken for the police to come, but when they did, they had found her with her fists clenched on the arms of her chair, her knuckles white, her eyes tightly shut. Bert had gone to the back door to let them in. They hadn't made her return upstairs but had moved her to one of the police cars.

It was warm in the back of the car. She had unclenched her fists and looked at her hands. They hurt and were covered in blood. Four small incisions were on each of her palms from where her own nails had cut the flesh. She studied them for some time, flicking the tiny flaps of skin back and forth.

The police had explained that she was needed at the station for questioning. Better to do it there than in the back of the car, they said. Cathy hadn't argued with anything. She felt completely empty. She had nothing left inside. At the police station, she heard all that they had said to her. It was only her and Bert left there in the practice, they told her. Everyone else had gone home. She answered all their questions, hearing her own voice almost as an outsider might. She was mildly interested in what she was saying but not enough to fully listen. Her mouth was moving but her words were like a droning noise. She had no feeling. She should have felt sad, or angry or upset but she had nothing at all. Just emptiness.

Cathy must have slept at the police station. She couldn't remember, but Suzalinna was there to collect her and take her home. The tips of her fingers were covered in dried ink. They must have asked for her fingerprints, but she couldn't remember that either.

'My car?' she asked Suzalinna. 'It's at the practice.'

'Sorted,' her friend answered, as she directed her to her own car which waited in a space close to the station.

'She was dead. Stabbed,' Cathy said and Suzalinna glanced sideways, her face full of concern. 'She had a knife in her. I saw it,' Cathy went on, her voice rising. 'Mark, and now her. Both dead.'

'I know, I know but it's alright now,' Suzalinna said as she opened the car door and ushered her in.

'Why are they letting me go? What if it was me? Maybe it was me,' Cathy said, fighting off Suzalinna's attempts to fasten a seatbelt around her. 'Did I kill them? I was there. Why was I first to get to them?' Cathy went on. She turned hurriedly to her friend. 'Suzalinna. It was me. I think it was me.'

Suzalinna's words cut her like a slap to the face. 'Jesus Christ, Cathy,' she said angrily. 'Jesus. You need to sleep. Stop struggling and put the bloody seatbelt on and let me get you home. They said you were talking nonsense.'

Cathy was so shocked by this sudden outburst that she forgot to fight off her friend's assistance and sat meekly and allowed herself to be restrained.

'They are letting you go, darling,' Suzalinna went on, more gently, 'because Bert, your handyman from the practice, has already helped them with their enquiries. The real killer was seen. Bert saw them running downstairs and out, although, at the time, he didn't realise that anything suspicious had occurred. You were simply a witness, darling. The first to arrive on the scene. Bert saw who really killed her, and presumably Mark too.'

'Who did Bert see then?' Cathy said. 'Who was the killer?'

Suzalinna looked uncomfortable. 'It's not good darling. The police said it was Fraser, the pharmacist.'

33

Over the preceding days, Fraser had been going through a period of mental anguish comparable to no other in his already turbulent existence. The day of his altercation with Jackson up in the coffee room, now seemed quite distant, although of course, it was not.

Having drank Jackson's coffee, Fraser, confused and frightened, returned to his room to await the results. By the second hour, he knew that he was not going to die. The realisation came, as a bitter disappointment. If it had been the poisoned mug, it must since have been washed and all traces of the hydrocarbon, removed. Fraser still couldn't understand how the mug might still be there unless the police had returned it, but why would they, he reasoned, if it was part of a murder investigation? Fraser sat for some time contemplating death and wondering what on earth had happened that day. Finally, he tortured himself with how those final moments must have felt for poor Dr Hope.

And then of course, there was Tracy. Fraser had thought that he was one of the last to leave the building that fateful evening. Stupidly, he had gone upstairs, and when he discovered the girl lying dead, he had run to his room without raising the alarm. What he had been thinking, he didn't know, but for that moment, he was sure that he couldn't be the first to find her. Already he felt that the net was closing in on him and it was only a matter of time before Jackson intimated his guilt, which he was sure he had given away through his bizarre behaviour that day. Fraser recalled the nurse's lifeless form. Oh God. He had then spun on his heel and left. Left poor, fragile Dr Moreland to discover her. When he heard the doctor's screams, he had got out of the place as quickly as he could, hoping to pass unseen.

Sarah had been waiting for him at home. He knew though, that it was only a matter of time before the police would arrive. The heaviest burden, throughout all of this, had been the need for vigilance. Fraser had found it exhausting, trying to keep up an outward appearance of calm, but inwardly festering inside with the knowledge that he had killed another man, watching everything he did or said. He had wanted to confide in Sarah a thousand times over, to tell her that he had made the gravest of mistakes. Oh, what a relief it would have been to unburden himself and to hear her sympathetic response, but increasingly he realised that for the very reason that he loved Sarah, he could not tell her. She was the epitome of innocence and kindness. If he told her what he had done, he might shatter this forever. Their love for one another would change and warp. If she stood by him, he would endlessly feel indebted to her; a fate he decided to be far worse than death itself.

So much of his life had changed since his decision to kill. Since Dr Hope's death, Fraser had found that his interest at work, something that had once been his life, was now completely impossible. Before, his occupation had given him such joy and purpose. He had found it stimulating and rewarding in so many ways, but now, he couldn't read a single page without his mind wandering. Decisions over even the smallest of matters were absolutely terrifying to him. It was insufferable, knowing that he was failing at his career so horribly.

On the evening of Tracy's death, Fraser had sat hunched and uncomfortable. The television was on and Sarah sat beside him sewing the hem of some garment or other and quietly murmuring the odd comment, although thankfully not expecting much from him in return. Perhaps she had known all along, Fraser considered, for when the doorbell rang, she did not seem unduly surprised despite the late hour.

'Don't answer it,' he had said automatically as she went to get up.

'Why ever not, Fraser?' It might be important.'

Sarah had gone to the door, shaking her head and smiling. 'You're so jumpy just now,' she had said.

Fraser felt that this moment might well be the pivotal one in his whole existence. When Sarah returned with the police officers, leading them through with a concerned expression on her face, Fraser could hardly bring himself to look at her. An icy hand seemed to close around his heart and he felt suddenly quite emotionless.

'I'll get my jacket. I know what this is about,' he said, getting up and walking to the door. 'Not here,' he heard himself saying to the police officer closest to him. 'Please, not here.'

⁓

'I UNDERSTAND that it's been a very distressing few hours for you, Mr Edwards, but if you'd just go through it again?'

Fraser sat with his head in his hands. The top two buttons of his shirt were undone, and his hair was ruffled. He looked up at the police detective, his eyes, bloodshot. 'How many times do I have to tell you?' he asked. His voice was flat. 'I've explained already, I had nothing to do with her death. Why won't you believe me?'

The police officer sighed. 'My colleague is currently interviewing someone else as we speak, and I must warn you, that their account might well implicate you further. Wouldn't it be better to tell the truth?'

Fraser remained tight-lipped.

'Let's go through your movements one last time. You said that you looked at the clock in your office at five-thirty. You'd been working there all afternoon. Remind me, was there a reason at all to leave your room that afternoon?'

Fraser sighed and shook his head.

'For the purposes of the recording, Mr Edwards has shaken his head,' the detective stated. 'Mr Edwards, think hard. You can't really expect me to believe that you had been in your office since lunchtime and you'd not even got up to go to the toilet? The rest of the practice seem to take a coffee break mid-afternoon. Perhaps you've forgotten a trip upstairs.'

'I didn't go upstairs for coffee with them. I'd stopped all that a while ago.'

'I see,' the detective said. 'And was there a reason for stopping that? A falling out? I must tell you that we have been interviewing the rest of the practice team and we do know that you and the now-deceased Dr Hope weren't on the best of terms.'

Fraser sighed. It was true. No-one had betrayed him in telling the police the facts. He stared straight ahead now and barely heard what the other man said.

'Mr Edwards?' the detective repeated.

Finally, when Fraser spoke, his voice sounded odd and choked.

'The truth is, that I am a coward,' he said.

The police officer didn't speak.

Fraser swallowed. It had to come out. 'I found her,' he said, feeling as if the words were lodged in his throat. He looked desperately from the detective to the police officer who stood by the door of the interview room.

The solicitor sitting by Fraser's side reached out a hand. 'Mr Edwards? Can I warn you ...?'

But Fraser shook his head forcefully. 'No, no. It's no use. They need to know,' he said, and then turning back to the detective: 'I did stay in my room all afternoon. It's quite true. I've been avoiding someone in the practice. I know you think it was Dr Hope I had a problem with, but you're wrong. I'll be the first to admit that the two of us didn't hit it off. He was a difficult man to work with. No doubt, you've heard that. But I wished him no harm at all. I was shocked, horrified when I heard he had died. And as for Tracy ...' Fraser sighed and looked skyward. His eyes suddenly filled with tears. 'Oh God!' he moaned. 'It was awful. She was lying there. I saw the blood.' He sniffed and wiped his nose on the sleeve of his shirt. 'I should have raised the alarm, of course I should. I did go upstairs, but far later. I panicked. It was foolish. It was a cowardly act, I realise that. What poor Dr Moreland must have thought then, going into the room and finding her ...'

Fraser ran his hands through his hair. His fingers were tense and his knuckles white. For some minutes, he was quite inconsolable. The detective glanced at the solicitor.

'Perhaps we should take a break,' the solicitor said.

The detective raised a forefinger in warning. 'Five more minutes,' he said softly.

They waited until Fraser had regained his composure.

'Mr Edwards, I can see how difficult you're finding this, but I must get it clear. Let's back-track from the actual day itself. You mentioned that you were avoiding someone in the practice. Can I ask who that person was?'

Fraser's lip trembled. He looked down at his hands, now clasped tightly in his lap.

Having spent the past endless days fighting to keep his secret safe, doing anything and everything to prevent his guilt from being realised, he knew it now had to come.

He met the other man's eyes and nodded.

The confession came surprisingly easily. A wave of profound relief swept over him.

'It was meant for Jackson,' he said, almost spitting the name out. 'I did kill Dr Hope, but it wasn't supposed to be him.' The words fell as almost a wail of despair. 'It was Jackson. It never should have happened that way. That animal was meant to be consulting alongside Dr Hope. The mug was his too. I don't know how Dr Hope came to drink from it.'

This, of course, led onto his reasoning as to why he wanted Jackson dead. Funnily enough, it was the historic crime of stealing hospital medication to satisfy Jackson's demands, that caused Fraser the greatest anguish.

He looked at the detective finally and waited for his judgement. The man remained tight-lipped. Fraser thought he would rather have had his disgust and outrage, than his passivity.

34

C athy slept late into the next morning. When she awoke, she was confused, and it took her a second or two to realise where she was. She had stayed over several times before of course, but that morning something seemed different. Cathy allowed her eyes to become accustomed to the glare filtering around the curtains' edges. It was only then that she remembered the reason for being in her friend's house, and she shuddered, recalling the previous evening's ordeal.

When she went downstairs, she found that the house was empty, but Suzalinna had left a note on the kitchen counter telling her to stay put, to help herself to food, and that she would be home from work at six. Cathy opened the fridge door, but she couldn't face eating. Even the mug of tea that she prepared was more for the comfort of the ritual that the actual desire to drink. Having showered and dressed, she felt a little better. She saw her car keys next to the fruit bowl and assumed that Saj must have collected her car from the practice the previous night. Impulsively, she decided that she couldn't just sit around waiting for her friend to return. Snatching up the keys, she left the house.

It was gone ten o'clock when she pulled into the practice

carpark and abandoning her car parked at a jaunty angle, called out to him as she crossed towards the back door.

'I believe I have you to thank for my release from the police last night?' she said to the old man.

Bert was semi-stooped; his overalls engulfed his body and he had an oversized plastic backpack slung on his back. It seemed to weigh heavily on his shoulders, causing him to move with greater deliberateness that usual. He turned and smiled but continued to work. Cathy wondered if he had heard what she said. In his hand, he held a nozzle which was connected to the container on his back. His hands were gloved. Cathy saw that he wore surgical gloves rather than work ones. A fine spray of clear liquid shot from the outlet. Bert it seemed, found great satisfaction in such work. He moved slowly from patch to patch, painstakingly attending to the weeds that had begun to spring up around the carpark over the last few weeks. He finished with a crack in the paving by Cathy's feet, that seemed to have grown particularly wild, and gave her a sideways glance.

'Police?' he said smirking. 'Those fools don't know anything.'

'But it looks as if it was Fraser all along,' Cathy said. 'He killed Dr Hope and then, I suppose, rejected by Tracy, or afraid that she had seen something, he killed her too.'

The old man lifted the nozzle and looked into it speculatively. 'They need to start asking the right people,' he said elusively, shaking the plastic tubing. The old man's attention was drawn to an unwanted plant in his peripheral vision. Swivelling from Cathy, he aimed and shot at it with the clear fluid. The fine spray settled on the unfortunate vegetation. 'They need to ask the right questions,' Bert went on, 'and then they'll know,' he said.

'Bert,' Cathy said suddenly. 'Is that weedkiller kept in the practice?'

Bert chuckled as if she had just told him a hilarious joke.

'It's about time someone asked me about what's kept here instead of just rifling around in my cupboard,' he said ambiguously.

Cathy gave up this line of questioning and hurried on inside. Going to her room, she could feel her thoughts beginning to race. Was it the practice's weedkiller that had been used then to kill Mark? Could it have possibly been in the coffee? Cathy recalled Fraser's talk on poisons only the week before Mark died. She began to quickly rummage through the papers by the side of her desk. It had to be here somewhere. Finally, she found what she was after: the print-out from Fraser's talk. She flicked through the slides that he had annotated. The police had said it was hydrocarbon poisoning. Cathy ran her finger down the list of domestic hydrocarbons that were listed as risks for accidental poisoning. Weedkiller wasn't on the list, it was itemised under organophosphates, probably an equally horrible class of toxin, but not the one Mark had swallowed. Cathy looked at the list again, and only then she saw what she was after. Of course. It had been there in front of her all along.

But did it mean that it was still Fraser? Could the practice pharmacist really be a viable perpetrator of such a heinous crime? In truth, Cathy still wasn't convinced. Anyone at the practice meeting that night, who had heard Fraser's talk, could have been inspired to use poison to kill. Mentally, Cathy ran through motives, but everyone seemed to have a loose reason to want Mark out of the way. The man wasn't exactly liked within the practice. Granted, Cathy still couldn't see a palpable purpose to kill, and what of Tracy? Cathy thought of the silly girl standing only the day before in the front reception. The nurse had sounded as if she knew something about Mark's death. Cathy tried to recall exactly what she had said but found that she couldn't. Was that the reason for her death also? Cathy sat down and frantically thought. Who then had opportunity?

James came into her room at that moment without knocking. The door had been ajar, and Cathy sat hunched at her desk with her jacket still on. She looked up.

'James,' she said, almost confused to see him there. 'Free at last. I can't believe they thought it was you in the first place and then, I think they might have wondered if it was me. What a mess.'

James bent down and hugged her awkwardly, he rarely showed signs of affection. His arms fell once more to his sides and Cathy saw that his suit jacket was creased.

'Listen, James,' she said, her voice beginning to rise. 'I'm trying to work it all out, and I think I'm onto something. I'm not sure it was Fraser after all. Bert's in the carpark with weedkiller and it made me think, you know?'

Cathy was almost shouting in her excitement and James sat down next to her.

'Oh Cathy, my dear, dear friend, Cathy. You have been under a lot of strain recently. Dealing with Mark's death and then the practice while I was away, and the horror of finding that girl.' James shook his head sadly. 'All of that on top of your own diagnosis. You've been so unwell, Cathy. I think we've asked too much.'

'I know. I know, but listen to this, James,' Cathy went on. 'It was in the coffee. Remember the talk? You took the coffee down to him and it must have been poisoned already. Someone had done it before you got the cup. It must have been in the coffee room. Someone in the coffee room did it.'

James smiled. 'Cathy, the police have been through all of this with me already, while I was in the station. Do you think they've been just sitting twiddling their thumbs this whole time? The postmortem showed that poor Mark had been poisoned and yes, we all know it was some domestic hydrocarbon.'

'I know, I know,' Cathy almost shouted again. 'They said it at the inquest!'

'But Cathy, listen,' James went on. His voice was smooth and slow. He sounded as if he had said the words a thousand times before. 'Mark's coffee cup was sitting by the sink in his room. It was washed up, I grant you, he was a meticulous, obsessive-compulsive idiot, but the police said that they couldn't detect any trace of poison in that cup. Cathy, there was no hydrocarbon in Mark's coffee that day.'

Cathy took a moment to digest this new piece of information. 'Well,' she finally said, 'that just means he cleaned the cup extremely well. Nothing more. He always washed up after his coffee.'

James shook his head once more, but still, she went on.

'Listen, Bert has a whole cupboard full of potential poisons for cleaning and painting. Anyone, anyone could have gone in and taken something and squirted it in the cup.'

She let out a sigh and flopped back in her chair.

'Oh God, James, why aren't you listening? I even tested it out. I managed to squirt tap water into Julie's mug without anyone spotting it the other day. I was sure that was the way it had been done, before you even touched the mug. I know I'm right. Anyway James, what did you say to him that morning when you took him the coffee? What did you talk about?'

James sighed. He looked as if he was considering what to say. When he did explain, he spoke in the same level tone, but Cathy knew it must pain him. 'I told him I was resigning,' James said. 'I said that I was going to take early retirement. I'd had enough. It was for the greater good of the practice.'

Cathy moved forward in her seat. 'What did he say?'

'He just sat there and sipped his coffee. He didn't seem surprised.' James shook his head.

He looked so tired, Cathy thought. 'So, now what?' she asked.

James shifted and re-crossed his legs. 'Well, I need to sort this mess out before I even consider early retirement.' He smiled. 'I'm not jumping ship just yet, Cathy, don't panic.'

Brenda walked in looking flustered. A strand of her usually neatly pinned hair had come awry and inexplicably, the dishevelled look of her practice manager made Cathy want to laugh.

'You are not going to believe this,' Brenda said dramatically, unaware of Cathy's inner turmoil. 'The police have been on the phone again, asking me all sorts of questions about Fraser and our plans to begin methadone prescribing.'

Cathy looked at her sharply. 'What? But we haven't even set up the methadone clinic yet,' she said.

Brenda rubbed the back of her own neck. 'I don't know what it's all about, Cathy. They aren't releasing him though they said.'

'Are they charging him with murder then?' Cathy asked.

'Well, they'd hardly be likely to tell me that, would they?' Brenda snapped. Cathy grimaced and the practice manager lowered her voice. 'They're coming in soon and will want to speak to you about the plans for the clinic.'

'Jesus,' Cathy exploded.

Brenda looked acutely uncomfortable and hastily shut the door completely with a bang.

'Cathy,' she hissed. 'I'm sure it's been a very difficult time for you, what with finding Tracy and all that's happened.' Cathy rolled her eyes, but Brenda continued. 'And I'm sorry to be the one to hit you with the news about Fraser today also, but while James is here, I need to let you know that we've had a serious complaint from a patient. It came in just this morning,' Brenda said, turning to James who now sat with his head in his hands. Brenda turned back to Cathy. 'Cathy, I'm afraid the complaint is about your professional conduct.'

Cathy slapped the table. 'What? Who?' and then in sudden realisation, it came to her. 'That bloody drug seeker,' she said. 'He tried to blackmail me into giving him dihydrocodeine. I might have guessed. Mark saw through his little routine. He was the last patient he saw before he died.'

'Cathy,' Brenda said as unemotionally as she could, 'that's really not the point. You know how we deal with serious complaints and with your past history, we have to be even more stringent.'

Cathy had spun in her chair and was now surveying the carpark through the blinds, but the shapes were blurred with her tears. When she spoke again, she refused to look at Brenda.

'Are you for real, Brenda?' Finally, she turned on James who still sat, seemingly unable to intervene. 'James are you going to seriously sit there and allow this to happen?'

'Cathy,' he said, and when words failed him, he shook his head once more. 'We thought perhaps a bit more time off. I know we're struggling for staff but –'

'What, so you have discussed this already? Together? Without me?' Cathy spat. 'You've been talking about this while I've been tripping over dead bodies and being questioned by the bloody police?'

James looked wretched. 'Cathy. Just a few days off until –'

'No,' she said with finality. 'I have patients to see. Get out of my room, both of you. I will have a full surgery tomorrow morning.' She turned to her senior partner. 'James, if you seriously think that I'm not capable of doing my job, then call the bloody GMC. Get me struck off for bad language, or malpractice, or whatever. All for shouting at a manipulative drug addict. I stuck up for you when Mark was making your life a misery, and this is how you repay me? Jesus.' Brenda still hovered by the door, but she was not to be spared. Cathy met her gaze and saw a pathetic figure of a woman, but still, she went on. 'Brenda, I can't believe you. You of all people. You and I have kept things going together with all this going on and this is what you do? I thought you had more sense. We were meant to be a team.' Cathy was now openly sobbing, and her words came out in heaves. 'Get out. Leave me alone, both of you.'

35

Cathy stewed in her room for the rest of the morning. She worked solidly through the lab results, making rapid decisions about her patient's health. Over one-hundred-and-five decisions made in thirty-nine minutes.

At three o'clock the police arrived.

'Sorry to interrupt your surgery, Doctor,' DCI Rodgers said as he sat down in the chair offered. 'We'll try to be as quick as we can. We just had a couple of questions about the drug clinic you and Mr Edwards were planning to set up.'

DS Milne sat down next to his colleague, his pen and notepad ready.

Cathy frowned. 'Yes,' she said, 'I heard you had been asking about the methadone prescription plans.'

The two policemen watched her closely and Cathy felt herself flush. She was normally in control of the consultation and was annoyed to find she was nervous talking to the police in her own room. Her mouth was dry, and her tongue stuck to the roof with certain syllables.

'As you know, we currently have Mr Edwards in for questioning with regard to the unexplained deaths of Dr Hope and

Ms Steele,' DCI Rodgers said with gravity. 'Clearly, we have looked a little into Mr Edwards's past movements before coming to your practice. He has been here for how long now?'

Cathy tried to think. 'A month or so, maybe? Brenda would know exactly,' she said.

'Of course,' the police officer said.

Cathy caught the patronising edge to his voice. She leaned forward and rested her elbows on the desk as he continued to speak.

'And what was the process for employing the practice pharmacist? Did you put out an advert and then interview?'

Cathy's eyebrows knotted in confusion.

'To be honest, Doctor,' the policeman went on, 'I had never heard of a practice having a pharmacist working in-house so to speak.'

Cathy smiled. 'Sure,' she said. 'It's something the Health Board are actively encouraging. The idea is to have a highly trained pharmacist in individual practices as part of the multi-disciplinary team. Their job is to oversee the general prescribing and to make recommendations and changes to the systems we have in place.' Cathy looked from one officer to the other. DS Milne paused with his pen hovering and then looking up, met her gaze. 'Really they're there to keep the GPs up to date with the new drugs and educated in the best possible practice,' Cathy continued. 'Of course, each practice can choose what they ask their attached pharmacist to do. Fraser has been helping tidy up some of the chronic disease management prescriptions. Repeat prescriptions that haven't been updated in years.'

'And you interviewed a list of candidates?' the detective asked.

Cathy nodded. 'Fraser put in his application and we short-listed him for an interview. No-one else came close. He was local and presented himself very well. We asked Brenda to do a couple of referee checks. We heard that he was a bit of a loner but otherwise, he seemed faultless. He was very impressive when he came to interview, as it happens. It was a unanimous decision. As far as I'm aware, since appointing him he has only continued to prove his worth,' she said glancing across at the computer screen as an alert came up saying a patient was waiting to be seen.

'I take it you had heard about the death of a local drug addict about six months ago? The man in question belonged to your practice and I assume that you had heard of Fraser's involvement in dispensing methadone to the man?' asked DCI Rodgers.

Cathy nodded. 'Of course,' she said. 'It wasn't a deal-breaker for us. Fraser had been essentially exonerated of any blame. Has something further come out?'

DCI Rodgers turned to his colleague and after a silent exchange, returned to Cathy. 'No,' he said. 'But Mr Edwards does seem to have gotten himself into somewhat of a muddle. When we took him in, he was convinced that he had killed Dr Hope, although, to be quite honest, his story doesn't seem to add up at all with the facts as we know them. He denied having anything whatsoever to do with the death of your practice nurse, though. The man is in a fragile state, to say the least. Fraser admitted to a whole host of other crimes alongside Dr Hope's murder, some of which date back many years and seem quite petty, but he appears determined to make a clean break of things.'

Cathy sat back in her seat, shocked at this new information.

'I assume that you had no concerns regarding Mr Edwards's mental health at any time while he was working for you?'

Cathy shook her head. 'None at all. He seemed very distressed by the death of Dr Hope, as we all were.'

'No that's fine. He will, of course, be assessed by our own police surgeon and if it comes to it, a psychiatrist in due course, but I have to tell you that currently, we have little to go on. As I say, his story does not add up at all. Now to clear up a final point, Dr Moreland, as I can see that you're very busy. Brenda – Ms Ingram, told us that you and Fraser were planning to start up a clinic for drug users. Can you briefly tell me a bit about that, please?'

Cathy looked down at her fingers as she answered. She still had that ink on her fingertips despite scrubbing at them in the shower and her hands trembled slightly.

'Of course,' she said, 'but I have no idea why you want to know. The psychiatric services in the area are stretched to breaking point right now and general practices are being encouraged to take on some of the more stable drug misuse patients.' She glanced from one to the other and they both waited expectantly. 'Currently, the drug misusers have to go to a psychiatric outpatient clinic to get simple weekly methadone prescriptions. We, as a practice, have been discussing taking on a limited number of patients for a trial period for a weekly methadone clinic. Fraser and I had begun to think it through, but what with everything going on, it fell by the wayside somewhat.' Cathy smiled sardonically. 'Anyway,' she continued, 'I'm sure you know that drug misusers don't have a great reputation for engaging in mainstream services, so we have had to think carefully about how we might run the clinic. Our idea was to have it on a single afternoon using a two-hour slot when no other patients would be in the building to limit any difficulties.'

The detective nodded. 'And you were planning on prescribing the methadone yourself? Pharmacists aren't able to prescribe, are they?'

'Yes,' Cathy said. 'I would prescribe, and no they can't. Pharmacists don't have that power. I have a bit of experience in dealing with drug and alcohol misuse patients. It is a special interest of mine. Fraser, though, has a wealth of experience from his shop pharmacy days and he was to work alongside me to advise me regarding reducing methadone doses or increasing if we had to.'

'So, he would have had some control over the doses himself?'

Cathy couldn't understand where this was going. 'Well, I would be writing the prescriptions,' she reiterated. 'but I would have taken his advice on board, of course. I'd have been stupid not to.'

DCI Rodgers shifted in his chair, uncrossing his legs and then re-crossing them. Cathy looked at DS Milne and wished this would end.

'Look,' she said. 'I don't know what you want me to say.' There was silence. 'I have patients waiting,' she went on desperately. 'I'm sorry to be rude but you still haven't even told me what this line of inquiry is all about. Why are you asking me all these questions about the methadone clinic?'

DCI Rodgers got up and rebuttoned his suit jacket. 'As I said, Doctor, we're looking into Mr Edwards's background. We've spoken to him regarding the deaths at this practice and another drug-related issue that has arisen. I'm sure you can understand that I can't say any more for now.'

Cathy sat for some minutes alone in her room when they had gone. What on earth did it all mean? When she finally roused herself enough to continue consulting, her mind was only half on the job. She knew she gave her patients a poor service that afternoon and by the time her last appointment came and went, she felt very relieved to have survived the day. She had three messages on her computer screen saying that a Dr Bhat had been trying to call her. She would have to deal with Suzalinna's wrath later. No doubt her friend would be furious that she had come into work at all that day. A danger to herself and her patients she would tell her, when she was so over-wrought. Thankfully, neither James or Brenda had spoken with her again, and it seemed that they had not decided to report her to the GMC just yet anyway.

She listened to the rest of the practice packing up for the day once more. In James's room next to her, she could hear the movement of a chair and then the light being switched off and his door locked. She knew that he paused outside her own room, but clearly thinking better of it, continued out of the building. What a bloody mess. Perhaps there really was no going back with James. But despite all of this, she felt determined to get to the bottom of things.

36

Suzalinna shook her head. 'I can't actually believe what you're telling me, Cathy,' she said as she sat on the floor beside Cathy's chair.

'I know,' Cathy replied. 'It's like some horror story, isn't it? They've released him though. Said they were continuing to pursue enquiries regarding minor drug offences from years back, but that there was no concrete evidence to link him with the deaths.' Cathy leaned back against the wicker chair in her friend's conservatory and sighed. 'That's not the worst of it though,' she continued. 'They said that they needed to speak frankly with me, and that they were taking my own account of things at face value for now. They said that they had no reason to believe that I knew about Fraser's past, but that it would be imprudent to continue with my plans to take on those methadone patients. Can you believe it? They suggested strongly that I should leave the whole thing.'

Suzalinna's forefinger traced a pattern in the woodwork. Round and round a notch in the floorboard her hand moved. Cathy watched her, but Suzalinna didn't look up.

'Listen, I'm sorry for not answering your calls earlier,' Cathy said. 'I know you only have my best interests at heart, but you do understand that I had to go into work.'

Suzalinna scrunched up her face and sniffed.

'Well?' Cathy said, knowing that there was more to this than her friend was saying.

Suzalinna sighed. 'Darling,' she began and stopped. She looked up into Cathy's eyes and Cathy found it hard to maintain her stare.

'Darling, you know yourself it's wrong. This whole methadone prescribing nonsense,' Suzalinna sighed again as if waiting for a response, but when none came, she continued. 'After what you've been through, I'm surprised that you're even suggesting it. I thought James would have quashed the whole thing by now. You've been very lucky, Cathy.' Suzalinna touched her arm and Cathy froze. 'No, darling, but you have been. You've been diagnosed with a serious mental illness. Bipolar disorder is no laughing matter. But before that, you were so unwell that you did self-medicate. Oh, please, don't look like that Cath. If I can't say it to you, then no-one can.' Suzalinna shook her head. 'As a doctor, you have a duty of care to your patients. You also must be of sound enough mind, to recognise your own weaknesses. You took drugs from the store at your own work. You did, darling. You took them and you self-medicated. You became, perhaps not physically, but certainly mentally, addicted to them. Now then. Tell me how you would be strong enough, or detached enough, to deal with other addicts having been in that position yourself. Tell me darling. I know you can offer them empathy, but that's not enough.'

Cathy couldn't speak. She knew what her friend said was true.

'Can't you leave all of this to the police now?' Suzalinna asked. 'This investigating nonsense is all well and good, but you're making yourself ill. You'd only want me to be honest, and at the moment you're lurching from one lead to the next.' Suza-linna smiled. 'I know you hate me saying it, but it's true. You've hardly noticed how you look yourself, but as your friend, and as a doctor, I have to say it.'

Cathy shook her head. She felt exhausted. It was true, that since this business had begun, she had lost even more weight. She had always been slim, but her joints now seemed oversized compared to her limbs.

'Just leave it,' Suzalinna repeated. 'The police are doing their job just fine without you butting in. Have a bit of faith. They'll find out who did it eventually. Your job is to stay safe and healthy. You know what they told us back at med school? Look after number one and practise self-care, because if you become ill, it impacts a lot of other people.'

Cathy groaned.

'I know it sounds corny,' Suzalinna agreed. 'But it is true.'

That had been the previous evening and Cathy had thought of little else. For a time, she did consider jacking the whole thing in and leaving it to the police, but it was hard when she had already come so far.

Cathy drummed her fingers on the desk between patients or strode about the room, going over the conversation with the police the day before. She found herself standing on the scales, not bothering to look at her weight, then fidgeting with the blinds on her window. How was Mark killed that day? How did he drink the poison and what of Tracy? Did someone else run down the stairs following Tracy's death, someone who Bert failed to notice?

After finishing with a particularly simple prescription review and seeing that she had twelve minutes until her next patient was due in, she got up and quietly went to Mark's room. The door was still locked but she had her own key, one which opened all the doors on the corridor. They had been told by the police that they were now finished examining the room, so she knew she would not be in trouble. She heard James's voice as she passed, barely a muffled sound, but unmistakably him; slow and methodical. No-one was in the passageway, so she opened the door and slipped in, closing it silently behind her.

There had been something they'd all missed. There had to be. She wished she had been more attentive that morning. She had been so caught up in her own worries, what with only just coming back to work. Surely if she had been more observant, she would have seen. Cathy did, however, recall with at least some clarity, the afternoon before Tracy's death. She could picture the young nurse, standing in the front reception area, her bottom lip petulant and pouting. What had Tracy noticed that no-one else had? Cathy had considered this to be a wild exaggeration on the silly girl's part at the time, but had what she said, scared the murderer into acting again? It certainly seemed likely now.

Cathy looked around. She wondered what Mark had done that morning. Perhaps by reviewing his movements, she might come to some new conclusion. She sat at his desk and considered the facts. That morning, having been brought his coffee by James, they had spoken briefly, with the senior partner announcing his planned early retirement. James had mentioned that he had seen Mark drink at least some of his coffee. Cathy got up and went to the sink, as he must have done that day. She turned on the tap and allowed the water to swirl, eddying round and into the plughole. He must have washed his mug out having drunk the coffee as he always did. It had been found at the side of the sink by the police. He had then taken in his next patient. She turned off the tap, half afraid that someone might hear and discover her sneaking around. She had no reason to feel this way, she told herself. She was committing no crime in simply looking. The answer must surely lie in Mark's room, but aware that she should still be seeing patients, she gave it up for the time being. Frustrated, she left, glancing around one last time before relocking the door behind her.

Cathy ushered her final patient out having completed her list. Her mind had been preoccupied. Still, she felt she had been stupid somehow and had missed something obvious. Someone had said something to her, and she had missed the significance. As she turned to go back into her room, she looked up the corridor and saw Bert's cupboard door slightly ajar.

'Bert, can I come in?' she said as she stood outside, almost afraid to intrude. She didn't want to go in at all. In fact, she hoped he would come out and talk to her.

There was a shuffling from inside and Cathy heard something clang. When he opened the door, she realised that he must have dropped his metal thermos on the floor. He now held the lid in his hand.

'Wait a bit,' he said, and he shuffled back inside, tidying something or other, before fully opening the door.

'What's up Doc?' he asked and smiled at his unintentional joke.

'I need to speak to you,' Cathy said. It had taken her far too long to come to Bert. He must surely be the only person who might know the truth. Who was better placed than he, to have seen what happened that day? Who else could have heard or seen the comings and goings in the corridor the morning of Mark's death? How could she have been so slow? Cathy smiled at the handyman. She had always liked him. 'You seem to be the only person round here who knows what's going on,' she said. 'Do you want to come to my room? It's maybe a bit cramped in there to talk.'

Bert followed her slowly down the corridor. She shut the door behind the old man and gestured for him to sit. It seemed to take him an eternity to fold his frame into a seated position, but despite his ailing physical form, Cathy noted his mental vigour. He grinned at her.

'More detecting?' he asked conspiratorially.

Cathy grimaced. 'They all think I'm going crazy in this place; both Brenda and James now, but I think I'm onto something. I still don't know how, but I thought you might have seen.'

Bert returned her gaze steadily, but didn't answer.

'Bert, the metal cleaner in your cupboard,' she went on. 'You had been using it to scrub the graffiti on the doctors' name plaque out at the front there. Had it been moved at all, or had any of it been used? I feel sure that's where the poison came from. It had to be from here.'

The old man rubbed his chin. The rough skin on stubble sounded like sandpaper. 'Maybe moved, I'd say,' the old man said contemplatively, 'But sometimes stuff moves around though in that cupboard.'

Cathy had hoped for more positive confirmation, but she continued. 'Right, so it could have been moved though, and your cupboard door? Is it open at all times? No lock?'

'I like to lock it up sometimes and keep people from poking and taking things,' Bert said. There was a long pause and then he announced loudly: 'Someone's had some of my custard creams!'

Cathy sighed. Maybe this wasn't such a great idea after all.

'Bert,' she continued with an air of desperation now. 'I know the police have asked you all of this, but just tell me again about what you saw the night Tracy was killed. You were still here. It was just the two of us. You said it was Fraser that you saw, is that right?'

'I saw him, like I told them, I saw that Fraser lad leaving, just after you had gone upstairs. I poked my head out and saw you going up. That was when he left.' Bert said.

There was no arguing with the certainty of his evidence. 'But

Bert,' Cathy went on. 'There's a chance there could have been someone else. Wait a minute. As I was going upstairs, I heard a sound outside in the carpark. Do you think you might have seen the person who left before I went up? You see, I'm not sure it was just you, me and Fraser in the building. I think someone else had just slipped out the back door. I'm positive I heard someone. Might they have driven off when I was carrying on having discovered Tracy's body?'

Having said this, Cathy found herself holding her breath. She watched the old man as he scratched his forearm.

'Maybe,' he said, but he suddenly seemed to grow impatient with the conversation 'Look,' he said, 'I didn't say the pharmacist had killed her. It was those stupid policemen who jumped to that reasoning. I suppose maybe someone else did go past but I'm not saying anything now, not even to you,' he said leaning forward. 'You saw what happened to the nurse girl when she said too much. I'm old, but I'm no fool.'

'But if you know Fraser wasn't the last person to see Tracy, then why would you let the police take him in for questioning? You haven't told them the full story. Someone else is free to kill again and Fraser might be wrongly accused.'

'Look, Doctor,' Bert said with finality. 'Here's the honest truth. I saw the young lad leaving that evening. But the fact is, I didn't see anything else because I was busy tidying my cupboard. The next thing I knew was you were screaming and hollering out. That's the truth, I swear.'

Cathy was utterly defeated. She didn't know what to believe now. The old man got up to go.

'How's your wife doing Bert?' Cathy asked, almost as an afterthought.

'Fine' he said, contradictorily shaking his head.

He shuffled past her as she held open the door, and coughed

twice, it was dry rasping cough and she smelt the stale, sweet coffee on his breath.

It was only then, that it finally dawned on her and Cathy realised how Mark must have been poisoned.

'How could I have been so stupid?' she said aloud.

Bert snorted, unaware of her sudden realisation. She could have kissed the man. And she, Cathy, had had the answer all the time for she would have been the only person in a position to notice. She was the one working on Mark's airway during the resuscitation attempt. What a fool she had been. Cathy now knew with certainty what Tracy had seen missing from Mark's room, a comment that had sealed the nurse's own fate. She knew how Mark had been poisoned and the reason for that particular way of killing him meant that only four people could have done it. Before anything else, she had to speak to Fraser.

37

During the hours of isolation, while locked in a cell awaiting his next round of questions, Fraser had found himself thinking of his parents. His mother was now quite infirm and it was many months since he had last communicated with her. For this, he felt immense sorrow. As he sat waiting, his mind returning to his childhood and his mother's encouraging words. He replayed memories that he had long since forgotten and wept for the unconditional love his mother had felt, that he had not repaid or recognised. He thought also of his father, now passed many years. The irony of his father's profession in law, and Fraser's current predicament, was not lost even on Fraser. He sat and spoke with the dead man and begged for his absolution but above all, his guidance.

When the police finally came and told him that currently, he would face no charges, Fraser was stunned. He was led from the cell and after collecting his belongings, he left the police station, his path tentative and uncertain. It felt as if he was learning to walk for the first time.

He let himself into his home, but he knew that his job, his relationship, and the life he had previously known, was long since lost. Despite this realisation, he found himself, feeling lighter. The police had more work to do, they had told him. As yet, nothing he had said, fitted with the facts as they knew them. Fraser didn't understand what this had meant. How many times he had to tell them that he had accidentally killed a man, he didn't know.

Sarah had repeatedly tried to call his mobile, but knowing that he could not face her, he had ignored it. She had come to the house in the end, of course, and let herself in with the key he had given her.

Standing in the hallway, she had waited and then gone to him with her arms outstretched. 'Fraser? Oh, my poor darling. What did they do to you? Fraser, please? They've released you. I knew it was all a mistake.'

She took another step towards him, but he turned, unable to look at her face.

'Fraser?' she repeated, her voice cracking. 'Talk to me.'

He shuffled through to the living room and she followed.

'I'll make you something to eat,' she said. 'Let's get the heating on and make the place a bit more comfortable. I'm not due in today, I've already called them to say.'

He allowed her to fuss in the kitchen, and listened to her chatter, of how he'd feel a good deal better after something warm was in his stomach and he'd had a hot shower. But when the practicalities were taken care of, and they sat together, he knew he couldn't mislead her any longer.

He looked at her with great sadness. Of all the things he regretted, deceiving her had been the most dreadful. As he attempted to compose himself, she smiled shyly, encouragingly, and his heart could have broken. What he had to tell her, would shatter both her innocence, and her love for him, but he must do it all the same.

The house was still when she left. Fraser looked around the

place. The colours from the matching cushions that Sarah and he had chosen together, seemed to have faded along with his hopes.

Fraser barely realised himself shakily moving about during those solitary hours. Now that his conscience was clear though, he could face death, if not easily, then gladly. He sat in the front room for some time, with his eyes closed. The sunlight was coming through the branches of the tree outside, and the warmth played a lattice across his pale countenance.

It was here in his favourite chair, that his exhausted body rested.

When the doorbell rang, Fraser did not move. The bell rang again, more insistently and then someone began beating at the front door with their fists.

38

Cathy was about to smash a window. She had run around the side of the house and peeping in the front, she had seen him. His figure looked unnaturally stiff and with a feeling of horrified disbelief that she might be about to discover a third body, Cathy raised her hand to the pane of glass. She hadn't thought of the pain of doing so, but thankfully instinct made her momentarily pause and then she saw with great relief, Fraser's eyelids flutter. Oh, thank God, he was alive.

'Open the door, Fraser,' she yelled. At first, she thought that she might still be too late, for he closed his eyes once more. 'Now!' she screamed, 'or I'm smashing my way in.'

Slowly, Fraser seemed to shift his weight, and then unsteadily, he raised himself and made his way from the room. Cathy watched through the window and then when he was out of sight, she went around to the front door. She heard him fumbling with the lock while she impatiently waited.

When the door swung open, the practice pharmacist seemed barely half the man he had been all but a few days ago. Cathy pushed past him, afraid that he might refuse her entry.

'Before we go any further,' Cathy said sternly. 'If you have taken anything, I need to know now. It will save me a good deal of bother later.'

Fraser shook his head.

'Well?' she said, not satisfied. 'I'm serious, Fraser. I know you've had a rough time of things what with being hauled in by the police, but if you've swallowed something and decided to end it, tell me.'

Fraser led her through to the front room. 'I've not,' he said. 'I came close, and I still might have if you'd not turned up. I'm so tired.' He sat down in the chair she had seen him in, through the window. Cathy walked further into the room and sat down herself.

'Fraser,' she said and shook her head. 'Has it really come to this?'

The man smiled sadly and looked at his hands. 'You don't know the half of it,' he said.

'Well, how about you start telling me. I have a meeting up at the practice in just over an hour,' Cathy said, looking at her watch. 'You're coming to the meeting with me, by the way, so you'd better buck up bloody quickly and start talking, or I'm going to look a bit of a fool going in there, amn't I?'

Fraser shrugged wearily. 'I can't help. They don't believe what I've told them anyway, the police. I told them that I killed Dr Hope, but they wouldn't listen. Oh God, what a mess I've made of it all.'

'Start at the beginning,' Cathy said, her voice softening. 'It's far better that you tell me. I've guessed some of it already, I think. You didn't intend to kill Dr Hope at all, did you? It was someone else.'

The whole story came out. How Fraser had been overjoyed at getting the job, but then, when he thought his life was settled, a face from the past came back to haunt him. He told Cathy of the dreadful torment he had suffered at Jackson's hands all those years before as a junior pharmacist, and with the threat of losing all he had worked for, he had gone half-mad. In some crazed state, he had swilled paint-thinner around the thermos mug that Jackson alone used, knowing that come the following morning at coffee time, the man who might ruin him, would make his coffee in it and receive the fatal dose.

'It was callous, to say the least,' Fraser said. 'I'll never forgive myself for it. And then Jackson called in sick. I have no idea how the mix-up with the cups occurred. No-one else used that horrible mug. It was Jackson's choice simply because he went out the back to smoke and it kept his coffee warm.'

Cathy cast her mind back to Mark's room that fateful day as she crashed through the door and discovered her partner lying there. She had tried to picture it a thousand times before when she was attempting to recall what Tracy had seen was missing. Now, in her mind's eye, Cathy saw the sink area and the cup beside it, that Dr Hope had only minutes before washed, having drunk his coffee.

'It wasn't a thermos mug, but an ordinary china one,' she said breathlessly. 'You didn't kill Mark at all, Fraser. In fact, it had nothing whatsoever to do with the coffee. Your poisoned mug, I assume was loaded into the dishwasher along with the rest of the mugs and cups left lying around at the end of the day. Fraser, do you hear what I'm saying? You didn't hurt anyone. You're blameless.'

'But what about Tracy then?' Fraser asked. 'I was seen fleeing the building. It looks grim. As it happens, I didn't kill her. I found her; you know? I'm so sorry I wasn't man enough to deal with it, and then I let you go on in there and ... Oh God, what a mess. What must you think of me?'

Cathy sighed. 'Bloody hell, this is self-indulgent, isn't it? I thought you'd be delighted to be in the clear and here you are weeping and wailing about some of the finer details. Fraser, listen to me. The main thing is that you are not a murderer, right? Yes, you didn't exactly act with the highest regard for others. I suspect you might well have to face some repercussions over the previous drug offences if the hospital pharmacy has any record of missing tablets, but as far as I can tell, you've done nothing wrong other than that. Yes, yes, I know you had the intention to harm, but it never actually came to it, thank God. Jackson himself has a few questions to answer too, I should say. I hardly think he's general practitioner material. Certainly not at our practice, that's for sure. Blackmail is a criminal offence. If you press charges, he might well lose his licence to practice as a doctor at all. I wonder if he did come looking for you, or if it was coincidence.'

Fraser snorted, and Cathy was glad to see that the colour had begun to come to his cheeks. 'Oh, he came for me. He said as much upstairs the other day. What a gift, it must have been to get a training position in the same practice too.'

'Well, let's put that behind us now,' Cathy said brusquely. 'Time to get yourself sorted, Fraser. You're needed at the practice now. We have a full-team meeting and you are part of that whether you like it or not. After today, we can discuss your employment arrangements. I think we'll need you more than ever when this is over, but of course, it'll depend on what the police allow. As far as I'm concerned, it's done with now. You've already made a huge difference to our practice; Fraser, and we'd be quite lost without you. Right, don't just sit there, get washed or changed, or whatever you have to do. We need to get back to the practice, and fast.'

39

Michelle and Julie were already in the meeting room. 'I hope this isn't going to go on for too long,' whispered Julie, squeezing Michelle's arm. 'I've got a stack of labs to sort out and we have to see to the house visits still.'

'Brenda said it was just a quickie,' Michelle replied. 'She didn't look best pleased this morning though. Face like thunder coming out of her office.'

The office girls perched on the sideboard at the end of the room, allowing their legs to dangle, knocking on the wood below.

The door opened and Irene, the sole practice nurse now, and Linda, who had taken on more shifts than she probably really wanted, came in. Both looked tired, and if anyone had taken the time to notice, they would have seen that poor Irene's hand trembled as she drew back a chair to seat herself at the table beside James who had preceded them shortly before.

'Brenda's on her way up,' the GP said. He too looked as if he could have well done without the meeting. He sat in his usual chair, his hair perhaps greyer than it had been a month or so ago. The last time they had all been gathered here was when Mark had still been alive. So much had happened since then, and yet it was only a matter of weeks before.

Cathy was the last to arrive, accompanied by Fraser to everyone's surprise. All eyes were on the young pharmacist, but Cathy gave him a reassuring nod and indicated that he should sit beside her. James smiled at the practice manager as she shuffled her papers, but she had been looking at her notes which she had drawn up that morning; a list of topics she must discuss and points she must cover. It wasn't going to be pleasant, any of it.

'Right, shut the door, Irene, if you don't mind and we can get on,' said Brenda. The practice manager settled in her chair and Cathy saw in front of her was a stack of patient notes and a notepad. She clicked her pen irritably a couple of times. The gesture reminded Cathy very much of poor Mark.

Cathy was still at a loss as to why Brenda had called the meeting in the first place. The practice manager had sent an email around first thing. No excuses for absentees, everyone must attend, it had said. For Cathy, it felt like the one opportunity to say her own piece. First, though, she would allow Brenda to say whatever it was that she needed to. The practice manager clearly had to get something off her chest.

Cathy looked around at the faces of her colleagues wondering if she really knew any of these people. Over these last weeks, even mild-mannered James had changed in her opinion. She looked across at her senior partner, his face creased, the skin tanned and weathered. The past few years must have been torture for him. Losing his wife and then day-in-day-out coming to work to serve his community, but at the cost of working alongside someone who he obviously despised. Cathy now knew that James had it in him to take a life. It changed her perception of him slightly. Everything had changed following her conversation with James's old partner, Dr Clark. A mercy killing was still wrong. Cathy recalled the oath she swore to when she had qualified as a young doctor; first, do no harm. James had violated that pledge. Even if it was out of compassion, he had played God.

'Right,' Brenda said, and Cathy turned to look. Brenda, who was flushed in the cheeks, had picked up her notepad and was reading from it. 'I've called this meeting,' she said, 'to quash a few rumours and to allow us to unite as a team at this difficult time.' She glanced around the room, taking in all of the staff in turn. 'I have just come off the phone from the police,' she continued, 'and unfortunately, they are still dragging their heels over making an arrest. Fraser,' Brenda said turning to the man, 'I hope you'll understand that we cannot have you here until this business is completely cleared up. I'm not accusing you of anything, but you can see how things are. The police are still clearly trying to gain solid evidence. They said that themselves.' Brenda looked around once more. 'I was going to use this meeting to talk about how we were all going to deal with handling members of the public, our patients, at this uncertain time. I think we need to be prepared. I myself am going to be taking some leave from things, so I need your support ...' The practice manager trailed off as she saw Cathy's reaction.

'Take some leave from things? This is all wrong Brenda,' Cathy said. She had her hands on the desk in front of her and as Brenda paused, Cathy got to her feet, scraping her chair back. Slowly, she looked around at all of them. Irene stared back at her and Linda squirmed in her seat. Only the office girls seemed to be enjoying the drama.

'How can you all just sit back and agree that it must have been Fraser?' Cathy said. 'How can any of you really believe that?' Cathy turned to Fraser who could not look at any of them. 'No,' Cathy repeated. 'It's not right.'

There was a stunned silence. Surprisingly, it was Michelle who first spoke.

'Well the police certainly believed it when they took him in,' the girl said. 'Killed Dr Hope because he was in love with Tracy, or had humiliated him or something, and then probably when she turned him down, he stabbed her.' Michelle seemed satisfied with this version of events anyway. 'He was the one who knew about poisons,' she went on, growing in confidence. 'And then, he was the one who was seen running away that evening before Tracy was found. He was going to set up some drug thing at the practice too to make money.'

Cathy grew exasperated. She shook her head. 'But listen,' she said, 'it's all wrong, can't you see?' They stared back at her with blank expressions. 'Jesus,' Cathy exclaimed. 'What's the matter with all of you?'

It was the first time he had spoken, and the sound of his voice seemed to shock them all. 'And this,' James said quietly, 'is another reason for the meeting.' Brenda seemed to nod, and the senior doctor continued. 'Dr Moreland, Cathy, we know you have been under some extreme strain lately, and we have given you some leeway for that.' He hesitated and Cathy stood opened mouthed. 'But,' James continued, 'the team, well, Brenda and I, feel that a break would be best for the practice as a whole.'

Cathy could have spat at him. 'James,' she said, losing herself completely. 'Shut the hell up and listen to me. Kick me out after I say all this, fine, but let me just speak!'

James sat back and gestured to Brenda that he was defeated.

'OK,' Cathy said, trying to speak levelly, 'so we know that Mark was poisoned that morning and we all thought it must have been done in the coffee room before James took the mug from Michelle and went downstairs to say his piece about resigning.' There was a murmur of surprise from those members of staff who had not heard this small piece of intrigue, but Cathy ploughed onwards. 'I'm sorry James,' she said, 'but I'm sure it's hardly in doubt that some of us may have, along with the police, assumed that the killer was you. You had the opportunity to tamper with the coffee.' James raised his hands in acceptance of the fact. 'The truth was though,' Cathy went on, 'that anyone in the building that morning could have put the poison in that cup.' Cathy looked around at all the faces turned to her. 'It's true,' she said, 'you all had the chance. While you were all milling around upstairs making your teas and coffees that dreadful day, any one of you could have taken a syringe-full of poison from your pocket, quickly squirted it into the mug while everyone was busy gossiping, and it would be done. By the way, it was a metal cleaner that was used. Highly toxic and awful stuff, but readily available and easy for anyone to obtain from Bert's cupboard.' Cathy paused but knew that she must plough on. 'None of you noticed the other day when I came upstairs for coffee with you,' Cathy said. 'As an experiment, I filled a five-millilitre syringe with water in my room. I put it in my pocket and came up. You all faffed around talking and getting in each other's way while you were making your coffee. No-one was paying any attention to me and my syringe of water. Two seconds was all it took. I squirted it into your mug, Julie. I don't think it'll have done you any harm,' Cathy said, smiling now at Julie's look of disbelief. 'Maybe just cooled your drink down a bit,' Cathy continued. 'So, in theory, it was possible that someone in the building that morning spiked the coffee. Do you all agree?'

Cathy looked around the room beseechingly, desperate for at least one of them to nod. Nothing.

'I must admit that for a while I was confused. It seemed to me that Mark was definitely the intended victim, but I couldn't forget that he had been doing a dual clinic alongside his trainee that morning, or rather he should have been if Jackson had turned up.' Cathy looked across at the trainee with distaste. He had, up until now, sat quietly alongside the receptionists. Cathy had seen him attempting to make eye contact with Fraser, but the pharmacist was too intent on studying his own hands to be drawn. 'In fact, there might well have been an accident had Jackson come in that day, but his thermos mug, having been left carelessly on the kitchen worktop, had already been cleaned the night before, so any residual unpleasantness might have been washed away. No, Jackson was a red-herring. We'll have a chat later about things,' Cathy said to the trainee. 'Now's not the time, but I think you might agree that general practice is not the best place for you.'

Cathy ignored the man's look of disgust and began again. 'We all knew from Fraser's talk that domestic cleaners were occasionally taken in attempted suicides and we all knew that that the ones containing hydrocarbon were unpleasant and oily but could be swallowed without much problem. Half an hour to an hour later though, you would start to know about it. Usually, the oesophagus would rupture and it would cause extreme respiratory distress, pulmonary oedema and death.'

Cathy saw the blank expressions on all the non-clinical members of the team and explained: 'Gullet gets big holes in it and breathing packs up.'

Michelle and Julie looked horrified.

'Sorry,' she said but was secretly glad to have at least elicited some kind of a reaction.

'What I didn't understand was why Mark's mouth was such a mess, remember James?' Cathy continued, turning to her partner. 'If he had just drunk the poison straight down, then why was his mouth as blistered as it was?' James shrugged and looked as if he was going to intervene, so Cathy quickly turned and began again. 'So, I went into Mark's room this morning. Don't look like that Brenda. I was trying to see what Tracy had spotted that none of the rest of us had. She stood in the front reception, remember? And she said that something was missing from his room. I couldn't work it out, I'll be honest,' Cathy said ruefully. 'That was until I spoke to Bert.'

'I thought he might be involved,' Brenda said under her breath.

'Shut up Brenda and listen,' Cathy replied rudely. She was beyond reasoning now and any thought of maintaining public niceties was long gone. 'It wasn't what Bert said to me that helped, it was when he coughed. His breath, you see? It stank of coffee. It was only then that I realised that that was what Mark's breath should have smelled like too. It should have smelled of coffee as it was the last thing he had drank. It didn't though,' Cathy said vehemently. 'And I was probably the only one in a position to be to close enough to know. I was the one who tried to intubate him. I was literally peering down his mouth.' Cathy shook her head in reminiscence of that awful morning. 'He didn't smell of coffee though,' she went on, 'he smelled minty.'

The rest of the room looked astonished.

'The mouthwash,' Cathy exploded, slamming her hand down on the table, making them jump. 'The poison was in his bloody mouthwash! We all knew about his obsession with perfection and cleanliness. It was his routine to freshening up after his coffee. Tracy noticed. She was the only smart one amongst us all. She saw that the mouthwash bottle, that he kept by the sink, had gone.'

'So, why go to all the fuss to put it in the mouthwash when it could have just as easily been put it in the coffee before it was taken down to him? I don't understand,' Irene said. 'What was the significance of the mouthwash?'

'Alibi.'

Cathy let that hang for a moment or two and then went on.

'So, the person who really killed Mark,' Cathy said, 'thought they were on to a sure thing. James was in the police station still helping with their enquiries and the police appeared to be no closer to working out how Mark was actually given the poison.' Cathy looked grimly around the room. 'But then Tracy went and ruined it all. She could be horribly boastful. Even all the nonsense about inheriting Mark's money was a lie. I hear that Mark hadn't left her the house or any of his money. It was to go to his distant relatives all along. Anyway, the foolish girl announced, for all to hear, that she had spotted something missing in Mark's room. She even suggested that she had an idea of who the killer really was. It was a stupid thing to say, even for her.' Still, no-one spoke. 'None of us could believe that James was involved, but we couldn't be sure,' Cathy continued. 'I don't really know if Tracy knew who the killer was for certain, but she had to throw that bit of a threat out there and wait and see if anyone bit.'

'So, Fraser saw his opportunity,' Brenda interjected, 'and went to see the silly girl. But then what? It all keeps coming back to Fraser.'

'No hold on Brenda,' Cathy said raising a hand in protest. 'Fraser did go upstairs, but that was after she had been killed. He found her, and panicking, he ran. I heard someone else leaving that evening and stupidly it didn't click until later. Of course, had I looked out of my window; I might have seen the car of the real murderer driving away.'

'But you didn't,' said Irene. Cathy turned to the practice nurse and raised her eyebrows. Irene looked back defiantly. 'I'm sorry, Dr Moreland, but even the police will say that you thinking you heard someone else leaving, isn't strong enough evidence to clear Fraser of the crime. All roads still lead to him.'

'No, Irene. That's where you're wrong,' Cathy said, glancing at Fraser who was now picking at the skin around his finger-nails. 'The murderer knew they had to speak to Tracy in person that late afternoon. It was imperative that they find out what she knew. I think it was pretty much luck that the killer and Fraser didn't pass each other on the stairs. It was a terrible risk for the killer to take, when any one of us might have walked in and caught them, but they had no choice. Tracy had shown her hand and grabbing the only thing within easy reach, they stabbed her. Bert, as you all know, had seen Fraser running away but even he admits that he might have missed someone else.'

'So, the murderer stabbed her to keep her quiet and let Fraser take the blame?' Linda asked.

'Yes Linda,' Cathy said, looking at the GP locum, who had saved them from so much disruption by stepping up to the mark these past few weeks and taking on extra shifts. Cathy had in the past found Linda both tiresome and irritating. If she was honest, she had been jealous of the young GP, after she had filled Cathy's shoes so easily while she herself had been off sick. Cathy smiled at her own insecurity. 'But here we are left with a problem, Linda, everyone,' she said, looking around the room. 'Fraser is still very much a suspect for murder. The murderer, I assume, would be happy to let that suspicion just hang. The police might still find enough evidence to incriminate Fraser even now. The DCI hinted as much to me on the phone earlier.' Cathy looked almost rueful. 'Fraser's career seems in tatters. So does mine, for that matter, Fraser, so you're in good company.' The practice pharmacist smiled slightly but didn't look up. Cathy continued. 'Fraser was there at the scene of the crime on both occasions. He was the one with superior knowledge about hydrocarbons. The case looks bleak against him.' Cathy saw James raise his eyebrows.

'But let's just go back to Mark's death and that word; Alibi,' she said. 'Why should the murderer go to all that trouble to poison the mouthwash and then have to hide the poisoned bottle and dispose of it later? Isn't that what you wanted to know, Irene?'

Irene shifted uncomfortably and re-crossed her legs.

'The murderer,' Cathy said, 'could have been caught out doing just that. Surely it was a foolish and dangerous plan. So unnecessary. The reason for all the over-complication was, that they hoped that the police, and all of us, for that matter, would assume that Mark had been poisoned that morning. He did ingest the poison that morning, but it wasn't actually put there that day. That is the important point. The morning that Mark died; the killer wanted to distance themselves from the practice as far as possible. They were conveniently away and out of the building, attending a meeting on the other side of town.' Cathy smiled again and ran the palm of her hand across the smooth surface of the table. 'Alibi,' she repeated.

Irene, Linda and Brenda looked troubled as all eyes fell upon them, the only people that this applied to. Cathy didn't make eye contact with any of them. She knew if she did, she might falter.

'I didn't know who had done it until ten minutes before I came into this meeting. It finally clicked when I parked the car, having been to check on Fraser, who I thought might well be a danger to himself. Bert had been out earlier spraying some of the weeds in the carpark. He was doing a very careful job, from what I saw, but then I noticed that one of the rose bushes had been apparently accidentally sprayed also. The leaves were black, and the flowers had fallen off. It was then that it dawned on me, that rather than Bert being careless, this was how the remaining poison had been disposed of. The killer, desperate to rid themselves of any connection with the crime, had tossed the oily liquid out. The container, they had put in the recycling bin. It's possible that the police might still find it there along with the killer's fingerprints, with any luck. It was an impulsive thing to do, but the dead rose bush, now clear for all to see, marks the killer's room as it is right outside their window.'

And then, the chair scraped back. Her face was the picture of rage. Her eyes, grey and staring. For that second, Cathy thought that she looked almost blind.

'You little bitch,' she screamed.

She made it to the door with surprising speed.

And then everything was chaos. People were getting up and shouting.

She got to the top of the stairs. Bert was there as Cathy had instructed him to be, and there was a scuffle. Falling heavily down the two flights, she came to rest at the bottom, her right leg twisted at an impossible angle.

40

'Thanks for all your help with things Bert,' said Cathy later in the day. Although she had spent the majority of the afternoon speaking with the police, she couldn't go home without talking to him. It felt as if there was unfinished business.

Cathy still couldn't understand how Brenda might have allowed either James or Fraser to take the blame for her crimes. She could only assume that the practice manager was in so deep that she had lost sight of what she was doing.

Bert was in the corridor outside his beloved cupboard when she came across him.

'Did you know it was Brenda all along then, Bert?' Cathy had asked.

'I had an idea it might be,' the old man said. 'They say she's broken her leg but that's the least of her worries now, I suppose. Why did she do it, though? That's what I can't understand.'

'Oh, money it seems,' Cathy said 'Mark had caught her embezzling practice funds. She was desperately trying to scrape some if it back by economising. Remember all the lectures about saving energy and turning off lights? She even disconnected the CCTV to the practice to save money. Our own practice manager. Someone we trusted to keep the place safe. She was in a real fix, actually. Mark would have shown her no mercy after the misappropriation of practice funds. He would have told me and James at the next meeting for sure.' Cathy saw the old man shake his head. 'Then, Tracy sealed her own fate by trying to do a bit of blackmail,' Cathy continued. 'I don't know if Mark had been indiscreet enough to tell her what was going on. I guess we'll never know that. Tracy was far more observant than the rest of us though and ultimately that was what did for her.'

'And Brenda deliberately took advantage of that pharmacist's mistake and used it for her own ends. It was a coincidence him choosing the same time to put oil in a mug upstairs thinking it might make that dreadful trainee sick. How did she get rid of the poisoned mouthwash afterwards?' asked Bert. 'I understand that she chucked the stuff out the window and then got rid of the empty bottle at her leisure, but how did she get past all of us, carrying it, without being seen?'

'That was easy,' Cathy laughed. 'She knew there'd be a massive commotion with the discovery of his body and rightly supposed that in the time after us finding him, and him being taken away, she'd have a chance alone in the room to nip in and take it. She probably used a bag or ring-binder to slip it inside, in case she met anyone in the corridor. The irony is that it was probably hidden in her room the whole time the police were sitting there, interviewing folk. Then she could dispose of it whenever she liked afterwards. Clever, you see?'

'Ah well,' Bert said sighing. Cathy thought the old man was tired of the conversation already. 'I suppose that pharmacist lad's off the hook now?' he asked.

'Fraser? Yes and no,' Cathy said. 'The police had a few other issues to clear up with him. He'll take a bit of time to sort himself out, but I've told him the door's open. He said that he had a lot of explaining to do to someone very important. I hope he sorts it out with his girlfriend. He seemed determined to explain everything and start afresh.'

'Always the best way,' the old man said. 'And you, Doc?'

'Oh, I'm not going anywhere, Bert. I think the practice needs a bit of stability just now, don't you?'

Turning back, she smiled at him.

'Bert, you know the petty vandalism? The graffiti on the practice sign next to Dr Hope's name?'

A slow smile crept across the old man's face. Cathy couldn't be sure, but she thought he winked at her. Turning, Bert shuffled away. Cathy knew that the handyman never had got on with Mark after the GP had failed to recognise his wife's multiple sclerosis. She had only recently discovered that it was Linda who had made the diagnosis. Perhaps the girl was partnership material after all.

THE END.

ACKNOWLEDGMENTS

Many thanks to Amanda Horan for all the editing advice. To my parents, I thank you for your love, support and encouragement. Yuen, I am forever indebted to you for your unerring faith in me, and for putting up with it all.

THANK YOU!

I do hope you enjoyed reading my debut novel: *Murder and Malpractice,* I certainly had a blast writing it! If you're interested in reading future books in the *Dr Cathy Moreland* series, please visit my website: http://mairichong.com and join my mailing list. I'll let you know when any new titles are coming out. Please say hello on twitter @mairichong. Thank you once again.

Lightning Source UK Ltd.
Milton Keynes UK
UKHW011819010320
359582UK00001B/18